The Courage Consort

The Courage Consort

THREE NOVELLAS

Michel Faber

LARGE PRINT

This large print edition published in 2004 by
RB Large Print
A division of Recorded Books
A Haights Cross Communications Company
270 Skipjack Road
Prince Frederick, MD 20678

Published by arrangement with Harcourt, Inc.

Publisher's Cataloging In Publication Data
(Prepared by Donohue Group, Inc.)

Faber, Michel.
  The courage consort : three novellas / Michel Faber.

    p. (large print) ; cm.

ISBN: 1-4193-2253-2

1. Psychological fiction, English. 2. Excavations (Archaeology)—Fiction. 3. Vocal
ensembles—Fiction. 4. Twins—Fiction. 5. Large type books. I. Title.

PR6056.A27 C68 2004b
823/.914

Printed in the United States of America

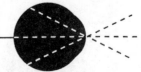

**This Large Print Book carries the
Seal of Approval of N.A.V.H.**

CONTENTS

THE COURAGE CONSORT

*To all those who sing lustily and with good
courage, and to all who only wish they could*

O n the day the good news arrived,
Catherine spent her first few waking
hours toying with the idea of jumping out
the window of her apartment. Toying was perhaps
too mild a word; she actually opened the window
and sat on the sill, wondering if four storeys was
enough to make death certain. She didn't fancy
the prospect of quadriplegia, as she hated hospi-
tals, with their peculiar synthesis of fuss and
boredom. Straight to the grave was best. If she
could only drop from a height of a thousand
storeys into soft, spongy ground, maybe her body
would even bury itself on impact.

"Good news, Kate," said her husband, not raising
his voice though he was hidden away in the study,
reading the day's mail.

"Oh yes?" she said, pressing one hand against
the folds of her dressing gown to stop the chill
wind blowing into the space between her breasts.

"The fortnight's rehearsal in Martinekerke's
come through."

Catherine was looking down at the ground far
below. Half a dozen brightly dressed children were

1

loitering around in the car park, and she wondered why they weren't at school. Then she wondered what effect it would have on them to see a woman falling, apparently from the sky, and bursting like a big fruit right before their eyes.

At the thought of that, she felt a trickle of mysterious natural chemical entering her system, an injection of something more effective than her antidepressants.

"Is . . . is it a school holiday, darling?" she called to Roger, slipping off the sill back onto the carpet. The Berber plush felt hot against her frigid bare feet, as if it had just come out of a tumble dryer. Taking a couple of steps, she found she was numb from waist to knee.

"School holiday? *I* don't know," her husband replied, with an edge of exasperation that did not lose its sharpness as it passed through the walls. "July the sixth through to the twentieth."

Catherine hobbled to the study, running her fingers through her tangled hair.

"No, no," she said, poking her head round the door. "Today. Is today a school holiday?"

Roger, seated at his desk as usual, looked up from the letter he was holding in his hands. His reading glasses sat on the end of his nose, and he peered forbearingly over them. His PC's digital stomach emitted a discreet *nirp*.

"I wouldn't have the foggiest," he said. At fifty-two years old, a silver-haired veteran of a marriage that had remained carefully childless for three decades, he obviously felt he'd earned the right to be hazy on such details. "Why?"

Already forgetting, she shrugged. Her dressing gown slipped off her naked shoulder, prompting one of his eyebrows to rise. At the same moment, she noticed *he* wasn't in pyjamas any longer, but fully dressed and handsomely groomed. Hitching her gown back up, she strained to recall how she and Roger had managed to start the day on such unequal footing. Had they got up together this morning? Had they even slept together, or was it one of those nights when she curled up in the guest bedroom, listening to the muted plainsong of his CDs through the wall, waiting for silence? She couldn't remember; the days were a chaos in her brain. Last night was already long ago.

Smiling gamely, she scanned his desk for his favourite mug and couldn't spot it.

"I'll put the kettle on, shall I?" she offered.

He produced his mug of hot coffee out of nowhere. "Some lunch, perhaps," he said.

Determined to carry on as normal, Roger picked up the telephone and dialled the number of Julian Hind.

Julian's answering machine came on, and his penetrating tenor sang: "*Be-elzebub has a devil put aside for me-e-e . . . for me-e-e . . . for meeeeeeee!*"— the pitch rising show-offishly to soprano without any loss of volume. Roger had learned by now to hold the telephone receiver away from his ear until the singing stopped.

"Hello," said the voice then, "Julian Hind here. If *you* have a devil put aside for me, or anything else for that matter, do leave a message after the tone."

Roger left the message, knowing that Julian was probably hovering near the phone, his floppy-fringed head cocked to one side, listening.

Next, Roger dialled Dagmar's number. It rang for a long time before she responded, making Roger wonder whether she'd gone AWOL again, mountain climbing. Surely she'd have given that a rest, though, in the circumstances!

"Yes?" she replied at last, her German accent saturating even this small word. She didn't sound in the mood for chat.

"Hello, it's Roger," he said.

"Roger who?" There was a hornlike sonority to the vowels, even on the telephone.

"Roger Courage."

"Oh, hallo," she said. The words were indistinct amid sudden whuffling noises; evidently she'd just clamped the receiver between jaw and shoulder. "I was just talking to a Roger. He was trying to sell me some thermal climbing gear for about a million pounds. You didn't sound like him."

"Indeed I hope not," said Roger, as the nonsense prattle of Dagmar's baby began to google in his ear. "This is to do with the fortnight in Martinekerke."

"Let me guess," said Dagmar, with the breezily

scornful mistrust of the State—any State—that came to her so readily. "They are telling us blah-blah, funding cuts, current climate, regrets . . ."

"Well, no, actually: it's going ahead."

"Oh." She sounded almost disappointed. "Excellent." Then, before she hung up: "We don't have to travel together, do we?"

After a sip of coffee, Roger rang Benjamin Lamb.

"Ben Lamb," boomed the big man himself.

"Hello, Ben. It's Roger here. The fortnight in Martinekerke is going ahead."

"Good. Sixth of July to twentieth, yes?"

"Yes."

"Good."

"Good . . . Well, see you at the terminal, then."

"Good. 'Bye."

Roger replaced the receiver and leaned back in his swivel chair. The score of Pino Fugazza's *Partitum Mutante*, which, before the calls, had been glowing on his PC monitor in all its devilish complexity, had now been replaced by a screen saver. A coloured sphere was ricocheting through the darkness of space, exploding into brilliant fragments, then reassembling in a different hue, over and over again.

Roger nudged the mouse with one of his long, strong fingers. Pino Fugazza's intricate grid of notes jumped out of the blackness, illuminating the screen. The cursor was where Roger had left it, hesitating under something he wasn't convinced was humanly possible to sing.

"Soup is served," said Catherine, entering the room with an earthenware bowl steaming between her hands. She placed it on his desk, well away from the keyboard as she'd been taught. He watched her as she was bending over; she'd put a T-shirt on underneath her dressing gown.

"Thanks," he said. "Any French rolls left?"

She grinned awkwardly, tucking a lock of her greying hair behind one ear.

"I just tried to freshen them up a bit in the microwave. I don't know what went wrong. Their molecular structure seems to have changed completely."

He sighed, stirring the soup with the spoon.

"Five to ten seconds is all they ever need," he reminded her.

"Mm," she said, her attention already wandering outside the window over his shoulder. Meticulous though she could be with musical tempos, she was having a lot of trouble lately, in so-called ordinary life, telling the difference between ten seconds and ten years.

"I do hope this château is a *cheerful* place," she murmured as he began to eat. "It would have to be, wouldn't it? For people in our position to bother going there?"

Roger grunted encouragingly, his face slightly eerie in the glow of the monitor through the haze of soup steam.

★   ★   ★

Roger Courage's Courage Consort were, arguably, the seventh-most-renowned serious vocal ensemble in the world. Certainly they were more uncompromising than some of the more famous groups: they'd never sunk so low as to chant Renaissance accompaniment to New Age saxophone players, or to warble Lennon/McCartney chestnuts at the Proms.

A little-known fact was that, of all the purely vocal ensembles in the world, the Courage Consort had the highest proportion of contemporary pieces in their repertoire. Whereas others might cruise along on a diet of antique favourites and the occasional foray into the twentieth century, the Courage Consort were always open to a challenge from the avant-garde. No one had performed Stockhausen's *Stimmung* as often as they (four times in Munich, twice in Birmingham, and once, memorably, in Reykjavik), and they always welcomed invitations to tackle new works by up-and-coming composers. They could confidently claim to be friends of the younger generation—indeed, two of their members were under forty, Dagmar Belotte being only twenty-seven. Fearlessly forward-looking, they were already signed up for the Barcelona Festival in 2005, to sing a pugnaciously postmillennial work called *2K+5* by the enfant terrible of Spanish vocal music, Paco Barrios.

And now, they had been granted two weeks' rehearsal time in an eighteenth-century château in rural Belgium, to prepare the unleashing of Pino

Fugazza's fearsome *Partitum Mutante* onto an unsuspecting world.

Come the sixth of July, the early-morning English air was still nippy but the Belgium midday was absolutely sweltering. The message from God seemed to be that the Courage Consort shouldn't be deceived by the brevity of the plane and train journeys or the trifling difference in geographical latitude: they had crossed a boundary from one world into another.

In the cobbled car park outside Duidermonde railway station, an eleven-seater minibus was waiting, its banana-yellow body dazzling in the sun. Behind the wheel, a smart young man was keeping an eye out for British singers through a pair of very cool granny specs. He was Jan van Hoeidonck, the director of the Benelux Contemporary Music Festival. Spotting his overdressed guests disembarking from the train, he flashed the headlights of the minibus in welcome.

"The Courage Consort, yes?" he called through the vehicle's side window, as if to make perfectly sure it wasn't some other band of foreign-looking travellers lugging their suitcases through the railway barriers.

Benjamin Lamb, towering over the others, waved in salute. He was grinning, relieved there had been no turnstiles to squeeze through—the bane of his travelling life. The mighty scale of his obesity was easily the most identifiable feature of the Courage

Consort, though if anyone who'd never met them before asked for a pointer, Roger would always tactfully advise: "Look out for a man with silver-grey hair and glasses"—himself, of course.

"But aren't there supposed to be five of you?" asked the director as Roger, Catherine, Julian, and Ben approached the side of the minibus.

"Indeed there are," said Roger, rolling open the sliding door and heaving his wife's huge suitcase inside. "Our contralto is coming under her own steam."

Jan van Hoeidonck translated this idiom into Dutch instantaneously, and relaxed behind the wheel while the Consort lugged their belongings. Catherine thought he seemed a friendly and intelligent young man, but was struck by his apparent lack of motivation to come out and help. *I'm in a foreign country,* she told herself. It hadn't been real to her until now. She always slept like a corpse on planes and trains, from the moment of departure to the instant of arrival.

Having loaded his luggage next to hers, Roger walked jauntily round the front of the vehicle and got in next to the director. He consulted no one about this. That was his way.

Catherine climbed into the banana-yellow bus with her fellow Courage Consort members. In true British fashion, each of them sat as far away from the others as possible, spreading themselves across the nine available seats with mathematical precision. Ben Lamb needed two seats to himself, right enough, for his twenty stone of flesh.

Catherine looked aside at Julian. It had been three months since she'd seen him, or so Roger said. It seemed more like three years. In profile, his heavy-lidded, supercilious face, superbly styled black hair, and classic cheekbones were like a movie star's, with the same suggestion of jaded, juvenile naughtiness. He might have been the older brother she never had, contemptuously running ahead of her to the haunts of grown-up vice but never quite escaping her memories of him in short trousers and shopping-centre haircut. Yet he was only thirty-seven, and she was ten years older than that.

As the bus pulled away from the station, Catherine reflected that she almost always felt much younger than other people, unless they were clearly minors. This wasn't vanity on her part; it was inferiority. Everyone had negotiated their passage into adult-hood except her. She was still waiting to be called.

Jan van Hoeidonck was talking to her husband in the front. The director spoke as if he'd been facilitating cultural events since World War II. But then they all spoke like that, Catherine thought, all these cocky young administrators. The chap at the Barbican was the same—born too late to remember the Beatles, he talked as if Peter Pears might have cried on his shoulder when Benjamin Britten died.

Self-confidence was a funny thing, when you thought about it. Catherine squinted out the window, stroking her own shoulder, as the bus ferried them into a surreally pretty forest. Chauffeured like this, towards a nest prepared for her by admirers, she still managed to feel like a fraud; even under a shimmering sun, travelling smoothly through placid woodland, she felt a vapour of fear breaking through. How was that possible? Here she was, an artist of international standing, secretly wondering whether she looked dowdy and feeble-minded to Jan van Whatsisname, while he, a fledgling bureaucrat with the pimples barely faded from his pink neck, took his own worth for granted. Even Roger listened respectfully as Jan explained his plans to steer the ship of Benelux art into new and uncharted waters.

"Of course," Jan was saying, as the minibus delved deeper into the forest, "multimedia events are not so unusual with rock music. Have you seen Towering Inferno?"

"Ah . . . the movie about the burning skyscraper?" Roger was more of a Bergman and Truffaut man himself.

"No," Jan informed him, "they are a multimedia music group from England. They have performed a piece about the Holocaust, called *Kaddish,* all over Europe—and in your own country also. The piece used many video projections, an orchestra, the Hungarian singer Marta Sebestyén, many things like this. I hope this piece *Partitum Mutante* will do something similar, in a more classical way."

11

The director slowed the vehicle and tooted its horn, to scare a pheasant off the road. They had encountered no other traffic so far. "Wim Waafels," he went on, "is one of the best young video artists in the Netherlands. He will visit you here after a week or so, and you will see the projections that you will be singing under."

Julian Hind, listening in, remarked, "So, we'll be the Velvet Underground, and this video chap will be Andy Warhol's *Exploding Plastic Inevitable*, eh?"

Roger glanced over his shoulder at Julian in mute incomprehension, but the director nodded and said "Yes." Catherine had no idea what any of this was all about, except that Roger didn't like being shown up on matters musical.

Catherine's chest tightened with disappointment as, true to form, her husband took his paltry revenge. She tried to concentrate on the lovely scenery outside, but she couldn't shut her ears to what he was doing: moving the conversation deftly into the area of European arts bureaucracy, a subject Julian knew next to nothing about. He reminisced fondly about the French socialist administration that had made the 1985 Paris Biennale such a pleasure to be involved with, and expressed concern about where the management of the Amsterdam Concertgebouw was heading just now. Catherine's irritation softened into boredom; her eyelids drooped in the flickering sunshine.

"So," interrupted the director, evidently more concerned about where the conversation was heading than the fate of the Concertgebouw. "This Consort of yours is a family affair, yes?"

Catherine's ears pricked up again; how would her husband handle this? Nobody in the ensemble was actually a Courage except her and Roger, and she tended to cling to her maiden name as often as she could get away with it, for sheer dread of being known as "Kate Courage". She couldn't go through the rest of her life with a name like a comic-book superheroine.

Suavely, Roger more or less evaded the issue.

"Well, believe it or not," he said, "the Consort is not specifically named after me. I regard myself as just one member of the ensemble, and when we were trying to think of a name for ourselves, we considered a number of things, but the concept of courage seemed to keep coming up."

Catherine became aware of Julian's head tilting exaggeratedly. She watched an incredulous smirk forming on his face as Roger and the director carried on:

"Did you feel maybe that performing this sort of music needs courage?"

"Well . . . I'll leave that to our audiences to decide," said Roger. "Really, what we had in mind was more the old Wesleyan adage about hymn singing, you know: 'Sing lustily and with good courage.'"

Julian turned to Catherine and winked. "*Did* we have that in mind?" he murmured across the seats to her. "I find myself strangely unable to recall this momentous conversation."

Catherine smiled back, mildly confused. While meaning no disloyalty to her husband, she couldn't recall the conversation either. Turning to look out the window of the minibus, she halfheartedly tried to cast her mind back, back, back to a time before she'd been the soprano in the Courage Consort. Hundreds of neat, slender trees flashed past her eyes, blurring into greeny-brown pulsations. This and the gentle thrumming of the engine lulled her, for the third time today, to the brink of sleep.

Behind her, Benjamin Lamb began to snore.

For the last couple of miles of their journey, the château was in plain, if distant, view.

"Is that where we're going?" asked Catherine.

"Yes," replied Jan.

"The wicked witch's gingerbread house," murmured Julian for Catherine to hear.

"Pardon?" said the director.

"I was wondering what the château was actually called," said Julian.

"Its real name is 't Luitspelershuisje, but Flemings and visitors call it Château de Luth."

"Ah . . . Château de Luth, how nice," repeated Catherine, as the minibus sped through the last mile—or 1.609 kilometres. When the director parked the car in front of the Consort's new home-away-from-home, he smiled benignly but, again, left them to deal with their own baggage.

The Château de Luth was more beautiful, though rather smaller, than Catherine had expected. A two-storey cottage built right next to the long straight road between Duidermonde and Martinekerke, with no other houses anywhere about, it might almost have been an antique railway station whose railway line had been spirited away and replaced with a neat ribbon of macadamised tar.

"Luciano Berio and Cathy Berberian stayed here, in the last year they were together," said the director, encouraging them all to approach and go inside. "Bussotti and Pousseur, too."

The house was in perfect condition for its age, except for the artful tangle of stag horns crowning the front door, which had been eaten away some-what by acid rain in the late eighties. The red brick walls and dark grey roof tiles were imma-culate, the carved windowframes freshly painted in brilliant white.

All around the cottage, lushly tasteful woodland glowed like a high-quality postcard, each tree apparently planted with discretion and attention to detail. Glimpsed among the straight and slender boughs, an elegant brown doe froze to attention, like an expensive scale model of a deer added as a pièce de résistance.

Catherine stood gazing while Roger took care of her suitcase somewhere behind her.

"It all looks as if Robin Hood and his Merry Men could trot out of the greenery any minute," she said, as the director ambled up.

"It's funny you say this," he commented. "In the sixties there was a television series filmed here, a sort of French Robin Hood adventure called *Thierry la Fronde*. This smooth road through the forest was perfect for tracking shots."

The director left her deer spotting and hurried off to unlock the front door, where the others stood waiting. They were arranged in a tight trio around their bags and cases, Ben at the back and the shorter men in front, like a rock group posing for a publicity shot.

Jan worked on the locks, first with a massive, antique-looking brass key and then with a couple of little stainless-steel numbers.

"Presto!" he exclaimed. Never having seen a conjurer at work, Catherine took the expression as a musical directive. What could he want them to do *presto*? She was in a somewhat *adagio* state of mind.

The château's magnificent front room, all sunlight and antiques, was obviously the one where rehearsals would take place. Julian, as he was wont to do, immediately tested the acoustic with a few *sotto voce* Es. He'd done this in cellars and cathedrals from Aachen to Zyrardów; he couldn't help it, or so he claimed.

"*Mi-mi-mi-mi-mi*," he sang, then smiled. This was a definite improvement on Ben Lamb's rather muffled sitting room.

"Yes, it's good," smiled the director, and began to show them round.

Catherine had only been inside a couple of minutes when she began to feel a polite unease finding a purchase on her shoulders. It wasn't anything to do with the atmosphere of the place: that was quite charming, even enchanting. All the furniture and most of the fixtures were dark-stained wood, a little sombre perhaps, but there was plenty of sunlight beaming in through the many windows and a superb smell, or maybe it was an *absence* of smell: oxygen-rich air untainted by industry or human congestion.

All conveniences, both mod and antique, were on offer: Giraffe upright piano, electric shower, embroidered quilts, microwave oven, fridge, a concert-sized xylophone, an eighteenth-century spinning wheel, two computers, a complete prewar set of Grove's *Dictionary of Music and Musicians* (in Dutch), an ornate rack of wooden recorders (sopranino, descant, alto, tenor, plus a flageolet), several cordless telephones, even an assortment of slippers to wear around the house.

No, it wasn't any of these things that troubled Catherine as she accompanied her fellow Consort members on their guided tour of the château. It was entirely to do with the number of bedrooms. As the director escorted them from one room to the next, she was keeping count and, by the time he was showing them the galley kitchen, a burnished-wood showpiece worthy of Vermeer, she appreciated there wasn't going to be any advance on four. One for Ben, one for Julian, one for Dagmar, and . . . one for herself and Roger.

17

"The shops are not so accessible," the director was saying, "so we've put some food in the cupboards for you. It is not English food, but it should keep you alive in an emergency."

Catherine made the effort to look into the cupboard he was holding open for their appraisal, so as not to be rude. Foremost was a cardboard box of what looked, from the illustration, exactly like the vegetation surrounding the house. BOERENKOOL, it said.

"This really is awfully sweet," she said, turning the almost weightless box over in her hands.

"No," said Jan, "it has an earthy, slightly bitter taste."

So there were limits to his ability to understand his visitors from across the channel, after all.

It was around nine o'clock in the evening, almost nightfall, when Dagmar finally showed up. The director had long gone; the Courage Consort were busy with unpacking, nosing around, eating corn-flakes ("Nieuw Super Knapperig!"), and other settling-in activities. It was Ben who noticed, through an upstairs window, the tiny cycling figure approaching far in the distance. They all went to stand outside, a welcoming committee for their prodigal contralto.

Dagmar had cycled from Duidermonde railway station with a heavy rucksack on her back and fully laden baskets on both the front and rear of her bicycle. Sweat shone on her throat and plastered her loose white T-shirt semitransparently against her black bra and tanned ribcage; it darkened the knees of her electric-blue sports tights and twinkled in the unruly fringe of her jet-black hair. Still, she seemed to have plenty of energy left as she dismounted the bike and wheeled it towards her fellow Consort members.

"Sorry I took so long; the ferry people gave me a lot of hassles," she said, her huge brown eyes narrowing slightly in embarrassment. Like all colourful nonconformists, she preferred to zoom past awed onlookers, leaving them gaping in her wake, rather than be examined at leisure as she cycled towards them over miles of dead flat road.

"Not to worry, not to worry, we've not started yet," said Roger, stepping forward to relieve her of the bicycle, but it was Ben she allowed to take it from her. Despite his massive size, unfeasible for cycling, she trusted him to know what to do with it.

Swaying a little on her Reebok feet, Dagmar wiped her face with a handful of her T-shirt. Her midriff, like all the rest of her skin, was the colour of toffee.

"Well, childbirth hasn't made you any less of an athlete, I see," commented Julian.

Dagmar shrugged off the compliment as ignorant and empty.

"I've lost a hell of a lot of muscle tone, actually," she said. "I will try to get it back while I'm here."

19

"Toning up!" chirped Julian, straining, as he always did within minutes of a reunion with Dagmar, to remain friendly. "That's what we're all here for, isn't it?"

The thought of Dagmar's eight-week-old baby roused Catherine from her daze. "Who's taking care of little Axel?" she asked.

"It's not a problem," Dagmar replied. "He's going to be staying here with us."

This revelation made Julian's chin jut forward dramatically. Accepting delivery of Dagmar had already sorely taxed him; the prospect of her baby coming to join her was just too much to take.

"I . . . don't . . . know if that would be such a good idea," he said, his tone pensive and musical, as if she'd asked him his opinion and he had deliberated long and hard before responding.

"Is that so?" she said coldly. "Why not?"

"Well, I just thought, if we're being given this space—this literal and metaphysical space—to rehearse in, far away from noise and distractions, it . . . well, it seems odd to introduce a crying baby into it, that's all."

"My baby isn't a very crying baby, actually," said Dagmar, flapping the hem of her T-shirt with her fists to let the cooling air in. "For a male, he makes less noise than many others." And she walked past Julian, to stake her own claim to the Château de Luth.

"Well, we'll find out, I suppose," Julian remarked unhappily.

"Yes, I guess we will," Dagmar called over her shoulder. On her back, nestled inside her bulging rucksack, a spiky-haired infant was sleeping the sleep of the just.

By the time the Courage Consort settled down to their first serious run-through of *Partitum Mutante,* dark had come. The burnished lights cast a coppery glow over the room, and the windows reflected five unlikely individuals with luminous clarity. To Catherine, these mirrored people looked as if they belonged together: five Musketeers ready to do battle.

If she could just concentrate on that unreal image, shining on a pane of glass with a forest behind it, she could imagine herself clinging onto her place in this little fraternity. The rehearsals were always the hardest ordeal; the eventual perform-ance was a doddle by comparison. The audience, who saw them presented onstage as if they were a projection from far away, knew no better than that they were a closely knit clan, and this allowed them to behave like one. The artificiality of the concert platform was insulated against disturbing events: no one argued, or sulked, or asked her questions she couldn't answer, or expected her to say yes to sex. All they did was sing, in perfect harmony. Or, in the case of Pino Fugazza's *Partitum Mutante,* perfect disharmony.

"F-sharp there, Kate, not F-natural."

"Honestly?"

"That's what's written. On *my* printout, at least."

"Sorry."

The trick was lasting the distance from now till the premiere.

Late on the first night in the Château de Luth, tucked up in a strange, soft bed next to Roger, Catherine turned the pages of Extended Vocal Techniques by the *Extended Vocal Techniques* Ensemble of California. It was a book she resorted to sometimes to put her to sleep, but tonight it had the additional purpose of keeping physical contact off the agenda.

Roger was reading a coffee-table book on Karel Appel, a Dutch artist, that he had found in a bookshelf downstairs—or rather he was looking at the pictures, she supposed; she didn't think her husband had managed to learn Dutch for this adventure. He *might* have done, but she imagined she'd have noticed something if he had.

Slyly she glanced at him from time to time, without moving her head. He was sinking farther down in the bed, inch by inch. Her almost invincible insomnia would give her the edge soon enough, she hoped. She read on.

> Vowels can be defined linguistically by the characteristic band of overtones each contains. These bands are narrowed to specific pitches, so that the singer's voice resonates in a way that reinforces a single

harmonic partial of the fundamental being sung. Such reinforced harmonics make it possible to write in eight parts for four singers.

Catherine wondered if, rather than losing her sanity, she was perhaps merely getting old.

"Crazy character, this Karel Appel," remarked Roger.

"Mm," she said, drawing her knees up a little under the quilted eiderdown to better support her book. She wished this new piece by Pino Fugazza didn't require her and Dagmar to do so many things that distorted normal perception. Other people might think it was terribly exciting when two females singing in thirds made the airwaves buzz weirdly, but Catherine was finding that her nerves were no longer up to it. Even the way a sustained A-flat tended to make an auditorium's air-conditioning hum gave her the creeps lately. It was as if her face was being rubbed in the fact that music was all soundwaves and atoms when you stripped the Baroque wrapping paper off it. But too much sonic nakedness wasn't good for the spirit. At least that's what she was finding lately, since she'd started coming . . . adrift. A bit of Bach or Monteverdi might be more healing than what this Pino Fugazza expected of her.

Cowardly sentiments, she knew, from a member of the Courage Consort.

When Roger finally fell asleep, it was long past

midnight. She didn't know exactly what time, because the only clock in the room was Roger's watch, hidden underneath his pillow as he breathed gently off the edge of the bed. It was strange the things you forgot to bring with you to a foreign place.

Catherine laid *Extended Vocal Techniques* gingerly on the floor, drew the eiderdown up to her chin, and switched off the bedside light. The silence that descended on her then was so uncompromising that she was unnerved by it. It was as if the whole universe had been switched off.

On the threshold of sleep, she found herself wondering how a person might go about killing herself in an environment like this.

At dawn, there were birds. Nothing on too grand a scale, just a few piccolo chirps and twitterings from species unknown. How strange that in London, in her flat near the half-dozen trees planted by the council, there should always be such a racket in the mornings from throngs of birds making the best of things, while here, in the middle of a forest, so few voices should be raised. Either there were only a handful of birds out there, chirping at the tops of their lungs in a hopeless attempt to fill the vacuum, or else there were millions and millions of them, all keeping silent. Sitting in the branches, waiting for the right moment.

Catherine was aghast to find herself becoming

afraid: afraid of all the millions of silent birds, infesting the trees, waiting. And, knowing how irrational this fear was, she despised herself. Surely she was too crazy to live, surely it was high time she cleaned herself off the face of the planet, if she'd sunk to feeling anxiety even at the thought of birds sitting contentedly in a forest. It was as if the frayed and tangled wiring of her soul, submitted to God for repairs, had been entrusted to incompetent juniors instead, and now she was programmed to see danger in every little sparrow, dire warning in music, deadly threat from the love of her own husband.

Roger was sleeping like a stone beside her. He might wake any second, though; he never snuffled or fidgeted before waking, he just opened his eyes and there he was, fully conscious, fully functioning. Catherine looked at his head on the pillow, the head she'd once been barely able to resist stroking and kissing in adoration. She'd been so grateful he wanted her, so in awe of his conviction that he could shape her into something more than just another lost and self-destructive girl with a pretty soprano voice.

"You've got it inside you," he'd promised her.

Yearning, terrified, she'd left her father's house at long last, and given herself over to Roger Courage instead.

Now she lay next to him in this strange soft bed in Belgium, and she wished she could breathe some magic odourless chloroform into his open mouth, to keep him safely asleep while she worked up the courage to face the day.

She mentioned the unearthly silence of the night to the others, over breakfast. She was light-headed with relief by then: she'd leapt out of bed and got herself ready before Roger was able to rouse himself from an unusually deep sleep. She was already in the kitchen, fully dressed, before he made his way down-stairs to join his fellow Consort members. She was cooking *havermout*—porridge by any other name—for a ravenous unshaven Ben, and generally behaving like a sound-minded person.

"Good morning, darling," she said, as her husband appeared. He looked a bit nonplussed, padding down the stairs in his herringbone-patterned socks. (All the men were in socks, actually, caught between the château's house rule against wearing shoes and their own reluctance to wear the leather clogs provided for them.)

Julian, bleary-eyed and elegantly dishevelled, was nursing a coffee without drinking it. As soon as Catherine mentioned the silence, he said he'd noticed it too, and that it wasn't natural. He'd lain awake all night because of it.

Catherine shuddered; the thought of her and Julian lying awake at exactly the same time in the same house, with only a wall between them, was disturbing somehow. It wasn't that she disliked him really, but she was so thin-skinned now-adays, so hypersensitive, that this simultaneous

26

insomnia in a shared darkness was like unwelcome intimacy.

"And the way there's hardly any birdsong, in this big forest: that's a bit unsettling, don't you think?" she suggested hesitantly, wary of stepping into the spotlight of mental frailty but enjoying the idea of communication with her friends.

Dagmar was cutting fresh bread on the kitchen worktop, her snoozing baby lying swaddled in a blanket on the same surface, right near the breadboard, as if she meant to slice him next.

"That silence is what you get if you climb a mountain," she said, referring to her favourite pastime. "I like it."

Having failed to get any joy from womankind, Catherine looked back to the men. Ben was now busy with the *havermout*, however, spooning it through his big soft lips, and Julian had turned his attention to his coffee, so that left only Roger.

Her husband searched his soul briefly for some appropriate observation.

"A vocal acoustic as silent as this must be very rare, when you think about it," he said. "I mean, just think of that recording of Hildegard songs by Gothic Voices . . . There you have Emma Kirkby singing like a lark, and in the background you can hear cars accelerating along the road!"

Julian had to disagree.

"That's because the sound engineers placed the microphones such a long way back from the singers," he said, "to try and get that monastery acoustic. They should have miked the singers close up, and put some reverb on later."

"You can't mean that," protested Roger. Catherine had ceased to exist, forgotten as she tried to make toast for him under the oven grill. "The acoustics of a place are unique and precious."

"For a live performance, yes," agreed Julian. "I've never sounded better than in that cellar in Reykjavik, with the stone walls and everything. But Gothic Voices weren't performing, they were making a record. Who needs the Church of St. Jude-on-the-Wall in Hampstead if at the flick of a switch or the push of a fader you can have a churchy acoustic, without the bloody Volvo vrooming up the road?"

A smell of burnt toast started to pervade the kitchen. Little Axel coughed uneasily and started flapping his arms gently on the kitchen worktop, as if trying to fly away to a fresher square of air.

"Sorry," said Catherine.

Partitum Mutante was sheer pleasure for at least one of its performers: Benjamin Lamb. Pino Fugazza was obviously very taken with the sonorous chanting of Tibetan monks, and had written oodles of something very similar for the bass parts of his own piece. While the other members of the Courage Consort had to learn complicated and athletic melodies in perverse keys, Benjamin was required to hum like an organ for bar after bar after bar. At the very beginning of the piece, his vocalisations were

28

intended to convey the birth of the universe, no less, and he tackled this with an eerie resonance worthy of a holy Himalayan—indeed, of several.

"*Mwoooooooiiiinnng, mwoooooooiiiiinnng, mwooooooiiiinnng,*" he sang, from deep within his huge belly.

Pino Fugazza was cunning, though: he'd timed low baritone swoops for Roger to cover Ben's pauses for breath, creating the illusion of a ceaseless foghorn of bass. And, just when it seemed that the music was going to remain abyssally dark forever, Julian came in with a high, pure voicing of the first articulate word: "God"—pitched in G major, of course.

The real trouble came with the entry of the females, a reflection no doubt on the Italian's philosophy of human relations as filtered through Judeo-Christian tradition. The manuscript became alarmingly complex at this point, the notes crowding the bar lines like dense troops of ants squashed wholesale on the way to something irresistible.

Dagmar and Catherine sang till the sweat was falling off their brows onto the pages. They sang until their throats ached. They sang until they both felt moved to stare at each other imploringly, like two plantation slaves willing each other not to collapse, for that would be to invite a far worse fate. The hours were passing, not in linear flow, but in endless repetitions of two minutes here, five minutes there, and then the same two minutes from before, over and over and over.

Finally, as night was again falling, the Consort reached the end of the piece, and, one by one, each of the singers faded away, leaving Catherine to bring *Partitum Mutante* to its close. The very last note was a very high C, to be reached over several bars from two octaves below, then sustained for fifteen seconds, increasing in volume, then diminishing to nothing. Ecstatic that the end was in sight, Catherine sang it with the purity and sureness of a fife.

For several seconds after she had ushered the last traces of the note into oblivion, the rest of the Courage Consort sat mute. In the extraordinary quiet of Martinekerke forest, they breathed like babies, no one wanting to be the first to speak.

"I was worried about that one, I must confess," said Roger, finally. "Well done."

Catherine blushed and concealed her throat behind one hand.

"I just seem to be able to hit higher and higher notes all the time," she said.

The silence moved in again, as soon as she'd finished speaking, so she pressed on, making conversation to fill the void.

"Maybe if I'd had one of those fearsome Svengali mothers pushing me when I was young I could have been a coloratura by now."

Dagmar was uncrossing her lotused legs with a wince of discomfort, wiggling her naked feet—her own solution to the house-slipper dilemma.

"So what sort of mother did you have?" she asked.

Catherine looked up at the ceiling, to see what might be written there about what sort of mother she'd had.

"She was a cellist, actually," she replied meditatively, "in the BBC Symphony Orchestra."

"But I meant what sort of person was she?"

"Umm . . . I'm not really sure," murmured Catherine, her vision growing vague as she stared at the delicate mosaic of cracks in the paint overhead. "She was away a lot, and then she committed suicide when I was twelve."

"Oh, I'm sorry," said Dagmar.

It sounded odd, this effete Britishism, coming at robust volume from the German girl. The sharpness of her accent made the condolence sound like something else altogether, and yet there was nothing insincere in her tone: in fact, it was Dagmar's sincerity that really struck the discord. The phrase "Oh, I'm sorry" must have been composed by the English to be softly sung in a feminine cadence.

"Not your fault," said Catherine, lowering her gaze to smile at Dagmar. A ghostly blue after-image of the ceiling lamp floated like an aura around the German girl's face. "It was me who found her, actually. Me or I?—which is it, Roger?" She glanced at him, but not long enough to notice his frowning, eyebrow-twitching signal for her to stop talking. "She did it in her bed, with sleeping pills and a polythene bag over her head."

Dagmar narrowed her eyes and said nothing, imagining the scene and how a child might have taken it in. Julian couldn't contain himself, however.

"Did she leave a note?" he enquired.

"No," said Catherine. Roger was getting up,

31

rustling papers at the periphery of her attention. "Though the polythene bag wasn't a plain one. It was a UNICEF one, with pictures of smiling children all over it. I always wondered about that."

Even Julian couldn't think where to take the conversation from there.

"Tragic business," he said, getting to his feet to follow Roger into the kitchen.

Dagmar wiped her forehead with one arm. As she did so, the fabric of her top was pulled taut against her breasts, alerting her to the fact that she had leaked milk from her nipples.

"Excuse me," she said.

"How long has it been, do you think," enquired Roger in bed that night, "since we last made love?" Leading a singing group, he'd learned to hide his fault-finding under a consultative guise.

"I don't know," she said truthfully. "Quite a long time, I suppose." It would have been . . . undiplomatic to suggest otherwise, obviously.

The spooky silence of Martinekerke forest was back with them in the inky-black bedroom. Catherine wondered what had become of the moon, which she could have sworn was almost full last night. There must be clouds hiding it just now.

"So, do you think we might have a problem?" said Roger after a while.

"I'm sure it's nothing that won't come good," said Catherine. "The doctor did say that the anti-depressants might suppress . . . you know . . .

desire." The word sounded cringe-makingly romantic, a Barbara Cartland sort of word, or else a throwback to William Blake.

What is it that women do require?
The lineaments of gratified desire.

It was partly to save her from having to figure out what such terms as "lineaments" could possibly mean that Catherine had originally allowed Roger to pluck her out of St. Magdalen's College.

"Are you still listening to me?" he prompted now, in the vacuum of the noiseless night.

"Yes," she assured him. "I was just thinking."

"Thinking what?"

"I can't remember now." She giggled in embarrassment.

Roger lay still for another few seconds or minutes, then rolled onto his side—facing her. Not that she could see his face, but she could feel his elbow digging into the edge of her pillow and could sense, in the centre of the bed near her own thighs, the warmth of his . . . well, his desire.

"You're still a good-looking woman, you know," he said in a quiet, deep voice.

Catherine laughed out loud, unable to control herself. The faint praise, offered so solemnly, so seductively, at a time when neither of them could see a bloody thing, struck her as unbearably funny somehow.

"I'm sorry, I'm sorry," she whispered, mortified

lest Julian hear them through the wall. "It must be the antidepressants."

Roger slumped onto his back with an emphasis that rocked the bedsprings.

"Maybe you should stop taking them now," he suggested wearily. "I mean, have you felt suicidal lately?"

Catherine stared out of the window, relieved to see a pale glow of moonlight seeping into the sky.

"It comes and goes," she said.

Hours later, when he was asleep, Catherine began to weep in the silence. She wished she could sing to herself, something sweet and tuneful, a little Schubert *lied* or even a nursery rhyme. "Twinkle, Twinkle, Little Star" would do fine. But of course it wasn't possible. Her throat was sore from singing *Partitum Mutante,* and she lay in dread of waking her husband, in a strange bedroom in a forest in Belgium, with that wicked Julian Hind listening through the wall for her every snuffle. Oh my God, how had things come to this?

Suddenly, she heard a short, high-pitched cry from somewhere quite far away. It wasn't Axel, she didn't think; that boy slept like an angel all night through and, during the day, hardly uttered a sound unless you set fire to a slab of Belgian bread right near his nose.

Catherine's skin prickled electrically as the cry came again. It didn't sound human, or if it was, it was halfway toward something else. She wished she could slide across the bed, into the big protecting arms of someone who could be trusted to do nothing to her except keep her warm and safe. Such people were hard to find, in her experience.

Instead, she drew the bedclothes up to her mouth and lay very still, counting the cries until she fell asleep.

In the morning, she didn't manage to make an appearance at breakfast. She'd hoped to be there, bright-eyed and bushy-tailed, each morning before Roger, but the previous night's insomnia caught up with her and she slept till midday. Roger was long gone by the time she awoke. Score—Roger: one; Catherine: zero, then.

The sun was pouring in through the window, its heat boosting her body's metabolism to an itchy simmer. Just before waking, she'd been having a nightmare of suffocation inside a humid trans-parent sac; anxiously conscious at last, she fought her way out of the clammy bedclothes and sat up, drenched with sweat.

She showered and dressed, hearing nothing except the sounds she was making. Perhaps the others were sitting around downstairs, waiting to sing, but lacking their soprano. Perhaps they'd gone exploring together, leaving her alone in the Château de Luth with its spinning wheels and antique recorders and a bed she didn't know if she could bear to lie in again.

She needn't have worried. Arriving in the kitchen, she found Ben still in his XXL pyjamas, looking slightly sheepish as he sat alone at the sunlit bench, browsing through a four-year-old *Times Literary Supplement*.

He was such a strange man, Catherine thought. The oldest of them all, he was as baby-faced at fifty-five as he'd been when the Courage Consort first formed. He'd always been immense, too, though perhaps marginally bigger now than a couple of decades ago. Quietly competent and poised in every sphere of life, he had just this one area of weakness, his Achilles' stomach. Each concert tour brought more surprises from his store of hitherto unsuspected talents—last year he'd dismantled the engine of a broken-down tour bus and got it going with a necktie and two wedding rings—but he just wasn't terribly good at feeding himself.

"Hello," he said, and a rumbling noise not a million miles removed from the moans he contributed to *Partitum Mutante* issued from somewhere inside him.

Catherine had no doubt he could have solved whatever physical and intellectual challenges a cooking pot and a box of oats might pose, but, plainly, there was some reason why he couldn't bring himself to tackle them. He looked at Catherine, his eyes sincere in their supplication. He was telling her, with that look, that he loved his own wife dearly, but that his wife was in London and Catherine was here with him, and what were they going to do about it?

"Would you like some porridge, Ben?" she asked him.

"Yes," he immediately replied, colour rising to his great cheeks.

"Then I'll make us both some," she said.

It turned out that the Courage Consort had already been lacking its contralto even while its soprano slept the morning away. At first light, Dagmar had cycled off into the forest with Axel, and had not yet returned. Perhaps she'd gone to Martinekerke or Duidermonde to fetch more supplies; perhaps she was merely exercising. She was gone, anyway, so Roger was typing correspondence on one of the computers, Julian was reading a paperback in the sitting room, and Ben had been waiting around for someone to offer him breakfast.

"Say 'whoa,'" said Catherine as she began to pour the milk.

"Whoa," he murmured regretfully, when the bowl threatened to overflow.

Overhearing the sounds of nurture, Julian found his way back to the kitchen, where he'd fed himself on tinned rice pudding and coffee a few hours earlier. He was dressed in black jeans, a black Tshirt, black socks. From the top of his blow-dried head to where his ankles began, he looked like a French film star.

"Morning," he grinned, still holding his book aloft, as if he'd just glanced up from his reading and noticed the kitchen had sidled up to him.

"Hello, Julian," said Catherine, trying not to be sour-faced as the moment of benign simplicity—the bowl of hot oatmeal, herself as provider, Ben Lamb as mute recipient—was ruined. As Julian stepped casually between herself and Ben, she noted that the book spreadeagled in his elegant hands was some sort of thriller with a frightened female face on the cover, and she suddenly thought, *I really, really dislike this man.*

"Julian, would you like some porridge?"

During the first five words of her question his eyes lit up, but they dulled in disappointment when she reached the end.

"No thanks," he said. "There's nothing . . . ah . . . more substantial is there?"

"I don't know," said Catherine, gazing wistfully at Ben spooning the steaming *havermout* into his mouth. "Porridge is quite filling, isn't it?"

"I was thinking of eggs, actually," confessed Julian.

"Perhaps Dagmar will bring some back with her."

"Mm." Plainly, for Julian, the prospect of asking Dagmar to share food with him was not a realistic one.

Scraping the remnants of the *havermout* into a bowl for herself, Catherine asked Julian how he'd slept.

"Lay awake half the night again," he grumbled, settling himself on a stool. His paperback nestled on his lap, its glossy image of a wide-eyed beauty staring up from between his slim black thighs.

"You heard the cries, then?" said Catherine.

"Cries?"

"Cries, out there in the forest somewhere."

"Probably Dagmar's baby," he suggested. "Or bats."

She could tell he hadn't heard anything really.

"I definitely heard them," said Catherine. "Human. But terribly forlorn and strange. Just cries, no words."

Julian smiled indulgently.

"An infant crying in the night, / an infant crying for the light, / and with no language but a cry, eh?" he said, deadpan.

Catherine stared at him in uneasy puzzlement. Julian often came out with this sort of thing: a tantalising quote from one of her favourite Victorian or Romantic poets, delivered with a shrug as if it were an arch soundbite from a TV commercial or an election slogan of yesteryear made tacky, or poignant, or poignantly tacky, by hindsight.

Elsewhere in the house, a telephone rang.

"Ghostbusters," quipped Julian.

The call was from a young woman called Gina. She wanted to know if it was convenient for her to drive over this afternoon and clean 't Luitspelershuisje, change the bed linen, that sort of thing.

Catherine was relieved when Roger told her this. She hadn't expected domestic help somehow; after the director's indifference to their baggage, she'd assumed it wouldn't be Dutch. But if someone could come and do something about the sweat-soaked sheets on the bed she'd have to share with Roger tonight, that would make a big difference.

Minutes after Roger passed on the message about the maid, Dagmar returned from her adventures, hot and bothered. She barged into the kitchen, plastic bags in each fist, Axel still on her back. He was whimpering and grizzling.

"*Moment mal, moment mal,*" she chided him, dumping groceries on the kitchen bench. The *Times Literary Supplement* was obscured by yoghurts, fresh apricots, crispbreads, cheeses, avocados, cold meats, coffee, cartons of "Vla met echt fruit!," plastic flip-top containers of baby-wipes—and eggs.

Roger was already gone; Ben Lamb followed him gracefully, recognising that there wasn't room in the kitchen for all this bounty, Catherine, Dagmar, Julian, and himself as well. Julian hesitated, his eyes on the eggs. He was thinking he might be able to put up with the irritating noise of the baby if there were omelettes on the horizon.

But Dagmar sat heavily on a stool right opposite him and hoisted Axel over her shoulder, depositing him on her lap. Then, hitching her T-shirt up, she uncupped one breast and guided her baby's mouth to the nipple.

"Excuse me," said Julian, leaving the women to it.

Catherine sat at the kitchen bench, staring abstractedly into Ben's porridge bowl. It was so clean and shiny it might have been licked, though she imagined she would have noticed if that were the case. She herself tended to half eat food and then forget about it. Roger didn't like that for some reason, so, back home in London, she'd taken to hiding her food as soon as she lost her appetite for it, in whatever nook or receptacle was closest to hand. *I'll finish this later*, she'd tell herself, but then the world would turn, turn, turn. Days, weeks later, ossified bagels would fall out of coat pockets, furry yoghurts would peep out of the jewellery drawer, liquefying black bananas would lie like corpses inside the coffins of her shoes.

She hoped she wasn't doing it here in the Château de Luth, though chances were that she was. Roger was probably cleaning up after her, refraining from saying anything because of the other people. Could she perhaps be getting Alzheimer's instead of going crazy? At forty-seven she doubted it was very likely . . . Still: there was something so very blameless and . . . nonnegotiable about Alzheimer's. Nobody would think of telling you to pull yourself together, or get impatient for you to return to your sex life. You wouldn't have to take Prozac anymore, and if somebody found a hoard of half-eaten apples behind the television, well, they'd understand.

And when you died, you wouldn't even know what was happening. You'd just dither absent-mindedly into the next world, blinking mildly in the light of the Almighty.

Catherine's eyes came into focus on the *Times Literary Supplement,* from which she had removed the food and neatly put it away in refrigerator and cupboards minutes ago. The *TLS* was open at the letters pages, and nine distinguished academics from all over Britain and the USA were arguing about the dedicatee of Shakespeare's sonnets, taking it all very personally. *Correspondence on this matter is now closed,* warned the editor, but after nigh-on four hundred years it was pretty obvious that the sonnets argument, like all arguments, would run forever without resolving anything. As for Catherine, she had no opinion, except that it would be nine different kinds of hell to be married to these men.

"You can eat any of the food that you want," Dagmar said.

Catherine had forgotten the German girl was there, and looked up with a start.

"Oh . . . thank you," she said.

"Except if I'm the only one of us who's going to be shopping, I'll need to have some extra money soon," added Dagmar. Her baby was still sucking at the breast, placid as a sleeping kitten.

"Just mention it to Roger, he'll take care of it," said Catherine. She hadn't signed a cheque or set foot in a bank in years. Latterly she had a little plastic card which gave her money out of a slot in the wall, providing she could remember a four-digit number—and the card, of course. There was nowhere in Martinekerke forest where that little plastic card could be inserted.

"How did you sleep last night, Dagmar?" asked Catherine, carrying Ben's bowl to the sink.

"Perfect," said Dagmar.

"You didn't hear anything unusual, in the small hours of the morning? Like a cry from the forest?"

"Nothing wakes me," said Dagmar, looking down at Axel, "except him, of course."

This seemed unlikely, given the child's almost noiseless functioning, but Dagmar must know what she was talking about. Catherine was struck by how, when the German girl was looking down at the baby at her breast, her slim, taut-skinned face acquired a double chin, adding five years to her age. There was a pale scar on Dagmar's fore-head, too, which Catherine had never noticed before. Wrinkles of the future, cicatrices of the past, all the million marks recording a private life that no outsider could ever understand.

"Are you enjoying yourself here?" asked Catherine.

"Sure," Dagmar replied. "It's good they provide us with this space. I've been a professional musi-cian now for ten years, and I have a kid; it's about time somebody pays for us to rehearse, yeah?"

"But the place itself, and the piece itself—are you enjoying those?"

"I don't care at all about Pino Fugazza's music," shrugged Dagmar, removing Axel from her breast. Saliva gleamed on her nipple and areola, prompting immediate loss of eye contact from Catherine. "I want to sing it well. If I get too bored with the music put in front of me, I should get off my ass and compose some of my own, yeah?"

Catherine, still embarrassed at her own queasiness about the spittly nipple, was even more thrown by this turn the conversation was taking. The American-accented "ass" instead of "arse" emphasised Dagmar's foreignness even more than her German accent usually did, and her frank indifference to the commission that had brought them all here was startling. Strangest of all was this notion that you could compose yourself, if you were dissatisfied with the music you were given.

"You write music?" At the bottom edges of her vision, Catherine registered that the T-shirt was coming down, covering the perturbing swell of flesh.

"Sure," said Dagmar, finding a more convenient spot to lay her boy's wispy head. "Don't you?"

Catherine had never once dreamt of composing a note. She played the piano competently, could get by on the flute, could hear a piece of music playing in her head just by reading the score—though not as accurately as Roger could hear it, of course. When it came to score reading, she imagined her brain as an old radio, fading out now and then, and Roger's brain as a CD player, extracting every nuance with digital efficiency. As for the prospect of making her *own* marks on the staves: no, that was inconceivable. The only times she ever sang a note that was different from what had been written for her,

Roger was always there to say, "F-sharp, Kate, not F-natural," or whatever.

"I'm sure I don't have what it takes," she told Dagmar.

The German girl wasn't passionately motivated to disagree, her brown eyes as dark and opaque as Belgian mocha chocolate.

"If you think so." She shrugged.

Catherine flinched inwardly: she'd been hoping for reassurance. How strange these Germans were, not understanding that a declaration of unfitness was really a plea for encouragement. Perhaps it was a good thing they hadn't won the Battle of Britain.

"I haven't had the right training, for a start," Catherine said. "People like Pino Whatsisname have studied composition for years and years."

Dagmar was plainly unawed by this reminder of Pino's credentials.

"Humming to yourself in the bath is composing, don't you think?" she said, hugging Axel up onto her shoulder. "I sing to myself when I'm out cycling, and to my kid. It's not *Partitum Mutante* I'm singing, that's for sure."

She grinned, and Catherine grinned, too. It was a nice, safe place to leave the conversation.

"I'm going to put Axel to bed now," said Dagmar. "You should go out for a walk, don't you think? Everything is perfect out there—the weather, the forest, everything."

"I'd like that," promised Catherine. "I really would. But maybe Roger wants us to start now."

The look she got from Dagmar then was enough to shame her into finding her shoes.

Gina the maid arrived in a little white Peugeot just as Catherine was stepping out the door—excellent timing, since it meant that Roger couldn't be angry about the delay in the rehearsals, could he?

Slightly awed at her own daring waywardness, Catherine cast off from the house without even explaining herself to anyone, hurried into the fringe of the forest, then peered through the sparse trees back at the château. Roger and Julian were competing to welcome Gina, who, contrary to expectations, was a blond twentysomething with a figure like a dancer and work apparel to match. Everything in the Netherlands was of better quality than you thought it would be. Even the vacuum cleaner that Gina was struggling to remove from her vehicle's backseat without the assistance of foreigners looked like a design award winner that could suck anything into its sleek little perspex body.

To the best of Catherine's knowledge, Roger had never been unfaithful to her. It wasn't his style. Once he made a commitment to something, he stuck with it and never let go, no matter what. No matter what. Nor was a sudden heart attack or stroke likely to take him from her. He was four years older than her, but very fit. They would be together always, unless she died first.

Catherine turned her back on the château and wandered deeper into the trees. As she walked she

46

kicked gently at the soft, rustling carpet of fallen leaves and peaty earth, to leave some sort of trail she could follow later if she got lost. The sky was clear, the breeze gentle. Her footsteps would remain, she was sure.

During the war, the Nazis had probably killed people in these woods. The war had come to Belgium, hadn't it? She was vaguely ashamed to concede that she wasn't sure. She didn't really know much about anything except singing. Roger had rescued her from postadolescent misery at St. Magdalen's College and, forever after, had taken responsibility for the world at large. He told her what he thought might interest her, vetted out what in his opinion she'd rather not know. Then again, she was terribly forgetful, especially lately. Roger possibly *had* told her about Belgium and World War II once, but she would have forgotten it by now.

Anyway, assuming there *had* been Nazis in this forest, this would have been a perfect spot to execute people. Catherine wondered what it would be like to be rounded up, herded to the edge of a communal grave, and shot. She tried to feel pity for those who didn't wish to die: women with children, perhaps. All she could think of was what a mercy it would be to have the burden of decision shouldered by someone else: a Nazi to lead you from prevarication to the grave, where he would shoot you in the back of the head, a place you couldn't reach yourself.

Then, a few years later, a French Robin Hood

and his Merry Men would ride their horses over your bones, twirling their colourful pennants, delighting children all over Europe.

After fifteen minutes or so, Catherine stopped walking and squatted against the mossy bough of a cedar, making herself comfortable on the forest bed. The ground was quite safe to rest her bottom—her ass?—on; it seemed to have been designed by Netherlandish scientists to nourish vegetation without staining trousers. The warmth of the sun, diffused by the treetops, beamed vitamin D onto her skin. All around her, pale golden light flickered subtly on the greens and browns, the leaves breathing out their clean, fragrant oxygen.

Composers are often inspired by nature, she thought. Beethoven's *Pastoral* Symphony, Vaughan Williams, Delius, that sort of thing. What did nature mean to her? She tried to decide, as if God had just asked her the question.

Nature meant the absence of people. It was a system set up to run without human beings, concentrating instead on the insensate and the eternal. Which was very relaxing now and then. But dangerous in the long run: darkness would fall, and there would be no door to close, no roof over one's head, no blankets to pull up. One wasn't an animal, after all.

Catherine stood up and slapped the leaves and fragments of bark off the seat of her jeans. She'd had enough nature for one day. It was time she was getting back to the house.

Walking back along the path she'd made, she became aware of all the birds that must be sitting in the trees all around and above her. A few were twittering musically, but the vast majority were silent. Looking down at her. It didn't bear thinking about; she concentrated on the sound of her own feet rustling through the undergrowth.

Her quickening breathing sounded amazingly loud in the stillness, and as she walked faster the breaths became more like voiced utterances, with an actual pitch and timbre to them. Exactly like avant-garde singing, really: the vocalisations of a terrorised soul.

She was almost running now, stumbling on loose branches and clods of earth she had kicked up earlier. The sunlight was flickering much too fast through the trees, like malfunctioning fluorescence, lurid and cold. Had she lost track of time again? Was she hours away from home?

What would she do if she heard the cry?

The thought came suddenly, like an arrow shot into her brain. She was alone in the forest of Martinekerke with whatever had wailed out to her during the night. Its eyes were probably on her right now, glowing through the trees. It was waiting for the right moment to utter that cry again, waiting until she had blundered so close that it could scream right in her ear, into the nape of her neck, sending her crashing to her knees in panic. Catherine ran, whimpering anxiously. She would be a good girl from now on, if only Roger would come and rescue her.

49

Breathless, half-blind, she broke into the clearing. For all the intensity of her dread, she'd taken only a couple of minutes to put the forest behind her; she hadn't strayed very far from home at all. The château was right there across the road, and the little white Peugeot parked outside spoke of the impossibility of supernatural cries.

"OK, time for *Partitum Mutante*," said Roger to her, as soon as she stepped across the threshold.

Rehearsals went badly that day. Ben, Dagmar, and Catherine were game enough, but Roger was irritable, strangely unsettled. Julian had his mind on something else and lost his place in the score at every small distraction—like Gina leaving the house, for example. He watched her through the sparkly clean windows as she loaded her equipment into her car, and his cue to sing the words of the Creator God went by unnoticed.

Politely hostile words between Julian and Roger were mercifully interrupted by another phone call. It was a journalist from a Luxembourg newspaper, trying to find a story in the Benelux Contemporary Music Festival.

Those members of the Consort who were not Roger Courage sat idle while Roger handled the enquiries, the first of which was evidently why Pino Fugazza's piece was called *Partitum Mutante*. This was one of many questions that Catherine had never thought to ask Roger, so she made the effort to listen to his reply.

"Well, my Italian is pretty rudimentary," he purred into the mouthpiece, implying quite the opposite, "but I gather the title isn't Italian as such, or even Latin. It's more a sort of multilayered pun on lots of things. There's a play on *partita*, of course, in the sense of a musical suite, as well as some reference to *partum*, in the sense of birth. *Mutante* then suggests mutant birth, or a mutant musical form . . ."

Catherine's attention wandered to the forest outside. A deer was grazing right near the window. It was really awfully nice out there, seen from indoors. She must go walking in the woods more often, face her fears, not be such a baby.

"I do think it's awfully important to give performers of newly commissioned music adequate rehearsal time," Roger was saying to the journalist from Luxembourg. "Too often when you go to a première of a contemporary vocal work, you're hearing singers flying by the seat of their pants, so to speak, on a piece they've only just learnt. There hasn't been time to master it fully, to capture the nuances and inflections. You have to remember that when a traditional vocal group does Handel's *Messiah* or some such chestnut, they can virtually sing it in their sleep. What we, in the Courage Consort, are trying to do with *Partitum Mutante* here in this splendid château is learn it to the point when we can sing it in our sleep. That's when the real work can begin."

Moments later, when Roger was off the phone

and sitting down with his fellow Consort members, Catherine said, "I thought it meant underpants."

Dagmar chuckled throatily, a release of tension. Roger looked at his wife as if he had every expectation that she would resume making sense very soon, if he only stared hard enough into her eyes.

"*Mutante*," Catherine explained. "I could've sworn it meant underpants."

"I'm sure it's to do with mutation, dear," Roger warned her mildly, rolling his eyes from side to side to remind her they were not alone in their apartment now. But she was not to be brushed off like that. She had been to Italy only last year, singing Dowland and Byrd. En route, she'd done a bit of shopping in Rome, thrilled and terrified to be off Roger's leash for an hour.

"I remember when I was in Rome," she said, "I needed some briefs. I was in a big department store and I didn't know how to ask. Obviously I couldn't show them my knickers, could I? So I looked up underpants in a guide book. I'm sure it said *mutante*." She laughed, a little embarrassed. "That's the sort of thing I do remember."

Roger smirked wearily.

"On that note," he said, "coffee, anyone?"

When they were all sitting together again, Roger informed them that Pino Fugazza himself would be paying a visit to them tomorrow, to see—or rather hear—how they were progressing with his masterpiece. What needed to be discussed before then, obviously, was which parts of *Partitum Mutante* they needed to rehearse most intensively, in order to make the best possible impression on the composer.

It was a tense discussion, at least among those of the Consort who had an opinion on the matter. Julian felt the tenor-rich passages were most under-developed, while Dagmar was sure that the contralto and soprano harmonics were far short of ideal; Roger tended towards the view that these weak-nesses could be improved at leisure within a binding framework woven by a clean and confident baritone line. An impasse was reached with no singing done. Julian went to the toilet, Roger went for a breath of fresh air, and Dagmar went to look in on Axel.

Left alone with Ben, Catherine said, "I've still got the briefs, actually. They lasted superbly. I might even have them on right now."

Ben rested his massive head on his hands and half closed his eyes, smiling.

In bed that night, Roger finally allowed himself to be badly behaved.

"You don't love me anymore," he said, as Catherine cringed beside him, rolling herself up into a ball.

"I don't know, I don't know," pleaded Catherine, her voice strangled to a squeak by tears and too much singing.

"Have you given any more thought to stopping the antidepressants," he enquired tonelessly, tugging at the blankets to cover the parts she had exposed.

"I've already stopped," she said. It was true. It

had been true for days. In fact, despite Roger's frequent gentle reminders, back in London, about all the items she should make sure she took with her to Belgium, she had somehow managed to leave those little pills behind. The cardboard box they lived in had got beetroot and mayonnaise soaked into it somehow, and she hadn't been up to fixing the problem. The box of pills, the spilled food, the handbag in which all this had happened: she'd left the whole caboodle under her bed at home. The bed she slept in alone, in the spare room.

"Really?" said Roger, lying right next to her in Belgium. "So how are you feeling?"

She burst out laughing. She tried desperately to stop, mindful of Julian in the next room, but she couldn't; she just laughed louder, sobbing until her sides were aching.

Later, when the fit had subsided, Roger lay with his head and one hand against her back.

"We have a big day tomorrow," he sighed, heavy with loneliness on the brink of sleep.

"I won't let you down," Catherine assured him.

No sooner had his breathing become deep and regular than the first cry echoed eerily in the forest outside.

"Come for a cycle with me," Dagmar invited her next morning after breakfast.

Catherine blushed, her hands trembling up to her throat. She could not have been more nonplussed if she'd just been asked to go skinny-dipping in Arctic waters with a bunch of fervent Inuits.

"Ah . . . it sounds lovely, Dagmar, really, but . . ."

She looked to Ben for help, but he was busy spooning up the *havermout,* content as a . . . well, a lamb.

"I haven't got a bicycle, for one thing," she pointed out gratefully.

"I found one at the back of the château," said Dagmar. "It's an old one, but sound construction. A good Dutch bike. But if you think you can't ride an old one, you can use mine."

Defeated, Catherine allowed herself to be led out of the house. The German girl's thighs and buttocks flexed like an Olympian's as she walked, the shiny aquamarine of her tights contrasting sharply with the pastel blue of Catherine's evenly faded jeans. There were the two bicycles already parked, side by side at the edge of the road, gleaming in the sun. There was no escape except to say *No, I don't want to,* which had always been impossible for Catherine.

"They say you never forget how to ride a bicycle," she said, approaching the machines warily, "but I've forgotten the most amazing things, you know."

"It's all right, we'll take it easy," said Dagmar, preoccupied with strapping on the Axel rucksack.

Catherine examined the seats of the two bikes, feeling the leather curves, trying to imagine how hard or soft each might be between her legs.

"Erm . . . which of these is better for someone who hasn't . . . you know . . ."

Dagmar shrugged, quite an achievement for a woman with a six-kilo human being on her back.

"One bike has about a hundred gears, the other has none," she said. "But travelling slow on a totally flat road, it makes very little difference."

And so it began. Catherine's anxiety turned to relief as she discovered she could still ride perfectly well. Her other fear, that Dagmar would speed ahead of her, was equally unfounded. The German girl cycled at a slow and even pace—not because she was making any special effort to be considerate, but because she had simply sent an instruction down to her legs to rotate at a certain number of revolutions per minute. Whatever the reason, Catherine was able to keep up, and, to her growing delight, found herself cycling along the dark smooth road, forest blurring by on either side, a breeze of her own creation blowing through her hair.

After a mile or two, she was even confident enough to speak.

"You know, I really am enjoying this terribly much," she called across to Dagmar.

Axel, nestled against his mother's back, his face barely distinguishable under a woollen cap, opened his eyes wide. He wasn't used to fellow travellers.

"You will sing better tonight," Dagmar asserted confidently. "It's good for the lungs, good for the diaphragm, good for everything."

"You'll have me going mountain climbing with you next!" It was the sort of comment you could make in the Low Countries, without fear.

"Great idea," called Dagmar. "There are some OK mountains just over the German border, in Eifel. Three hundred kilometres' journey, maximum."

Catherine laughed politely, possibly not loud enough for Dagmar to hear over the whirring of the wheels. In the distance, a church spire gave advance warning of Martinekerke.

It was a proud and glowing Catherine who cycled up to the front door of the Château de Luth an hour later. She had been exploring the big wide world, making a bit of a reconnaissance of the local facilities. Now she and Dagmar were bringing back the goodies.

The three men watched them mutely as they, two flushed and sweaty women, carried groceries into the kitchen.

Mind you, Catherine hadn't actually been able to carry much on the bicycle with her, having neglected to bring along any sort of bag. But she'd taken responsibility for the eggs, wrapping them up in a sweater she was too hot to wear, and nestling them safely in the basket of her strange Dutch bike.

"You may need another shower, dear," Roger suggested *sotto voce* as she was pouring a big glass of milk down her glistening throat. "Pino Fugazza will be here soon."

Abruptly, for no apparent reason, little Axel started bawling.

Of all the composers that the Courage Consort had ever met, Pino Fugazza proved to be the least charming. Perhaps they ought to have been forewarned slightly when they'd found out that his sizeable fortune derived not from the honest popularity of avant-garde music but was inherited from the family business of automatic weapons. However, in a spirit of not blaming the child for the sins of his parents, they reserved judgment. In any case, as Ben pointed out, Tobias Hume, a favourite composer of the Courage Consort's seventeenth-century repertoire, had actually been a professional killer in his time, and that didn't detract from the merit of the songs he'd written for the viol.

The image of a dashing Tobias Hume laying sword aside to pen the immortal "Fain would I change that note" was rudely extinguished by the very real arrival, in a black Porsche, of Pino Fugazza. He swanned into the château wearing a red Galliano shirt with dozens of little black ears printed on it, black Armani slacks jingling with loose change, and shoes with tassels on them. His smile was startlingly unappealing.

"How do you do," said Catherine, playing hostess, though she could tell at a glance that she had no desire to know the answer.

"*Prima, prima,*" exclaimed the composer, bounding into the house with a lightness of step possibly achieved by the feeble claims of gravity on his four-foot-eleven frame. Already bald at twenty-nine, he had a face like a macaque. Even Ben Lamb, who was usually most careful not to gape at people with physical peculiarities, couldn't quite believe what Fate had delivered.

Pino had parked his Porsche as close to the front door as possible without driving it into the house, and, as Signor and Signora Courage strove to make him welcome, he kept glancing through the window, as if worried that some delinquent forest animal was liable to drive off with his splendid vehicle.

Calmed at last, he spread his arms beneficently and invited the music to begin.

The Courage Consort sang *Partitum Mutante*—all thirty-one and a half minutes of it, without a break—and they sang it rather well, all things considered. As always, when it came to the challenge of a real performance to an audience—even an audience of one—they moved Heaven and Hell to overcome their differences. Julian managed nuances of some humility, Dagmar conformed for the greater good, Roger slowed his tempo when his wife faltered at one point, gathering her back into the fold. And, at the finish, Catherine sang the last notes with even greater virtuosity than she had before.

Arboreal silence settled on the house as the Courage Consort slumped, exhausted, on the farther shores beyond conventional harmony. They had swum a long way in turbulent sonic waters with barely a pause for breath. Rather disconcertingly, as they struggled up from the sea, they felt themselves being looked down on by a macaque in an infant's pyjama jacket.

"Bravo," the macaque leered.

Pino Fugazza was, briefly, lavish in his praise, then, at length, lavish in his criticism. As he spoke, he left the score unconsulted at his side; matters of mere pedantic detail did not seem to trouble him. Instead, it was larger issues that he felt the Consort were failing to grasp. Issues like the very essence and spirit of the piece.

Gesticulating balletically, Fugazza swayed before them, his slacks jingling as he strove to make himself understood in his own avant-garde version of English.

"It shoot be more extrème, but more soft also," he exclaimed after many abortive attempts. To illustrate some sort of sublime paradox, he threw his stubby claws violently up into the air, then let them float languorously down like dying squidlets. "Like somesing very lo-o-o-ost, from ze bottom of a well."

There was a pause.

"Quieter?" Roger attempted to translate.

Fugazza nodded, pleased that progress was being made at last.

"Yes, very much quieter," he said, "but wiz no losing of . . . of psychic loudity, you understand? Quiet, but loud inside ze ears . . . Like ze sound of water dripping from a . . . a . . ."

"Tap?"

"Faucet. Dripping in ze night, when everysing is quiet. So it's loud, yes? Silence, amplificated."

They all pondered this a moment, then Roger said:

"You think we should sing extremely quietly, but have microphones amplifying us?"

"No! No! No microphones!" cried Pino, plucking invisible offending objects from the air in front of him and casting them straight into a lake of fire. "Ze loudness comes from ze . . . ze intensity, yes?"

"Intensity of emotion?"

"Intensity of . . . of concentration. Concentrated like . . . like . . ."

"Chicken stock cubes?" suggested Dagmar in a poisonous murmur as she played with a strand of her hair.

"Like a bullet," affirmed the composer in triumph. "A bullet is very small, yes? But ze effect is . . . is . . ." He grimaced, betrayed yet again by a language so inferior to Italian.

Catherine, resisting the urge to leave her body and float up to the ceiling after her big exertion, tried hard to help him find the right word. She imagined the effect of a bullet entering someone's flesh—someone who didn't want to die.

"Dreadful," she said.

"I hate him," hissed Dagmar when he had driven away.

"It's probably a communication problem," said Roger spiritlessly.

"I hate him," repeated Dagmar, intently flicking her damp hair with her thumb and index finger. "That's what I'm communicating to you."

"Well," sighed Roger, "he has *his* idea of the piece, we have ours . . ."

Ben was padding around the house like a bear, going from window to window, opening them all wide. It wasn't until he was opening the biggest, nearest window that his fellow Consort members noticed the whole château stank of the sort of perfume probably derived from scraping the scrotums of extremely rare vermin.

United in their dislike of the composer, the Courage Consort devoted the next week to getting on top of *Partitum Mutante*. By day, they did little other than sing. By night, they slept deeply. Even Catherine was less troubled by insomnia than ever before. No sooner had the piercing, plaintive cry of the creature in the forest woken her up than she was drifting off again.

In the Château de Luth, she was developing a kind of routine, to which, amazingly for her, she was able to adhere religiously. She who had always seemed programmed to disappoint, abandoning the best-laid late-night plans in the suicidal torpor of dawn, was now getting up early every morning, cooking porridge for Ben, going off for a bike ride with Dagmar, then freshening herself up for a long afternoon's singing. Looking down at herself in the shower as the misty water cascaded over her naked flesh, she wondered if she was merely imagining a more youthful appearance, or if it was real.

Roger was retreating into a hard shell of professionalism, a state he tended to go into whenever a deadline was growing too near. It was by no means unattractive: Catherine liked him best this way. He focused utterly on the task at hand—in this case, the fiendish *Partitum Mutante*—and strove to understand the nature of his fellow singers' difficulties, keen not to dissipate their precious energy or fray their raw nerves. Rather than demanding endless repetition, he was tolerant when things went wrong. "Let's not waste our breath," he'd quip gravely, whenever an argument loomed. Afterwards, he'd lie flat on his back in bed at night thinking up ways to make the next performance run more smoothly. Catherine almost felt like embracing him when he was like this. If she could have been sure he'd stay flat on his back, she would have rested her head on his shoulder and stroked his frowning brow.

She wondered if Ben was happy. He was such a mountain of poise, but was he happy? Every night at 11:00 P.M. sharp, he would retire to his little room, to a bed that could not possibly be big enough for him. What did he do to make himself comfortable? Did he miss his wife? Was his own body, when he was horizontal, intolerably heavy, like an unwanted other person bearing down on him?

Before this fortnight in Martinekerke, it would never have occurred to Catherine to wonder about such things. Each Consort member had his or her separate life, mysterious to the others. Their personal happiness or unhappiness was irrelevant to the purpose that brought them together—at least, that was the way it had always been in the past. They would rendezvous at the Lambs' place in Tufnell Park, like five football fans who were going to sit down and watch a televised match together, and with barely a word spoken they would start singing a Josquin *Miserere* or whatever was on the agenda. Ben's wife would make herself scarce, cooking what smelled like very large quantities of Asian food in the kitchen. In all the years the Consort had been doing this, Catherine had never even got around to asking what nationality Mrs. Lamb was. She looked Vietnamese or something, and dressed like an American hair-care consultant. At intervals, she would serve her guests coffee and cake: apple and cinnamon slices subtly impregnated with stray aromas of prawns, turmeric, garlic, soy sauce. Now and then Catherine got a hankering to ask Ben a few questions about his wife, but as the years passed she tended to feel she might have missed the right moment to raise the subject.

Julian was an unknown quantity too, although there were signs that he might inspire complex emotions in more people than just his fellow singers. Once, while the Consort were rehearsing at the Lambs' house, a drunken man, shouting unintelligible abuse, had kicked dents into Julian's car parked just outside. Julian went white and sat

64

waiting stoically as the characteristic *bimff* of breaking windscreen resounded in the night air. Again, no one in the Courage Consort asked any questions. Julian's extramusical activities were his own affair. He could sing the pants off any tenor in England, that was the important thing.

Even Catherine's mental frailties were tolerated, as long as they didn't interfere with the music. Last year, she'd even been able to show up for rehearsals with both her wrists wrapped in snowy white bandage, and nobody had mentioned it. By contrast, if she dared to spend a few minutes too long in Heathrow's toilets when the Consort had a plane to catch, she was liable to hear an admonitory summons over the airport PA.

As for Dagmar, the most recent addition to the group, she'd stuck with the Courage Consort because they gave her fewer hassles than any of her many previous liaisons. After walking out on the Dresden Staatsoper because the directors seemed to think she was too sexually immoral to sing opera (her last rôle for them was Berg's prostitute Lulu, for God's sake!) she'd been a bit wary of these smiling English people, but it had turned out OK. They allowed her to get away with tempestuous love affairs, even illegitimate pregnancy, as long as she showed up on time, and this she had no trouble with. For nine months of ballooning belly she'd never missed a rehearsal; she'd given birth, prudently, during the lull between Ligeti's *Aventures* in Basle and the "Carols Sacred and Profane"

Christmas concert in Huddersfield. That was good enough for Roger Courage, who had sent her a tasteful congratulations card without enquiring after the baby's name or sex.

This strange fortnight in Martinekerke, though, was making them so much more real to each other as human beings, at least from Catherine's point of view. Living together as a family, cooking for each other, seeing the stubble on each other's faces— well, not on hers, of course—watching each other's hair grow, even . . . Catherine was finding it all really quite exciting. She could definitely see herself, before the fortnight was over, asking Ben about his wife, or cycling all the way to Duidermonde.

It was her impression, though, that Julian was not a happy man. As the days in the Château de Luth wore on, he was growing increasingly restless. Not restless in the sense of lacking ability to concentrate on the task at hand; he worked as hard on *Partitum Mutante* as any of the Consort. Nor restless in the sense of itching for physical exercise; he was quite content to let Dagmar and Catherine cycle daily to Martinekerke to fetch their supplies. No, it appeared he was restless sexually.

In London, Julian was a lone wolf, never actually seen with a partner. Roger and Catherine had always assumed he must be gay, what with the Freddie Mercury ansaphone message and the waspish comments he was wont to make, but in Martinekerke it became clear that, at the very least, he was prepared to stoop to females if nothing better was available.

Females were in limited supply in the forest, but Julian made the most of what strayed his way. The first time Gina had come to clean the château, Julian behaved (Roger told Catherine later) like a gallant lord of the manor receiving an impressionable guest. The girl's flat refusal to let him carry her equipment frustrated this line of approach and so he hurried back indoors to launch Plan B, leaving the formal introductions to Roger. When, less than two minutes later, the time came for Gina to be introduced to Julian Hind, "our tenor," he was already seated at the piano, playing a piece of Bartók's *Mikrokosmos* with serene intensity. He turned his cheekbones towards her and raised his eyebrows, as if he'd never glimpsed her before this moment, as if she'd just blundered, childlike, into a sanctum whose holiness she couldn't be expected to understand. He inclined his head in benign welcome but did not speak. Disappointingly, Gina did not speak either, preferring to get down to business. With the plug of the vacuum cleaner nestled in her hand, she nosed around the room, murmuring to herself: "Stopcontact, stopcontact"—the Dutch word for electrical outlet, apparently. Once the vacuum cleaner started its noisy sucking, Julian stopped playing the piano and settled for a more passive role. Then, all too soon, Catherine had returned from her walk in the woods, and it was time for *Partitum Mutante*.

The second time Gina came to the château, five days later, Catherine was actually there, privileged to witness the changes that Julian's growing discontentment had wrought on him. It was an extraordinary sight, an unforgettable testament to the power of accumulated sexual craving.

To begin with, he welcomed her at the door as if she were royalty—the English rather than the Dutch kind—and immediately tried to get her to sit down with him on the sofa. When she insisted that she had work to do, he followed her from room to room, raising the volume of his velvety tenor to compete with the noise of motorised suction and clanking, sloshing buckets. He guessed, correctly, that she was involved in the expressive arts and only doing this cleaning work as a way of supplementing a government grant. He guessed, correctly, her birth sign, her taste in music, her favourite drink, her preferred animal. Dashing into the bathroom to fetch her some Elastoplast when she'd cut her finger, he returned naked from the waist up and with water combed through his hair, complaining of the heat.

Catherine didn't dare follow them upstairs, so she made herself a cup of tea, wondering despite herself whether there was going to be some sexual activity in the château after all. By the time she saw Julian again, ten minutes later, he was installed on the sofa, fully dressed, glowering into a book. A strange sound—bed-springy, rhythmic—from upstairs was eventually decoded as Gina slamming an iron onto a padded ironing board.

Four days before the end of the fortnight, Jan van Hoeidonck dropped in to see how they were getting on. Reacquainting himself with Catherine Courage, he at first thought she must be the sporty German contralto he'd been told about, she was so tanned and healthy-looking. He'd fixed Catherine in his memory as a slightly stooped middle-aged lady dressed in taupe slacks and a waterproof, with a freshly washed halo of mousy hair; here she was in green leggings and a berry-stained T-shirt, standing tall, her hair shiny, plastered with sweat. She'd just been for a long cycle, she said.

The real German woman appeared moments later, cradling a sleeping baby in her arms. She shook Jan by the hand, supporting her infant easily in one arm as she did so.

"This is Dagmar Belotte," said Roger, "and . . . erm . . . Axel."

As a way of breaking the ice, Jan made the mistake of asking Dagmar, rather than Roger Courage, what the Consort's impression of Pino Fugazza had been.

"I hate him," she volunteered. "He is a nutcase and he smells bad."

"Extraordinary composer, though, of course," interjected Roger.

"Don't you check them out before you give them money?" said Dagmar.

The director smiled, unfazed. The German girl's

69

frankness made much more sense to him than the strange, twitching discomfiture of the pale Englishman.

"Pino is very crazy, yes," he conceded. "Sometimes crazy people make very good music. Sometimes not. We will find out."

"And if it's bad?" enquired Dagmar.

Jan van Hoeidonck pouted philosophically.

"Bad music is not a problem in our circles," he said. "Ten years later, it's completely disappeared. Biodegradable. It's not like pop music. Bad pop music lasts forever. Johann Strauss. Herman's Hermits. Father Abraham and the Smurfs. These things will never die, even if we put a lot of effort into killing them. But for bad serious music, we don't need to do anything. It just sinks into the ground and it's gone."

"But Jan, what do *you* think of *Partitum Mutante*?" asked Roger.

"I haven't heard it yet."

"You've seen the score, surely."

The director gratefully accepted the steaming cup of coffee being handed to him by Mrs. Courage.

"I am a facilitator of musical events," he explained carefully. "I read budget sheets. There are enough crescendos there, I promise you." His face was solemn as he said this, though there was a twinkle in his eyes.

Dagmar excused herself and the conversation moved on to more general matters, like the château and its facilities. Were the Consort enjoying their stay? How was the environment suiting them?

The big fat man called Ben Lamb, sitting in the far corner of the room, made a small gesture indicating no complaints. Roger Courage said something to the effect that concentration on a musical project made the outside world cease to exist, but that during the brief moments when his Consort was not beavering away at *Partitum Mutante*, the Château de Luth and its setting were very attractive indeed. Julian Hind deflected the question, preferring to discuss with the director the feasibility of a hire-car from Antwerp or Brussels.

"I was wondering," Catherine said, when Julian, appalled at the high cost of Netherlandish living, had retreated to his room. "You've had many artists staying in this château over the years, haven't you?"

"Very many," affirmed the director.

"Have any of them ever mentioned strange noises in the night?"

"What kind of noises?"

"Oh . . . cries from the forest, perhaps."

"Human cries?"

"Mmm, yes, possibly."

She and Roger were sitting together on the sofa. On the pretence of bending down to fetch his plate of cake off the floor, Roger knocked his knee sharply against hers.

"Excuse me, dear," he warned, trying to pull her back from whatever brink she was dawdling towards.

Unexpectedly, however, the director had no difficulty with her claims of mysterious cries in the night; in fact, he went pensive, as if faced with something that genuinely might lie outside the scope of art and arithmetic.

"This is a story I have heard before, yes," he said. "In fact, it is a kind of legend about the forest here."

"Really," breathed Catherine, gazing at him over the top of her steaming coffee mug. Roger was already fading away next to her.

"It began, I think, at the end of the war. A . . ." Jan van Hoeidonck paused, checking the Dutch-English dictionary in his head. "A mental defective mother . . . can you say this in English?"

"It's all right," said Catherine, loath to explain political correctness to a foreigner. "Go on."

"A mental defective mother ran away from Martinekerke with her baby, when the army, the liberating army, was coming. She didn't understand these soldiers were not going to kill her. So she ran away, and nobody could find her. For all the years since that time, there are reports that a baby is crying in the forest, or a . . . a spirit, yes?"

"Fascinating," said Catherine, bending forward to put her cup down on the floor without taking her eyes off Jan van Hoeidonck. His own gaze dropped slightly, and she realised, with some surprise, that he was looking at her breasts.

I'm a woman, she thought.

Roger spoke up, pulling the conversation back towards Pino Fugazza and his place in contemporary European music. Had the director, in fact, heard *anything* by the composer?

72

"I heard his first major piece," Jan replied, un-enthusiastically. "*Precipice*, for voices and percussion—the one that won the Prix d'Italia. I don't remember it so well, because all the other Prix d'Italia entries were played on the same night, and they also were for voices and percussion. Except one from the former Soviet Union, for flügelhorn and ring modulator . . ."

"Yes, but can you remember *anything* about Fugazza's piece?" pursued Roger.

The director frowned: for him, dwelling on musical events that were in the past rather than the future was obviously quite unnatural.

"I only remember the audience," he admitted, "sitting there after four hours of singing and whispering and noises going bang without warning, and finally it's over, and they don't know if it's time to clap, and soon they will go home."

Roger was getting politely exasperated.

"Well . . . if you haven't heard *Partitum Mutante*, what makes you think it'll be any better?"

Jan waved a handful of fingers loosely around his right temple.

"He has since that time had a big mental breakdown," he said. "This could be a very good thing for his music. Also, public interest in Fugazza is very high, which is good for ticket sales. He is very famous in the Italian press for attacking his wife with a stiletto shoe at the baggage reclaim of Milan Airport."

"No!" said Catherine incredulously. "Is she all right?"

73

"She is very fine. Soon I think she will be divorced and very wealthy. But, of course, the music must stand or fall on its own qualities."

"Of course," sighed Roger.

Later, when the director had left, Roger stood at the window, watching the yellow minibus dwindling into the distance, on the long black ribbon towards Brussels. As he watched, the sun was beaming through the windowpanes like a trillion-watt spotlight, turning his silver hair white and his flesh the colour of peeled apple. Every age line and wrinkle, every tiny scar and pockmark from as far back as adolescence, was lit up in harsh definition. Eventually the intensity of the light grew too much for him; he turned away, fatigued, blinking and wiping his eyes.

Noticing that Ben Lamb was still sitting in the shady corner of the room, and Catherine lying sweating and sleepy on the couch, he allowed himself to express his first pang of doubt about the value of the project they were all engaged on.

"You know, I'm really rather tired of this glamour that madness is supposed to have, aren't you?" he said, addressing Ben. "It's the little marks on the score that ought to be sensational, not the behaviour of Italian lunatics at airports."

Catherine, not happy at the disrespect with which madness was being tossed about here, said, "Couldn't this Pino fellow just be young and excitable? I wouldn't presume to judge if anyone was definitely mad. Especially an Italian I've only met once. He surely can't be *too* barmy if he drives a Porsche and wears Armani."

"Poetically put, dear—if somewhat mysterious in reasoning," remarked Roger.

"No, I meant, he's obviously not . . . um . . . otherwordly, is he?"

There was a pause as the men pondered the significance of this word.

"What do *you* think, Ben?" said Roger.

"I think we should sing as much as we possibly can in the next four days," said Ben, "so that, by the time of the premiere, we can at least be sure of being less confused than Mr. Fugazza."

And so they sang, as the sun blazed in the sky and the temperature inside the château climbed towards thirty degrees Celsius. It was worse than being under a full rig of stage lights; all five of them were simmering in their clothes.

"We'll end up performing this in the nude," suggested Julian. "That'll put some sensuality into it!"

The others let it pass, appreciating that he was a man on heat.

When, at last, they were all too tired to go on, Roger and Julian went to bed—not with each other, of course, though lately Julian looked as if he might soon consider anything, even his fellow Consort members, as a sexual possibility. His initial disgust at seeing Dagmar breastfeed had, with the passing days, softened to tolerance, and then hardened to a curiosity whose keenness embarrassed everyone except himself. Dagmar, usually indifferent to the petty libidos of unwanted men, grew self-conscious, and the feeding of her baby became an increasingly secret act, perpetrated behind closed doors. In Julian's presence, she tended to fold her arms across her breasts, protectively, aggressively. After half an hour staring Julian down, she would leap up and start pacing back and forth, a dark band across her bosom where her sweaty forearms had soaked the fabric of whatever she was wearing.

On the night of the director's visit, with *Partitum Mutante* finished off and Julian safely gone to bed, Dagmar sat slumped on the couch, Axel at her breast. Ben sat by the open window, staring out at a sky which, even at a quarter to eleven, still had some daylight left in it. The unearthly quiet was descending again, so that even the drip of a tap in the kitchen could be heard from the front room.

Oddly revived by having had her milk sucked from her, Dagmar decided to take Axel out for a walk in the forest. She did not invite Catherine; the older woman guessed this must be one of those times when Dagmar wanted to have the run of the world alone with her baby, explaining things to him in German.

"Be careful," said Catherine as they were leaving. "Remember the legend."

"What legend?"

"A mother and her child disappeared in that

forest once, at the end of the war. Some people say the baby is still out there."

Dagmar paused momentarily as she made a mental calculation.

"Well, if we meet a fifty-seven-year-old baby on our walk, maybe Axel will like to play with him," she said, and sauntered into the dark.

Left alone with Ben, Catherine weighed the pros and cons of going to bed. On the pro side, she was exhausted. But the house had absorbed so much heat that she doubted she would sleep.

"Do you want anything, Ben?" she offered.

"Mm? No, thanks," he replied. He was still sitting by the window, his white shirt almost transparent with sweat. For all his bearlike bulk, he had no body hair, as far as Catherine could see.

"How are you, anyway?" she asked. It seemed a faintly absurd question, this late in the night.

"Tired," he said.

"Me too. Isn't it funny how we've lived here together, day after day, and sung together endlessly, and yet we hardly say two words to one another?"

"I'm not much of a conversationalist."

He closed his eyes and leaned his head back, as if about to release his soul into the ether, leaving his body behind.

"You know," said Catherine, "after all these years, I know hardly anything about you."

"Very little to tell."

"I don't even know for sure what nationality your wife is."

"Vietnamese."

"I thought so."

Their communication eddied apart then, but not disturbingly. The room's emotional acoustic was not full of shame and failure, like the silences between her and Roger. Silence was Ben's natural state, and to fall into it with him was like joining him in his own world, where he was intimately acquainted with each sleeping soundwave, and knew no fear.

After a while, sitting in the golden-brown front room with Ben in the stillness, Catherine glanced at her watch. It was almost midnight. Ben had never stayed up so late before.

"Did you always want to be a singer?" she asked.

"No," he said. "I wanted to carry on coxing."

She laughed despite herself. "Carry on *what*?" She was reminded of those dreadful comedy films her father had never allowed her to see, even when she was old enough to be going out with Roger Courage.

"At university," Ben explained, "I was a coxswain in a rowing team. I called instructions through a loudhailer. I enjoyed that very much."

"What happened?"

"I became involved in the anti-Vietnam war movement. Cambridge wasn't the most left-wing place in those days. I lost most of my friends. Then I got fat."

You're not fat, Catherine wanted to reassure him,

as a reflex kindness, then had to struggle to keep a straight face in the moon face of absurdity. Reassurance is such a sad, mad thing, she thought. Deep inside, everyone knows the truth.

"What do you really think of *Partitum Mutante*, Ben?"

"We-e-ell . . . it's a plum part for a bass, I have to admit. But I don't see us singing it far into the twenty-first century somehow."

Again the silence descended. Minutes passed. Catherine noticed for the first time that there were no clocks in the Château de Luth, except for those inside the computers and the oven, and the wrist-watches worn by the human visitors. Perhaps there had once been splendid old timepieces which some previous guest had stolen—she imagined Cathy Berberian stealthily wrapping an antique clock up in her underwear as she was packing her suitcase to go home. Perhaps there had never been clocks on these walls at all, because the château's furnishers had understood that the sound of seconds ticking would have been maddening, intolerable, in the forest's silence.

Suddenly, there was a plaintive, inarticulate wail from outside, a cry that was more high-pitched and eerie than anything Axel was capable of. Catherine's flesh was thrilled with fear.

"There!" she said to Ben. "Did you hear that?"

But, looking across at him, she saw that his eyes were shut, his great chest rising and falling rhythmically.

Catherine jumped up from the couch, hurried to the front door. She opened it—very quietly so as not to wake Ben—and peered out into the night, which was impenetrably dark to her unadjusted eyes. The forest was indistinguishable from the sky, except that there were stars in one and not the other. Catherine was half-convinced that Dagmar and Axel had been consumed by some lonely demon, swallowed up into the earth, never to be seen again. It was almost disappointing when, minutes later, both mother and baby materialised out of the gloom and strolled up to the château, Dagmar's white trainers luminescing.

"Did you hear the cry?" said Catherine as Dagmar reached the threshold.

"What cry?" said Dagmar. Axel was wide-eyed and full of energy, but his mother was exhausted, overdue for bed. She swayed in the doorway, looking as if she might consider handing her baby over to Catherine for a while.

Next day, Roger telephoned Pino Fugazza, to tell him that there was a problem with *Partitum Mutante*. A technical problem, he said. They'd rehearsed it so thoroughly now, he said, that they were in a position to tell the difference between awkwardnesses that arose from unfamiliarity with the score and awkwardnesses that might be . . . well, in the score itself.

While Roger spoke, the other members of the Courage Consort sat nearby, wondering how Pino was going to react, especially as Roger was pushed, *poco a poco*, to be more specific about the nature of the problem—which was that, in a certain spot, Pino's time signatures just didn't add up. The Italian's daring musical arithmetic, a tangled thicket of independent polyrhythms, was supposed to resolve itself by the 404th bar (symbolising the 4,004 years from Creation to Christ's birth), so that Roger and Catherine were suddenly singing in perfect unison, joined in the next bar by Julian and Dagmar while Ben kept lowing underneath.

"The thing is," said Roger into the phone, "by the 404th bar, the baritone is a beat behind the soprano."

A harsh chattering sound came through the receiver, indecipherable to the overhearers.

"Well . . ." grimaced Roger, adjusting his glasses to look at the computer screen. "It's possible I've misunderstood something, but three lots of 9/8 and one lot of 15/16 repeated with a two-beat rest . . . are you with me?"

More chatter.

"Yes. Then, from the A-flat, it goes . . . Pardon? Uh . . . Yes, I see it right here in front of me, Mr. Fugazza . . . But surely thirteen plus eight is twenty-one?"

The conversation was wound up very quickly after that. Roger replaced the telephone receiver on the handset and turned to his expectant fellow members of the Consort.

"He gives us his blessing," said Roger, frowning in bemusement, "to do whatever we want."

It was a freedom none of them would have predicted.

Later that afternoon, while the Courage Consort were taking a break to soothe their throats with fruit juice, a car pulled up to the house. Roger opened the door and let in a grizzled photographer who looked like a disgraced priest.

"Hello! Courage Consort? Carlo Pignatelli."

He was Italian, but worked for a Luxembourg newspaper, and he'd been sent to cover the Benelux Contemporary Music Festival. He had already seen publicity material on the Consort, and knew exactly what he wanted.

Dagmar was nursing a glass of apricot juice alone in the front room while the English members of the group hung around the oven trying to make toast. Pignatelli made a beeline for the German girl, who was wearing black tights and a white cotton blouse.

"You're Dagmar Belotte, right?" He sounded alarmingly as if he'd learned English from watching subtitled cockney soap operas; in truth, he'd just returned to the bosom of the European press after ten alcoholic years in London.

"That's right," said Dagmar, putting her drink down on the floor. She was going to need both hands for this one, she could tell.

"You're into mountaineering, right?" said

Pignatelli, as if getting a few final facts straight after a gruellingly thorough interview.

"That's right," said Dagmar.

"You wouldn't have any of your gear with you, would you?"

"What for?"

"A picture."

"A picture of what?"

"A picture of you in mountaineering gear. Ropes." He indicated with his hairy hands where the ropes would hang on her, fortunately using his own chest rather than hers to demonstrate. "Axe." He mimed a small act of violence against an invisible cliff face.

"There are no mountains here," said Dagmar evenly.

The photographer was willing to compromise. Quickly sizing up the feel of the château's interior, his eyes lingering for microseconds on the rack of antique recorders, he said, "Play the flute?"

"No."

"Mind holding one?"

Dagmar was speechless for a moment, which he took as assent. Surprisingly fleet on his feet, he bounded over to the recorders and selected the biggest. Handing it over to her, he leered encouragingly, then drew his camera from its holster with a practised one-handed motion. Dagmar folded her arms across her breasts, clasping the recorder in one fist like a police baton.

"Could you put it in your mouth maybe?" suggested the photographer.

"Forget it," said Dagmar, tossing the instrument onto a nearby cushion.

"Is there a grand piano?" rejoined the photographer, quick as a flash. She surely wouldn't object to leaning in and fingering a few strings, canopied by the lid.

"No, it's a . . ." The word Dagmar was looking for refused to translate itself from German. She considered saying "erect" but decided against it. "Not grand," she said, her big eyes narrowing to slits.

Undaunted, the photographer peered outside to gauge the weather. Mercifully, a loud noise started up from somewhere inside the house, a disconsolate human cry that could not be ignored.

"Excuse me," muttered Dagmar as she strode off to find her baby.

The photographer turned his attention immediately to Catherine.

"Is it true," he said, picking up Dagmar's half-finished tumbler of juice, "a soprano can shatter glass?"

That night, when the singing was over, the château was even hotter than the night before. Catherine found herself alone in the front room with Julian, everyone else having gone to bed.

Julian was on his hands and knees in front of a bookcase, peering at the spines. He had finished everything he'd brought with him to Belgium, all the thrillers and exposés, and was now in the market for something else. He read no Dutch, so such tomes as *Het Leven en Werk van Cipriano de Rore (1516–1565)* didn't quite hit the spot, but he was fluent in French and—surprisingly, to Catherine—Latin.

"Really? Latin?" she said, as if he'd just revealed a facility for Urdu or Sinhalese.

"I don't know why you're so surprised," said Julian, his bottom—ass?—arse?—in the air as he studied the titles. "We sing Latin texts all the time."

"Yes, but . . ." Catherine cast her mind back to the last time she'd sung in Latin, and was surprised at the ease with which she recalled the words of Gabrieli's "O Magnum Mysterium." Something was happening to her brain lately, an unblocking of the channels, a cleaning of the contours. "We use translations. Or I do, anyway. Roger prints out parallel English and Latin texts for me, and that's how I learn what it all means."

"I don't need Roger to tell me what it all means," muttered Julian as he pulled an ancient-looking volume out of the bookcase. It slid smoothly into his hands, without the billow of dust Catherine might have expected—but then, Gina had dusted there only a few days ago.

"I think I'll go for a walk," said Catherine.

"You do that," said Julian. He was in a peculiar, intense state, as if he'd passed right through frustration into whatever lay beyond. Sitting cross-legged on the carpet, he was opening the fragile old book in his lap and bending his head towards its creamy pages, his damp black hair swinging down over his forehead. For Catherine, it was all indefinably unnerving, and her instinct was to get away.

Roger would still be awake, though, in the bed upstairs. Roger, Julian, and the dark forest of Martinekerke: she was stuck between the devil, and the devil, and the deep blue sea.

Catherine set off into the night, with a windcheater loosely draped over her T-shirt, and only a pencil torch to guide her through the dark. She didn't even switch it on, but kept it in the back pocket of her jeans, hoping that her sight would adjust to the starlight, the way the eyes of people like Dagmar evidently did.

Walking across the road, Catherine felt and heard, but could not see, her feet stepping off the smooth tarmac into the leafy perimeter of the forest. She rustled cautiously forward, trusting her body aura to warn her of approaching trees. Overhead, the sky remained black; perhaps the awful humidity meant that it was cloudy.

She removed the torch from her pocket and shone its thin beam onto the ground before her. A small circle of leaves and earth stood out from the darkness like an image on a television screen. It moved as she tilted her wrist, scooting back-wards and forwards through the trees, growing paler. After only thirty seconds of use, the batteries of the torch were getting tired already; the feeble power supply just wasn't up to the challenge of a whole forest full of night. She switched it off, and hoped for the best.

You know what you've come here for, don't you? challenged a voice from inside her. She wasn't alarmed: it was her own voice, intimate and patient, not the terrifying stranger who had once commanded her to swallow poison or slice through the flesh of her wrists. It was just a little harmless internal conversation, between Catherine and herself.

No, tell me: what am I here for? she asked in return.

You're waiting for the cry, came the answer.

She walked deeper into the forest, afraid and unrepentant. A breeze whispered through the trees, merciful after the trapped and stagnant heat inside the house. She was just getting a breath of fresh air, that was all. There was no such thing as ghosts: a ghost would always be revealed, in the clear light of day, to have been an owl, or a wolf, or one's own father standing in the door of one's bedroom, or a plastic bag caught on a branch, waving in the wind. The dead stayed dead. The living had to push on, without help or hindrance from the spirit world.

Catherine's eyes had adjusted to the dark by now, and she could see the boughs of the trees around her, and an impression of the ground beneath her feet. Wary of getting herself lost but wanting to stay in the forest longer, she wandered in circles, keeping the distant golden lights of the house in sight. She clapped her palms against trees as she passed them, swinging around like a child on a pole. The roughness of the bark was heavenly on her hands.

After perhaps half an hour she grew conscious of a full bladder—all those glasses of fruit juice!—and squatted in a clearing to pee. Her urine rustled into the leaves, and something unidentifiable scratched softly against her naked bottom.

I hope nothing jumps into me while I'm exposed like this, she thought, as, in the château, the lights went out.

Next morning, Ben Lamb, waiting for his *havermout*, looked up expectantly as someone entered the kitchen. But it was only Julian, come for his coffee.

"I made a real find last night," Julian said, as the kettle hissed sluggishly.

"Mm?" said Ben.

"An original edition of Massenet's songs, printed in 1897, including some I'm sure have never seen the light of day, just sitting there on the shelf. Never been looked at!"

"How do you know it's never been looked at?"

"The pages were still uncut. Just think! Totally . . . virgin."

"And did you cut them, Julian?"

"You bet I did," grinned Julian. "And it was a delicious sensation, I can assure you." He was peering into the refrigerator as Dagmar, fully dressed and with Axel already in her rucksack, passed by the kitchen.

"Save a few eggs for other people, please," she called over her shoulder.

Julian contorted his face into a gargoyle sneer, beaming malice in her direction as the front door slammed shut.

"*Jawohl, mein Kommandant!*"

Ben sighed. The Courage Consort were reaching the limit of their ability to coexist harmoniously, at least in such hothouse conditions. It was only 10:30 A.M. now, and the temperature was already stifling; not the best conditions for negotiating the treacherous vocal labyrinths laid out for them by Mr. Fugazza. According to an imported *Times* Dagmar had brought back from Martinekerke yesterday, rain was pelting down all over London and the Home Counties: when would the clouds break here?

Roger walked into the kitchen, a veteran of yet another telephone call.

"Wim Waafels, the video artist, is coming here this afternoon," he said, looking glum.

"Some problem?" enquired Ben.

Roger ran his fingers through his hair, large patches of sweat already darkening the underarms of his shirt, as he searched for a way to summarise his misgivings.

"Let's just say I don't imagine Dagmar is going to like him very much," he said at last.

"Oooh," camped Julian, "fancy that! A soulmate for me. You never know your luck in a big forest."

Roger shambled over to the stove, tired of holding his little family together, day after day. He poured himself a cup of tea from the kettle that had boiled, unnoticed.

"Has anyone seen our soprano?" he said, trying to keep his voice light.

Ben shook his head. Julian stared directly into Roger's face and saw there a look he had a special facility for recognising: the look of a man who is wondering where his wife slept last night.

"She went walkabout," said Julian. "After the witching hour."

Roger sipped at his tea, not a happy man.

Then, a few minutes later, the front door clattered open and footsteps sounded in the hallway. Julian's jaw hardened in anticipation of another German invasion.

Instead, Catherine walked into the kitchen. She walked slowly, dreamily, in no hurry to focus on the men. Her hair was a bird's nest of tangles, her skin was flushed, her eyes half closed. Tiny leaves and fragments of twig clung to the calves of her leggings.

"Are you all right, Kate?" said Roger.

Catherine blinked, acknowledging his existence by degrees.

"Yes, yes, of course," she responded airily. "I've been out walking, that's all."

She padded over to the stove, patting her

husband's shoulder as she passed because the poor thing looked so miserable.

"Would anyone like some porridge?" she said, finding Ben's face exactly where she expected it to be and contemplating it with a smile.

Though there were two hours to kill before Wim Waafels was due to arrive, the Consort did not sing. By unspoken mutual agreement, they were giving *Partitum Mutante* a rest while the weather did its worst. Ben sat by the window, nursing a headache and indigestion; the others mooched around the house, fiddling with the musical instruments, books, and ornaments. Julian played Beethoven's "Für Elise" on the piano, over and over, always getting stuck in the same spot; Catherine squatted at the spinning wheel, touching its various parts tentatively, trying to decide if it was meant to be functional or was just for show. Roger sat at the computer, browsing through the score of Paco Barrios's *2K+5*, reminding himself that there would be life after *Partitum Mutante*.

By the time Mr. Waafels ought to be arriving, the British members of the Courage Consort had—again by unspoken mutual consent—pulled together, resolved to be philosophical in the face of whatever the visit might bring. Only Dagmar was exempt from the prevailing mood. She sensed something in Roger's manner which made her suspect that the overextended strings of her tolerance were about to be twanged.

"You've talked to this man, have you?" she queried warily.

"On the phone, yes," said Roger.

"Is he a nutcase?"

"No, no . . ." Roger reassured her breezily. "He sounds quite . . . focused, really."

"So he is OK?"

"He . . . he has a very thick Dutch accent. Much thicker than Jan van Hoeidonck's, for example. He's very young, I gather. *Your* age, perhaps. Not an old fuddy-duddy like us, heh heh heh."

Dagmar's eyes narrowed in contempt. She'd always had a lot of respect for Roger Courage, but right now he was reminding her of the directors at the Dresden Staatsoper.

A vehicle could be heard approaching the Château de Luth, though it was half a mile away yet, invisible.

"That'll be him now," said Roger, smoothly making his escape from Dagmar to take up a position at the window. But when the vehicle came into view, it proved to be not a van or a car, but a motorcycle, roaring through the stillness of Martinekerke forest in a haze of benzine, its rider in grey leather, studded gloves, and a silver helmet, like a medieval soldier come looking for Thierry la Fronde and his band of merry men.

Once they invited him in, Wim Waafels proved to be, physically at least, a slightly more impressive specimen than Pino Fugazza; he could hardly fail to be. Then again, as he was taking off his helmet

92

and leather jacket in the château's front room, he did cause several members of the Courage Consort to meditate privately on the infinite scope of human unattractiveness.

He was a young man—twenty-five, reportedly, though he looked seventeen, with an overweight teenager's awkward posture. He wore ochre-coloured cords, military boots, and a large threadbare T-shirt on which was printed a much-enlarged still from Buñuel's *Un Chien Andalou*—the razor blade hovering above the woman's eye. Waafels's own eyes were bloodshot and deep-set, full of sincere but rather specialised intelligence. Perspiration and the odd pimple glittered on his pumpkin face; his head was topped with a bush of bleached white hair corrugated with gel.

"Erm . . . is it hotter or cooler, driving here on a motorcycle?" asked Catherine, struggling to make conversation as she handed him a tall drink of orange juice.

"Bose," he replied.

Though Wim's English vocabulary was good, his accent was so thick that he seemed to have been schooled by a different process from that used by all the other Dutch people they'd met—interactive CD-ROMs, maybe, or those little translator gadgets you saw in brochures that fell out of the *Radio Times*.

More worrying than his accent was the way he blushed and stammered when introduced to Dagmar: evidently he had a weakness for big-breasted young German women with muscular limbs, even if they did not look overly friendly. Perhaps he mistook Dagmar's glower for the mock-dangerous pout of an MTV babe.

"Hi. I'm Wim," he told her.

"Great. Let's see the video," said Dagmar.

Small talk having reached its apex, they all got promptly down to business. Wim had brought with him a video of his images for *Partitum Mutante*. On the spine of the cassette, in silver felt-tip, he had scrawled "PArTiTEm M!" This, more even than Mr. Waafels's appearance, caused alarm bells to toll inside the overheated skulls of the Courage Consort.

There was a slight delay as the television proved not to be connected to the video player. To Wim, this was an eyebrow-raising oddity, something that could only be explained in terms of the Courage Consort having fiddled with the leads and plugs while using digital samplers, MIDI keyboards, or other sophisticated technologies. He could not have guessed that the Courage Consort simply did not watch television.

Wim Waafels connected the machines with a practised, casual motion, the closest he came to physical grace. He then asked for the curtains to be drawn so the daylight wouldn't interfere with the clarity of his images. Roger obliged, or attempted to.

"Ken it not be moor dark den dis?" Waafels enquired uneasily, as the room glowed amber in the muffled sunlight.

Roger fiddled with the curtains, trying out one thing and another.

"That's as dark as we're going to get it," he said.

They all kneeled around the television, except for Ben, whose massive body did not permit him to kneel; he sat on the divan, insisting he could see perfectly well from a little farther back.

"OK," announced Wim. "De oddience is here, you are on de staitch, de lights go out—blekness!"

The tape started to whirr through the machine, and the screen, at first snowy, went perfectly black. It remained perfectly black for what felt like a very long time, though it was probably only thirty seconds—a minute, at most.

"You heff to imegine you are singing, of coorse," Wim Waafels counselled them.

"Of course," said Julian, moving a little closer to the television so that he couldn't see Dagmar's face.

The blackness of the screen was finally softening at its core, to a reddish-purple—or maybe it was an optical illusion brought on by eyestrain. But no: there was definitely something taking shape there.

"In de beginning, de ooniverse woss widout form, yes?" explained Waafels. "Darkness moofs on de face of de deep." The videotape as it passed along the machine's play heads made a faint squeaking noise which set Catherine's teeth on edge; she wished Ben could be making his sonorous Tibetan moans to give this gloomy void a human soundtrack.

After an eternity, the inky amorphous swirls

finally coalesced into . . . into what? Some sort of glistening mauve orifice.

"Now, do you know what iss it?" challenged Waafels.

There was an awkward pause, then Ben spoke up.

"I believe I do," he said, his voice calm and gently resonant. "It's a close-up of a larynx, as seen by a laryngoscope."

"Ferry goot, ferry goot!" said Waafels, happy to have found a soul on his wavelength. "In de beginning woss de word, yes? De word dat coms from widdin de focal cords of Got."

Another eternity passed as the larynx trembled open and shut, open and shut, twinkling in its own juices. Catherine felt queasiness accumulate in her stomach as the picture became lighter and pinker, and she glanced sideways at her companions, to see if they were feeling it too. Roger's face was rigid with concentration, loath to miss any crucial details if and when they should come. Julian and Dagmar, though they would probably have hated to be told so, looked strikingly similar: incredulous, open-mouthed, beautiful in their disdain. Catherine longed to turn and look at Ben, but she didn't want to embarrass him, so she reapplied her attention to the yawning aperture of flesh on the screen. Some sort of digital magic was being employed now to morph the larynx; the labia-like *plica vocalis* and *vallecula* were evolving, cell by cell, into the vulva of a heavily pregnant woman. Then, with agonising slowness, silent minute upon silent minute, the vagina dilated to reveal the slick grey head of a baby.

The Courage Consort spoke not a word as the *largo*-speed birth took its vivid and glistening course on the screen before them. They were all intimately aware, though, that the duration of *Partitum Mutante* was a shade over half an hour, and the timer on the video player kept track of every second.

When, at long last, the newborn Adam or Planet Earth or whatever he was supposed to be was squirming out into existence, his slow-motion slither almost unbearably eventful after what had gone before, the Courage Consort began to breathe again. Soon, they knew, the lights would go on.

"Of coorse," said Wim Waafels by way of qualification, "it's a total different effect like dis, on only a smol screen."

"I'm sure it is," said Roger.

"In de life performance, de immitch will be ferry ferry bik, and you will be ferry smol. It will . . . enfelope you."

"Mmm," said Roger, as he might have done if a Bedouin chieftain was watching him eat sheep's eyes at a politically delicate banquet.

"Mmm," agreed Catherine, suddenly glad to have her husband around to suggest *le mot juste*.

Then, with heavenly timing, little Axel started crying upstairs, and Dagmar's ascension from the room was a fait accompli before Wim Waafels had a chance to ask her what she thought. He looked a little crestfallen to have lost the only member of his generation so abruptly, but he turned to the older, less gorgeous members of the Consort without ill feeling.

"Dis giffs you an idea, I hope?" he said to Julian, plainly the next-closest to him in age.

"It does, it does," said Julian archly. "I'm sure no one who sees this extraordinary work of yours will ever be able to forget it. My only regret is that I shall be onstage rather than in the audience."

Waafels hastened to reassure him that this base was covered.

"I will make a video," he said, "off de performance."

"Splendid! Splendid!" crowed Julian, turning away from Roger Courage so as not to be inhibited by the older man's warning stare. "A video within a video. How very postmodern!"

Waafels smiled shyly as the grinning Julian slapped him on the back.

Later, when Wim Waafels had gone home and Julian had excused himself, the Courages turned to Ben, who was pensively examining the first couple of printed pages of *Partitum Mutante*'s score.

"Well, what do you think, Ben?" sighed Roger.

"I'm too old to claim to know anything about video art," Ben conceded graciously. "There is one little thing that worries me, though."

Still a bit pale and peakish from the slow-motion gush of afterbirth, Catherine waited in silence for him to give voice to his concern.

"While it's utterly dark, in the blackness before

the world is born," mused Ben, "how are we to see the music?"

The following day was the Consort's second-last in the Château de Luth, and they spent most of it arguing.

Things started off civilly enough, in the short-lived morning hours of freshness before the heat set in. Catherine made Ben his *havermout* breakfast as usual, serene with pleasure at this wordless routine of nurture. He ate, she watched, as the sun flowed in on both of them, making them glow like lightbulbs. When it got too bright for comfort, Catherine squinted but did not stop looking, and Ben kept his eyes lowered, smiling into the steam of his porridge.

Julian was holed up in his room, no doubt to avoid a reprise of last night's unpleasantness with Roger over the Waafels affair. Roger had disapproved of Julian's sarcasm on the grounds that Waafels, if he'd taken it to heart, would have regarded Julian as speaking for the Courage Consort as a whole; Julian retorted that he damn well hoped he *was* speaking for the Courage Consort as a whole and that if Roger had any deep-seated enthusiasm for singing inside a pair of labia the size of a barn door he'd better come clean with it immediately.

In the wake of this altercation, there'd been a curious change to the château's atmosphere, sonically speaking. Julian had removed the television from the public domain and carried it upstairs in his arms, claiming that if he was going to endure another sleepless night he needed something to keep him from going gaga. And, indeed, by midnight Catherine was hearing, from her own bed, the muted sounds of argument and tender Dutch reconciliation coming through the wall. It was a change from the uncanny silence, but not necessarily a welcome one.

This morning, although she couldn't hear any identifiable television sounds filtering down into the kitchen, Catherine had a feeling it was probably still chattering away to Julian in his room, because the purity seemed to have been taken out of the silence somehow. There was an inaudible fuzz, like the sonic equivalent of haze from burning toast, obscuring Catherine's access to the acoustic immensity of the forest. She would have to go out there soon, and leave that haze behind.

Inconveniently, Dagmar didn't want to go for a cycle. Looking fed up and underslept, she came into the kitchen with no discernible purpose except to check that Julian hadn't touched the eggs in the fridge.

"My nipples are cracking up," she grouched, causing Ben to blush crimson over his *havermout* behind her. "First, one was still OK, now it's both of them. Today, it must rain—must, must, must. And I don't understand why you people let that asshole Wim Waafels go without hurting him."

Having run out of non sequiturs, she slammed

the door of the refrigerator and tramped out of the kitchen.

Catherine and Ben sat in silence as they heard Dagmar ambush Roger in the next room and start an argument with him. The German girl's voice came through loud and clear, an angry contralto of penetrating musicality. Roger's baritone was more muted, his words of pained defence losing some of their clarity as they passed through the walls.

"There was never any suggestion," he was saying, "that we had any choice . . ."

"I'm a singer," Dagmar reminded him. "Not a doll for nutcases to play with."

Roger's voice droned reasonably: ". . . multimedia event . . . we are only one of those media . . . problem with all collaborations . . . compromise . . . I'm not a Catholic, but I sing settings of the Latin Mass . . ."

"This is the Dresden Staatsoper all over again!"

On and on they went, until the listeners ceased to take in the words. Instead, Catherine and Ben let the sound of the arguers' voices wallow in the background, an avant-garde farrago of *Sprechstimme*.

By and by, Julian came downstairs and, smelling blood, gave mere coffee and toast a miss and joined the fray instead.

This was too much for Roger: fearing unfair odds, he called a meeting of the Consort as a whole, and the five of them sat in the front room where they had sung *Partitum Mutante* so endlessly, and bickered.

"The way to stop this sort of fiasco ever happening again," declared Julian, "is to price ourselves right out of the loony market."

"What on earth do you mean by that, Julian?" sighed Roger.

"Sing much more popular repertoire and command higher ticket prices. Do more recordings, get our pretty faces known far and wide. Then, whenever we're offered a commission, we pick and choose. And keep some sort of right of veto. No Italian arms dealers, no gynaecology buffs."

"But," Roger winced, "hasn't our strength always lain in our courage?—that is, our . . . um . . . willingness to be open to new things?"

Catherine started giggling, thinking of the yawning vulva that was waiting to "enfelope" them all.

"Perhaps Kate is, in her own way, reminding us of the need for a sense of humour," Roger suggested rather desperately.

"No, no, I was just . . . never mind," said Catherine, still chortling into the back of her hand. Roger was staring at her mistrustfully, imploringly: she knew very well he was trying to decide how crazy she was at this moment, how badly she might let him down. He needed her to be on his side, mentally frail or not; he needed her to see things his way, however impishly her inner demons might prevent her articulating it sensibly. She didn't have the heart to tell him that there weren't any inner demons making her laugh anymore; she just had more important things on her mind right now than the Courage Consort.

"The King's Singers went across a bomb at the Proms," persisted Julian.

Roger bridled at this; it was a sore point with him. "Look, I didn't cast my boat out on the dangerous sea of a cappella music," he remarked testily, "to sing 'Obla-di, Obla-da' to a crowd of philistines in funny hats."

"A very *large* crowd," Julian reminded him. "How many people are going to be hearing us at the Benelux Contemporary Music Festival?"

"For God's sake, Julian, are you suggesting we sing Andrew Lloyd Webber and 'Raindrops Keep Falling on My Head' in motet style?"

"Oh bravo, Mr. Courage: *reductio ad absurdum*!" Julian was rearing up alarmingly, balletic with pique. "I'm merely hummmmmbly suggesting you give a *thought* to what might put some reasonably intelligent *bums* on seats. The Beatles, it may *astound* you to know, inspire greater love than Pino Fugazza and Mr. Waffle put together—if such a pairing can be imagined without an ejaculation"—he gasped for breath—"of vomit."

"Yes, but . . ."

"You know what would make a great encore for us?" raged Julian, quite crazed by now. "Queen's 'Bohemian Rhapsody,' arranged for five voices."

Dagmar snorted loudly.

"You think I'm joking?" exclaimed Julian, fizzing with mischief. "Listen!" And he burst into song, a snatch of 'Bohemian Rhapsody' showing off his own range from horrible faux-bass to fiercely accurate falsetto: "Bis-mil-lah! No-o-o-o! We will not let you go—Let him go-o-o-o! Will not let you go—Let him go-o-o-o! No, no, no, no, no, no, no—Mama mia, mama mia, mama mia let me go . . ."

Mercifully, Julian's fury dissipated before he reached the "Beelzebub has a devil put aside" section so familiar from his answering machine, and he slumped back onto his knees.

"You are insane," pronounced Dagmar, awed, as silence settled again on the sweltering room.

"What do *you* think, Ben?" pleaded Roger.

Ben breathed deeply, blinking as bad vibes continued to float through the thick air.

"I think one thing is not in question," he said. "We've been contracted to sing *Partitum Mutante* at the Benelux Contemporary Music Festival. If we do it, some people may question our judgment. If we refuse to do it, many more people will question our professionalism."

Dagmar shook a heavy lock of hair off her face in a paroxysm of annoyance.

"You are all so British," she complained. "You would kill yourself so the funeral company wouldn't be disappointed. Why can't we tell the Benelux Music Festival to shove their Fugazzas and Waafels up their ass?"

"Aahh . . . Perhaps we should approach this from the other end, so to speak," said Roger, with grim optimism. "We all seem to be assuming that the fallout from this event is going to be bad for our reputation—but who's to say it won't be the best thing that ever happened to us? If *Partitum Mutante* outrages everybody and gets the press steamed up, that'll generate a lot of word of mouth about the Consort. In that sense, whatever we may feel in our heart of hearts, the whole affair may push us up to another level of recognition."

"Oh, you slut, Roger," said Julian.

"I *beg* your pardon?"

"I meant it good-naturedly."

Plainly, the discussion was doomed to be all downhill from here, but unfortunately there were still many hours of the day to get through. On and on, inexorable as a body function, the argument spasmed blindly along. Catherine, though she was kneeling in the midst of the battle, watched it as if from a distance. She knew Roger wouldn't ask her opinion, not after she'd giggled; he'd be too afraid she'd disgrace him by chattering about underpants. Or he might be worried she'd just stare back at him in a soulless daze, as though he'd tried to summon her from the bottom of a deep, deep well. He didn't realise she was elsewhere now.

It didn't impress her, actually, all this bluster about *Partitum Mutante* and the Consort's future, and she took pleasure in the fact that it didn't impress Ben, either. As often as she could get away with it, short of embarrassing them both, she turned to look at him and smiled. He smiled back, pale with tiredness, while between him and Catherine the stinging voices ricocheted.

She thought: *Dare I do something that might lead to the end of two marriages?*

In the end, it was Axel who came to the rescue again. Strange how this unmusical little creature, this uninvited marsupial whom they'd all imagined would meddle constantly with the serious business of singing, had left them to commune with *Partitum Mutante* uninterrupted for two solid weeks, only making himself heard when he could exercise his preferred role as peace broker. Today, he'd allowed the Consort to argue the morning and afternoon away, content at first to impose no more ambitious restrictions than to remind them, every few hours, to take a short break for food and drink. However, when nighttime came and they were still hard at it, Axel decided that drastic intervention was needed. Screaming at the top of his lungs, his mission was to lure his mother to his feverish little body, which he'd marinated in sufficient puke and ordure to earn himself a bath. Dagmar, interrupted just as she was about to announce her defection from the Anglo-German alliance, swallowed her words, stomped upstairs—and did not return.

With her departure, some séance-like bond of hostility was broken, and the Courage Consort dispersed, exhausted. They had resolved nothing, and the rain still hadn't come. Julian slunk off to be comforted by the murmurings of Dutch television; Roger said he was going to bed, though the expression of wounded stoicism on his face suggested he might be going to the Mount of Olives to pray.

Catherine and Ben sat in the rehearsal room, alone. Through the windows, the trees of the forest were furry black against the indigo of the night sky.

After a time, Catherine said, "What are you thinking, Ben?"

And he replied, "Time is short. It would have been better if we'd done some singing."

Catherine nestled her cheek inside her folded arms, her arms on the back of the couch. From this angle, only one of her eyes could see Ben; it was enough.

"Sing me a song, Ben," she murmured.

With some effort he raised himself from his chair and walked over to a glass cabinet. He swung open its doors and fetched out an ancient musical instrument—a theorbo, perhaps. Some sort of lute, anyway, creaking with its own oldness, dark as molasses.

Ben returned to his chair, sat down, and found the least absurd place to rest the bulbous instrument on his bulbous body. Then, gently, he began to strum the strings. From deep inside his chest, sonorous as a saxhorn, came the melancholy lyrics of Tobias Hume, circa 1645.

Alas, poore men
Why strive you to live long?

To have more time and space
To suffer wrong?

Looking back at a lifetime devoted to warfare and music, dear old Tobias might well have left it at that, but there were many more verses; the music demanded to go on even if there was little to add to the sentiments. Ben Lamb sang the whole song, about nine minutes altogether, strumming its sombre minimalist accompaniment all the while. Then, when he had finished, he got up and carefully replaced the lute in its display case. Catherine knew he was going to bed now.

"Thank you, Ben," she said, her lips breathing against her forearm. "Good night."

"Good night," he said, carrying his body away with him.

An hour later, Roger and Catherine made love. It seemed the only way to break the tension. He reached out for her, his strange and unreachable wife, and she allowed herself to be taken.

"I don't know anymore, I don't know anymore," he moaned, lonely as she stroked his damp back.

"Nobody knows, darling," she murmured abstractedly, smoothing his hair with her hands. "Go to sleep."

As soon as he had drifted off, she uncovered herself, imagining she was glowing like an ember in the heat. The house was perfectly quiet; Julian's relationship with the television must have run its course. Outside in the forest, the smell of impending rain dawdled over the treetops, teasing.

At the threshold of sleep, she thought she was already dreaming; there were disturbing sounds which seemed to be inside her body, the sounds of a creature in distress, struggling to breathe, vibrating her tissues. Then suddenly she was roused by a very real cry from outside herself. A child's cry, frightened and inarticulate. She was pretty sure it was Axel's, but some instinct told her that it was being provoked by something Dagmar couldn't handle alone.

Roger was dead to the world; she left him sleeping as she threw on her dressing gown and hurried out of the room.

"*Hilfe!*" called Dagmar breathlessly.

Catherine ran into the German girl's room, but Axel was in there alone, squirming and bawling on a bed whose covers had been flung aside.

"Help!"

Catherine rushed into the room next door, Ben's room. Ben was sprawled on the floor next to his narrow bed, his pyjamas torn open to expose his huge pale torso. Dagmar was hunched over him, apparently kissing him on the mouth. Then, drawing back, she laid her hands on his blubberous chest, clasping one brown palm over the other; with savage force she slammed the weight of her shoulders down through her sinewy arms, squashing a hollow into Ben's flesh.

"Airway. Take over," she panted urgently, as she heaved herself repeatedly onto where she trusted the well-hidden sternum to be. Ben's mountainous chest was so high off the floor that with every heave her knees were lifting into the air.

Catherine leapt across the room and knelt at Ben's head.

"Roger! Julian!" she screamed, then pressed her lips directly over Ben's. In the pauses between Dagmar's rhythmic shoves, she blew for all she was worth. Filling her lungs so deep that they stabbed her, she blew and blew and blew again.

Please, please breathe, she thought, but Ben did not breathe.

Julian burst into the room, and was momentarily overwhelmed by the sight of the two women, Dagmar stark naked and Catherine in a loose gown, kneeling on the floor with Ben.

"Eh . . . ," he choked, eyes popping, before the reality dawned on him. He flew out of the room, bellowing, in pursuit of a telephone in the dark.

The light in the Château de Luth was dim and pearly on the day that the Courage Consort were due to go home. The weather had broken at last. Baggage cluttered the front room like ugly modern sculpture forcibly integrated with the archaic spinning wheels, recorders, leather-bound books, lutes.

Jan van Hoeidonck would be arriving any minute now, in his banana-yellow minibus, and then, no

110

doubt, after the house was safely vacated, Gina would come to clean it. A couple of items in the hallway had been badly damaged by the ambulance people as they'd pulled Ben's body out of the narrow aperture, but the owners of the château would just have to be understanding, that was all. Antiques couldn't be expected to last forever; sooner or later, the wear and tear of passing centuries would get to them.

Standing at the window, blindly watching the millions of tiny hailstones swirling and clattering against the panes, Roger at last raised the subject that must be addressed.

"We have to decide what we're going to do," he said quietly.

Dagmar turned her face away from him, looking down instead at her baby, cradled tight in her arms. She had a pretty good idea what she was going to do, but now was not the time to tell Roger Courage about it.

"The festival isn't yet," she said, rocking on Catherine's absurdly big plastic suitcase.

"I know, but it's not going to go away, either," said Roger.

"Give it a rest, Roger," advised Julian softly, hunched over the piano, stroking his long fingers over all the keys without striking any.

Roger grimaced in shame at what he was about to say, what he could not help saying, what he was obliged by his own personal God to say.

"We could manage it, you know," he told them.

"The bass part of *Partitum Mutante* is the most straightforward, by a long shot. I know a man called Arthur Falkirk, an old friend of Ben's. They sang together at Cambridge . . ."

"No, Roger."

It was Catherine speaking. Her face was red and puffy, unrecognisable from crying. Before she'd finally calmed down this morning, she had wept more passionately, more uninhibitedly, than she'd done since she was seven. And, as she'd howled, the torrent of rain had dampened the acoustic of the Château de Luth, allowing her lament to take its place alongside the creaking of ancient foundations, the clatter of water from drainpipes and guttering, the burring of telephones. Her voice was hoarse now, so low that no one would ever have guessed she sang soprano.

Roger coughed uneasily.

"Ben was very conscientious," he said. "He would've wanted . . ."

"No, Roger," repeated Catherine.

The telephone rang, and she picked up the receiver before her husband could move a muscle.

"Yes," she croaked into the mouthpiece. "Yes, the Courage Consort. This is Catherine Courage speaking. Yes, I understand, don't be sorry. No, of course we won't be performing *Partitum Mutante*. Perhaps Mr. Fugazza can find another ensemble. A recording might be a more practical option at this late stage, but I'm sure Mr. Fugazza can make up his own mind . . . A dedication?

That's very kind of you, but I'm not sure if Ben would have wanted that. Leave it with me, let me think about it. Call me on the London number. But not for a few days, if you would. Yes. Not at all. 'Bye."

Roger stood at the window, his back turned. His hands were clasped behind his back, one limp inside the other. Against the shimmering shower of hail he was almost a silhouette. Outside, a car door slammed; the others hadn't even heard Jan van Hoeidonck's minibus arrive, but it was here now.

Catherine sat next to Dagmar on the suitcase; it was so uselessly big that there was ample space on its rim for both of them.

"Thanks for travelling with us this time," she whispered in the German girl's ear.

"It's OK," stated Dagmar flatly. Tears fell from her cheeks onto her baby's chest as she allowed Catherine to clasp one of her hands, those steely young hands that had proved unequal to the challenge of punching the life back into Ben Lamb's flesh.

The sound of a rain-swollen front door being shouldered open intruded on the moment. A great gust of wet, fragrant, earthy air swept into the house, as Jan van Hoeidonck let himself in. Without speaking, he walked into the front room, seized hold of two suitcases—Roger's and Ben's—and began to lug them out the door. Dagmar and Catherine slipped off Catherine's suitcase and allowed Roger to trundle it away, though it might just as well have been left behind. It was full of clothes she hadn't worn and food she hadn't eaten. She would travel lighter in future, if there was a future.

Oh Christ, don't start that again, she thought. *Just get on with it*. And she hurried out into the pelting rain.

The yellow minibus was roomier than she remembered, even though, with the addition of Dagmar and Axel, there were more passengers than there'd been last time—in number, if not in mass. Roger sat next to Jan van Hoeidonck as before. The director pulled away from the Château de Luth, tight-lipped, concentrating on the view through the labouring windscreen wipers; the chances that he and Roger would take up the threads of their discussion on the future of the Amsterdam Concertgebouw seemed slim. Julian sat at the back of the bus, gazing at the cottage as it dwindled into perspective, a picture postcard again, misty behind the deluge.

They had not been driving five minutes when the sky abruptly ran out of rain, and the forest materialised into view as if out of a haze of static. Then, dazzlingly, the sun came out.

Radiating through the tinted glass of the minibus window, the warmth bathed Catherine's face, soothing her cheeks, stinging the raw rims of her eyelids. With the rain gone, the world's acoustic was changing again: the gentle thrum of the engine surfaced from below, and birds began to twitter all around, while inside the bus, the silence of Ben's absence accumulated like stale breath. It was awful, deadly.

Instinctively, to fill the void, Catherine began to sing: the simplest, most comforting little song she knew, an ancient round she had sung before she'd even been old enough to learn its meaning.

> *Sumer is icumen in*
> *Loude sing cuckoo,*
> *Groweth seed and bloweth mead,*
> *And spring'th the woode now.*
> *Sing cuckoo . . .*

Catherine's soprano came out of her hoarse throat shaky and soft, barely in tune. She stared out of the window, not caring what the others thought of her; they could brand her as a nutcase if they needed to. The terrible silence was receding, that was the main thing.

Beginning the second verse, she was bewildered to find herself being joined by Julian, a delicate tenor counterpoint offering its assistance to her faltering lead.

> *Ewe bleateth after lamb,*
> *Low'th after calfe cow,*
> *Bullock sterteth,*
> *Bucke verteth,*
> *Merry sing cuckoo.*

Roger had joined in by now, and Dagmar, though she didn't know the words, improvised a strange but fitting descant *sans paroles*.

> *Cuckoo cuckoo*
> *Well singst thou cuckoo,*
> *Ne swicke thou never now.*
>
> *Sing cuckoo now,*
> *Sing cuckoo,*
> *Sing cuckoo,*
> *Sing cuckoo now . . .*

On and on they sang, not looking at each other, heading home.

THE HUNDRED AND NINETY-NINE STEPS

So word by word, and line by line, The dead man touch'd me from the past . . .

—TENNYSON, "In Memoriam"

The hand caressing her cheek was gentle but disquietingly large—as big as her whole head, it seemed. She sensed that if she dared open her lips to cry out, the hand would cease stroking her face and clasp its massive fingers over her mouth.

"Just let it happen," his voice murmured, hot, in her ear. "It's going to happen anyway. There's no point resisting."

She'd heard those words before, should have known what was in store for her, but somehow her memory had been erased since the last time he'd held her in his arms. She closed her eyes, longing to trust him, longing to rest her head in the pillowy crook of his arm, but at the last instant, she glimpsed sideways, and saw the knife in his other hand. Her scream was gagged by the blade slicing deep into her throat, severing everything right through to the bone of her spine, plunging her terrified soul into pitch darkness.

117

Bolt upright in bed, Siân clutched her head in her hands, expecting it to be lolling loose from her neck, a grisly Halloween pumpkin of bloody flesh. The shrill sound of screaming whirled around her room. She was alone, as always, in the early dawn of a Yorkshire summer, clutching her sweaty but otherwise unharmed head in the topmost bedroom of the White Horse and Griffin Hotel. Outside the attic window, the belligerent chorus of Whitby's seagull hordes shrieked on and on. To other residents of the hotel (judging by their rueful comments at the breakfast tables), these birds sounded like car alarms or circular saws or electric drills penetrating hardwood. Only to Siân, evidently, did they sound like her own death cries as she was being decapitated.

It was true that ever since the accident in Bosnia, Siân's dreams had treated her pretty roughly. For years on end she'd had her "standard-issue" nightmare—the one in which she was chased through dark alleyways by a malevolent car. But at least in *that* dream she'd always wake up just before she fell beneath the wheels, whisked to the safety of the waking world, still flailing under the tangled sheets and blankets of her bed. Ever since she'd moved to Whitby, however, her dreams had lost what little good taste they'd once had, and now Siân was lucky if she got out of them alive.

The White Horse and Griffin had a plaque out front proudly declaring it had won the *Sunday Times* Golden Pillow Award, but Siân's pillow must be immune to the hotel's historically sedative charm. Tucked snugly under the ancient sloping roof of the Mary Ann Hepworth room, with a velux window bringing her fresh air direct from the sea, Siân still managed to toss sleepless for hours before finally being lured into nightmare by the man with the giant hands. She rarely woke without having felt the cold steel of his blade carving her head off.

This dream of being first seduced, then murdered —always by a knife through the neck—had ensconced itself so promptly after her arrival in Whitby that Siân had asked the hotel proprietor if . . . if he happened to know how Mary Ann Hepworth had met her death. Already embarrassed that a science postgraduate like herself should stoop to such superstitious probings, she'd blushed crimson when he informed her that the room was named after a ship.

In the cold light of a Friday morning, swallowing hard through a throat she couldn't quite believe was still in one piece, Siân squinted at her watch. Ten to six. Two and a bit hours to fill before she could start work. Two and a bit hours before she could climb the one hundred and ninety-nine steps to the abbey churchyard and join the others at the dig.

A bath would pass the time, and would soak these faint mud stains off her forearms, these barely perceptible discolorations ringing her flesh like alluvial deposits. But she was tired and irritable and there was a pain in her left hip—a nagging, bone-deep pain that had been getting worse and worse lately—and she was in no mood to drag herself into the tub. What a lousy monk or nun she would have made, if she'd lived in medieval times. So reluctant to subject her body to harsh discipline, so lazy about leaving the warmth of her bed . . . ! So frightened of death.

This pain in her hip, and the hard lump that was manifesting in the flesh of her thigh just near where the pain was—it had to be bad news, very bad news. She should get it investigated. She wouldn't, though. She would ignore it, bear it, distract herself from it by concentrating on her work, and then one day, hopefully quite suddenly, it would be all over.

Thirty-four. She was, as of a few weeks ago, over half the age that good old Saint Hilda reached when she died. Seventh-century medical science wasn't quite up to diagnosing the cause, but Siân suspected it was cancer that had brought an end to Hilda's illustrious career as Whitby's founding abbess. Her photographic memory retrieved the words of Bede: "It pleased the Author of our salvation to try her holy soul by a long sickness, in order that her strength might be made perfect in weakness."

Made perfect in weakness! Was there a touch of bitter sarcasm in the Venerable Bede's account? No, almost certainly not. The humility, the serene stoicism of the medieval monastic mind—how terrifying it was, and yet how wonderful. If only *she* could think like that, feel like that, for just a few minutes! All her fears, her miseries, her regrets, would be flushed out of her by the pure water of faith; she would see herself as a spirit distinct from her treacherous body, a bright feather on the breath of God.

All very well, but I'm still not having a bath, she thought grouchily.

Through the velux window she could see a trio of seagulls, hopping from roof tile to roof tile, chortling at her goose-pimpled, wingless body as she threw aside the bedclothes. She dressed hurriedly, got herself ready for the day. The best thing about hands-on archaeology like the Whitby dig was that no one expected anybody to look glamorous, and you could wear the same old clothes day in, day out. She'd have to smarten herself up when she returned to her teaching rounds in the autumn; there was nothing like a lecture hall full of students, some of them young males, scrutinising you as if to say, "Where did they dig *her* up?" to focus your mind on what skirt and top you ought to wear.

Before descending the stairs to the breakfast room, Siân took a swig from the peculiar little complimentary bottle of mineral water and looked out over the rooftops of Whitby's east side. The rising sun glowed yellow and orange on the terracotta ridges. Obscured by the buildings and a litter of sails and boat masts, the water of the river Esk twinkled indigo. Deep in Siân's abdomen, a twinge of pain made her wince. Was it indigestion, or something to do with the lump in her hip? She mustn't think about it. Go away, Venerable Bede! "In the seventh year of her illness," he wrote of

Saint Hilda, "the pain passed into her innermost parts." Whereupon, of course, she died.

Siân went downstairs to the breakfast room, hoping that if she could find something to eat, the pain in her innermost parts might settle down. It was much too early, though, and the room was dim and deserted, with tea towels shrouding the cereal boxes and the milk jug empty. Siân considered eating a banana, but it was the last one in the bowl and she felt, absurdly, that this would make the act sinful somehow. Instead she ate a couple of grapes and wandered around the room, touching each identically laid, melancholy table with her fingertips. She seated herself at one, thinking of the Benedictine monks and nuns in their refectories, forbidden to speak except for the reciting of Holy Scripture. Dreamily pretending she was one of them, she lifted her hands into the pale light and gestured in the air the mute signals for fish, for bread, for wine.

"Are you all right?"

Siân jerked, almost knocking a teacup off the table.

"Yes, yes," she assured the Horse and Griffin's kitchen maid, large as life in the doorway. "Fine, thank you." She sighed. "Just going batty."

"I don't wonder," said the kitchen maid. "All them bodies."

"Bodies?"

"The skeletons you've been diggin' up." The girl made a face. "Sixty of 'em, I read in the *Whitby Gazette*."

122

"Sixty graves. We haven't actually—"

"D"you 'ave to touch 'em? I'd be sickened off. You wear gloves, I 'ope."

Siân smiled, shook her head. The girl's look of horrified awe beamed at her across the breakfast room like a ray, and she basked shyly in it: Siân the daredevil. For the sake of the truth, she ought to disabuse this girl of her fantasy of archaeologists rooting elbow deep in grisly human remains, and tell her that the dig was really very like gardening except less eventful. But instead, she raised her hands and wiggled the fingers, as if to say, *Ordinary mortals cannot know what I have touched.*

"Braver than me, you are," said the girl, unveiling the milk.

To help time pass, Siân crossed the bridge from the less corrupted east side to the more newfangled west, and strolled along Pier Road towards the sea. Thinly gilded with sunlight, the façades of the amusement arcades and clairvoyants' cabins looked almost grand, their windows and shuttered doors deflecting the glare. Siân dawdled in Marine Parade to peer through the window of what, until 1813, had been the Whitby Commercial Newsroom. "The Award-Winning Dracula Experience" said the poster, followed by a list of attractions, including voluptuous female vampires and Christopher Lee's cape.

The fish quay, deserted just now, was nevertheless infested with loitering seagulls. They wandered around aimlessly in the sunrise, much as the town's young men would do after sunset, or simply snoozed on top of crates and the roofs of the moored boats.

Siân walked to the lighthouse, then left the terra firma of Aislaby sandstone to tread the timber deck of the pier's end. Careful not to snag the heels of her shoes on the gaps in the wood, she allowed herself the queasy thrill of peeking at the restless waves churning far beneath her feet. She wasn't sure if she could swim anymore; it had been a long time.

She stood at the very end of the west pier and cupped her hand across her brow to look over at the east one. The two piers were like outstretched arms curving into the ocean, to gather boats from the wild waters of the North Sea into the safety of Whitby harbour. Siân was standing on a giant fingertip.

She consulted her watch and walked back to the mainland. Her work was on the other side.

Ascending the East Cliff, halfway up the one hundred and ninety-nine stone steps, Siân paused for a breather. Much as she loved to walk, she'd overdone it, perhaps, so early in the day. She should keep in mind that instead of going to sit at a desk now, she was going to spend the whole day digging in the earth.

Siân traced the imperfections of the stone step with her shoe, demarcating the erosion caused by the foot traffic of centuries. On just this spot, this wide plateaulike step amongst many narrow ones, the townspeople of ancient Whitby laid down the coffins they must carry up to the churchyard, and had paused, black-clad and red-faced, before resuming their doleful ascent. Only now that tourists and archaeologists had finally taken the place of mourners did these steps no longer accommodate dead people—apart from the occasional obese American holidaymaker who collapsed with a heart attack before reaching the hallowed photo opportunity.

Siân peered down towards Church Street and saw a man jogging—no, not jogging, running—towards the steps. At his side, a dog—a gorgeous animal, the size of a spaniel perhaps, but with a lovely thick coat, like a wolf's. The man wasn't bad-looking himself, broad-shouldered and well-muscled, pounding the cobbled surface of the street with his expensive-looking trainers. He was dressed in shorts and a loose, thin T-shirt a shivery proposition in the early morning chill, but he was obviously well up to it. His face was calm as he ran, his dark brown hair, free of sweat, flopping back and forth across his brow. The dog looked up at him frequently as he ran, revealing the vanilla and caramel colouring in its mane.

I want, I want, I want, thought Siân, then turned away, blushing. Thirty-four years old, and still thinking like a child! Saint Hilda would have been ashamed of her. And what exactly was she hankering after, anyway: the man or the dog? She wasn't even sure.

Another glance at her watch confirmed there was still a little while to fill before the first of her colleagues was likely to roll up. They all slept soundly, she gathered, in spite of the dawn chorus.

"Hello-o!"

She turned. The handsome young man was sprinting up the hundred and ninety-nine steps, as easily as if he were on flat ground. His dog was bounding ahead, narrowing the distance to Siân two steps at a time. For an instant Siân felt primeval fear at the approach of a powerful fanged creature, then relaxed as the dog scudded to a halt and sat to attention in front of her, panting politely, its head tilted to one side, just like a dog on a cheesy greeting card.

"He won't hurt you!" said the man, catching up, panting a little himself now.

"I can see that," she said, hesitantly reaching forward to stroke the dog's mane.

"He's got an eye for the ladies," said the man.

"Nothing personal, then."

The man came to a halt one step below her, so as not to intimidate her with his tallness: he must be six foot three, at least. With every breath his pectorals swelled into his shirt in two faint haloes of sweat, and faded again.

"You're very fit," she said, trying to keep her tone the same as if she were saying, "You're out and about very early."

"Well, if you don't use it," he shrugged, "you lose it."

The dog was becoming quietly ecstatic, pushing his downy black brow up towards Siân's palm, following her fingers with his eyes, hoping she would get around to stroking the back of his head, the right ear, the left, the part of the right ear she'd missed the first time.

"What sort of dog is he?"

"Finnish Lapphund," said the man, squatting on his haunches, as if seeking to qualify for a bit of stroking himself.

"Beautiful."

"A hell of a lot of work."

She knelt, carefully so that he wouldn't notice any problem with her left leg. "Doesn't look it," she said, stroking the dog's back all the way to his plushly fringed tail. All three of them were eye to eye now.

"You bring out his contemplative side, obviously," the man remarked, grinning. "With me, it's a different story. I'll be an Olympic runner by the time he's through with me."

Siân stroked on and on, a little self-conscious about the ardour with which she was combing the creature's sumptuous pelt. "You must have known what you were taking on when you got him," she suggested.

"Well, no, he was actually my father's dog. My father died three weeks ago."

Siân stopped stroking. "Oh, I'm sorry."

"No need. He and I weren't close." The dog, bereft of caresses, was poking his snout in the air, begging for more. The man obliged, ruffling the animal's ears, pulling the furry face towards his. "I didn't like our dad much, did I, hmm? Grumpy old man, wasn't 'e?"

Siân noticed the size of the man's hands: unusually large. A superstitious chill tickled her spine, like a tiny trickle of water. She distracted herself from it by noting the estuary twang of the man's accent.

"Did you come up from London?"

"Yeah." He frowned a little, intent on proving he could please the dog as much as the next pair of hands. "To bury the old man. And to sort out the house. Haven't decided what I'll do yet. It's in Loggerhead's Yard, so it's worth a mint. I might sell it; I might live in it. As a building, it's a hell of a lot nicer than my flat in West Kilburn." He cast a deprecating glance back at the town, as if to add, *Except of course it's in bloody Whitby.*

"Did you live here as a kid?"

"Many, many, long, long years," he affirmed, in a querulous tone of weary melodrama. "Couldn't get out fast enough."

Siân puzzled over the two halves of his statement, and couldn't help thinking there was a flaw in his logic somewhere.

"I like this place myself," she said. It surprised her to hear herself saying it—given the nightmares and the insomnia, she had good reason to associate Whitby with misery. But it was true: she liked the place.

"But you're not *from* here, are you?"

"No. I'm an archaeologist, working at the dig."

"Cool! The sixty skeletons, right?"

"Among other things, yes." She looked away from him, to register her disapproval of his sensationalist instincts, but if he noticed, he didn't give a toss.

"Wow," he said. "Gothic."

"Anglian, actually, as far as we can tell."

Her attempt to put him in his place hung in the air between them, sounding more and more snooty as she replayed it in her head. She returned her attention to the dog, trying to salvage things by stroking the parts the man wasn't stroking.

"What's his name?"

He hesitated for a moment. "Hadrian."

She snorted helplessly. "That's . . . that's an exceptionally crap name. For *any* dog, but especially this one."

"Isn't it!" he beamed. "My dad was a Roman history buff, you see."

"And *your* name?"

Again he hesitated. "Call me Mack."

"Short for something?"

"Magnus." His pale blue eyes narrowed. "Latin for 'great.' Grisly, isn't it?"

"Grisly?"

"Sounds like I've got a big head or something."

"I'll reserve judgment on that. It's a fine, ancient name, anyway."

"You *would* say that, wouldn't you?"

The familiarity of his tone worried her a bit. What

delicate work it was, this business of conversing with strangers of the other sex! No wonder she hardly ever attempted it anymore . . .

"What do you mean?" she said.

"You know, being an archaeologist and all that."

"I'm not actually a fully fledged archaeologist. Still studying."

"Oh? I would've thought . . ." He caught himself before he could say "at your age" or anything like that, but the implication stabbed straight into Siân—straight into her innermost parts, so to speak. Yes, damn it, she didn't look like a peachy young thing anymore. What she'd gone through in Bosnia—and since—was written and under-lined on her face. 'It pleased the Author of our salvation . . .' Pleased Him to put her body and soul through hell. In order that her strength might be made perfect in weakness. In order that people she'd only just met would think she was awfully old to be studying for a degree.

"I would've thought archaeology was a hands-on kind of thing," he said.

"So it is. I'm a qualified conservator, actually, specialising in the preservation of paper and parchment. I just fancied a change, thought I should get out more. There's a nice mixture of people at this dig. Some have been archaeologists for a million years. Some are just kids, getting their first pay-packet."

"And then there's you."

"Yes, then there's me."

He was staring at her; in fact, both he and his dog were staring at her, and in much the same way, too: eyes wide and sincere, waiting for her to give them the next piece of her.

"I'm Siân," she said, at last.

"Lovely name. Meaning?"

"Sorry?"

"Siân. In Welsh, it means . . . ?"

She racked her brains for the derivation of her name. "I don't think it means anything much. Jane, I suppose. Just plain Jane."

"You're not plain," he spoke up immediately, grateful for the chance to make amends.

To hide her embarrassment, she heaved herself to her feet. "Well, it's nearly time I started work." And she steeled herself for the remaining hundred steps.

"Can I walk with you as far as the church? There's a run I can do with Hadrian near there, back down to the town . . ."

"Sure," she said lightly. He mustn't see her limping. She would do what she could to prevent his attention straying below her waist.

"So . . ." she said, as they set off together, the dog scampering ahead, then scooting back to circle them. "Now that your father's funeral's over, do you have much more sorting out to do?"

"It's finished, really. But I've got a research paper to write, for my final year of Medicine. So, I'm using Dad's house as a kind of . . . solitary confinement. To get on with it, you know. There's a lot of distractions in London. Even worse distractions than *this* fellow . . ." And he aimed a slow, playful kick at Hadrian.

"You're partaking of a fine Whitby tradition, then," said Siân. "Think of those monks and nuns sitting in their bare cells, reading and scribing all day."

He laughed. "Oh, I'm sure they got up to a hell of a lot more than that."

Was this bawdy crack, and the wink that accompanied it, supposed to have any relevance to the two of them, or was it just the usual cynicism that most people had about monastic life? Probably just the usual cynicism, because when they ascended to the point where the turrets of Whitby Abbey were visible, he said: "Ah! The lucrative ruins!" He flung his right arm forward, unfurling his massive hand in a grandiose gesture. "See Whitby Abbey and die!"

Siân felt her hackles rise, yet at the same time she was tickled by his theatricality. She'd always detested shy, cringing men.

"If the Abbey'd had a bit more money over the centuries," she retorted, "it wouldn't *be* ruins."

"Oh come on," he teased. "Ruins are where the real money is, surely? People love it." He mimicked an American sightseer posing for his camera-toting wife: "'Take a pitcha now, Wilma, of me wid dese here ruins of antiquiddy behind me!'"

Squinting myopically, acting the buffoon, he ought to have looked foolish, but his clowning only served to accentuate how handsome he was. His irreverent grin, and the way he inhabited his body with more grace than his gangly frame ought

to allow, were an attractive combination for Siân—
a combination she'd been attracted to before,
almost fatally. She'd have to be careful with this
young man, that's for sure, if she didn't want a
rerun of . . . of the Patrick fiasco.

"Antiquity *is* exciting," she said. "It's *good* that
people are willing to come a long way to see it. They
walk up these stone stairs towards that abbey, and
they feel they're literally following in the footsteps
of medieval monks and ancient kings. They see those
turrets poking up over the headland, and it takes
them back eight hundred years . . ."

"Ah, but that thing up there isn't the real Whitby
Abbey, is it? It's a reconstruction: some tourist
body's idea of what a medieval abbey should look
like."

"That's not true."

"Didn't it all fall down ages ago, and they built
it up in completely the wrong shape?"

"No, that's not true," she insisted, feeling herself
tempted to argue heatedly with a complete
stranger—something she hadn't done since Patrick.
She ought to dismiss his ignorance with the lofty
condescension it deserved, but instead she said,
"Come up and I'll show you."

"What?" he said, but she was already quickening
her pace. "Wait!"

She stumped ahead, leading him past Saint
Mary's churchyard, past the cliffside trail to
Caedmon's Trod—the alternative path back to the
town below, along which he'd meant to run with

Hadrian. Teeth clenched with effort, she stumped up another flight of steps leading to the abbey.

"It's all right, I believe you!" Magnus protested as he dawdled in her wake, hoping she'd come round, but she led him straight on to the admission gate. He baulked at the doorway, only to see his cheerfully disloyal dog trotting across the threshold.

"Bastard," he muttered as he followed.

Inside, there was a sign warning visitors that all pets must be on a leash, and there was a man at the admissions counter waiting to be handed £1.70. Siân, so used to wandering freely in and out of the abbey grounds that she'd forgotten there was a charge for nonarchaeologists, paused to take stock. Mack's running shorts, whatever else they might contain, clearly had no provision for a wallet.

"He's with me," she declared, and led the hapless Magnus past the snack foods and pamphlets, through the portal to antiquity. It all happened so fast, Hadrian was dashing across the turf, already halfway to the twelfth century, before the English Heritage man could say a word.

Siân stood in the grassy emptiness of what had once been the abbey's nave. The wind flapped at her skirt. She pointed up at the towering stone arches, stark and skeletal against the sky. The thought of anyone—well, specifically this man at her side—being immune to the primitive grandeur and the tragic devastation of this place, provoked her to a righteous lecture.

"Those three arches there," she said, making sure he was looking where her finger pointed (he was—and so was his dog), "those arches are originally from the south wall, yes, and when they were reconstructed in the 1920s, they were propped up against the northern boundary wall, yes. Rather odd, I admit. But it's all the original masonry, you know. And at least those arches are safe now. We'd love to restore them to their original position, but they're better off where they are than in a pile of rubble—or don't you think so?"

"I'm sorry, I'm sorry!" he pleaded facetiously. "I didn't know I was treading on your toes . . ."

"I have some books and brochures that explain everything, the whole history," she said. "You can read those—I'll give them to you. A nice parcel. Loggerhead's Yard, wasn't it?"

"Oh, but no, really," he grimaced, flushing with embarrassment. "I should buy them myself."

"Nonsense. You're welcome to them."

"But . . . but they're *yours*. You've spent money . . ."

"Nonsense, I've got what I needed from them; they're not doing me any good now." Seeing him squirm, she was secretly enjoying her modest subversion of twenty-first-century capitalism, her feeble imitation of the noble Benedictine principle of common ownership. "Besides, I can smell cynicism on you, Mr. Magnus. I'd like to get rid of that, if I can."

He laughed uneasily, and lifted one elbow to call attention to his sweat-soaked armpits.

"Are you sure it's not the smell of BO?"

"Quite sure," she said, noting that two of her colleagues were, at last, straggling into view. "Now, I think it's about time I started work. It was lovely to meet you. And Hadrian, of course."

She shook his hand, and allowed herself one more ruffle of the dog's mane. Nonplussed, Magnus backed away.

A few seconds later, when she was already far away from him, he called after her:

"Happy digging!"

That night, Siân fell asleep with unusual ease. Instead of spending hours looking at the cast-iron fireplace and the wooden clothes rack growing gradually more distinct in the moonlight, she slept in profound darkness.

I'm sleeping, she thought as she slept. *How divine.*

"Oh, flesh of my flesh," whispered a voice in her ear. "Forgive me . . ." And the cold, slightly serrated edge of a large knife pressed into her windpipe. With a yelp, she leapt into wakefulness, but not before the flesh of her throat had yawned open and released a welter of blood.

Upright in bed, she clutched her neck, to keep her life clamped safely inside. The skin was unbroken, a little damp with perspiration. She let go, groaning irritably.

It wasn't even morning: it was pitch-dark, and the seagulls were silent—still fast asleep, wherever it is that seagulls sleep. Siân peered at her watch, but it was the old-fashioned kind (she didn't like digital watches) and she couldn't see a thing.

Ten minutes later she was dressed and ready for going out. Packed in a shoulder bag were the books and pamphlets for Magnus: "Saint Hilda and her Abbey at Whitby", *A History of Whitby*, the Pitkin guide to "Life in a Monastery", and several others. She slung the bag behind her hip and shrugged experimentally to confirm it stayed put; she didn't want it swinging forward and tripping her up. Getting your neck slashed in a dream was one thing; *breaking* your neck while trying to get down a steep flight of stairs in the dead of night was quite another.

In the event, she managed without any problem, and was soon standing in the cold breeze of the White Horse and Griffin's side lane, cobbles underfoot. The town was so quiet she could hear her own breathing, and Church Street was closed to traffic in any case, yet still she ventured forward from the alley very, very carefully—a legacy of her accident in Bosnia. Even in a pedestrianised cul-de-sac in a small Yorkshire town at four in the morning, you never knew what might come ripping around the corner.

In the dark, Whitby looked strange to Siân—neither modern nor medieval, which were the only two ways she was accustomed to perceiving it. In the daylight hours, she was either working in the shadow of the abbey ruins, coaxing the remains of stunted Northumbrians out of the antique clay, or she was weaving through crowds of shoppers and tourists, that vulgar throng of pilgrims with mobile phones clutched to their cheeks or pop groups advertised on their chests. Now, in the unpeopled stillness of night, Whitby looked, to Siân, distinctly Victorian. She didn't know why—the buildings and streets were much older than that, mostly. But it wasn't a matter of architecture; it was a matter of atmosphere. The glow of the streetlamps could almost be gaslight; the obscure buildings and darkened doorways scowled with menace, like a movie backdrop for yet another version of Bram Stoker's *Dracula*. Any alleyway, it seemed to Siân, could disgorge at any moment the caped figure of the Count, or a somnambulistic young woman of unnatural pallor, her white nightgown stained with blood.

Gothic. That's what the word "Gothic" meant to most people nowadays. Nothing to do with the original Germanic tribe, or even the pre-Renaissance architectural style. The realities of history had been swept aside by Hollywood vampires and narcissistic rock singers with too much mascara on. And here she was, as big a sucker as anyone: walking down Church Street at four in the morning, imagining the whole town to be crawling with Victorianesque undead. Even the Funtasia joke shop, which during the day sold plastic vampire fangs and whoopee cushions, seemed at this godforsaken hour to be a genuinely creepy establishment, the sort of place inside which rats and madmen might be lurking.

The house in Loggerhead's Yard was easy to find; when she'd asked about it in the hotel, half a dozen people jostled to give her directions. Magnus's father had been well known in the town and all the locals took a keen interest whenever a death freed up a hunk of prime real estate. Only when Siân approached the front door did she have her first doubts about what she'd come here to do. An action which, in daylight with people strolling round about, would look like a casual errand, seemed anything but casual now—the eerie stillness and the ill-lit, empty streets made her feel as if she were up to no good. She could be a thief, a cat burglar, a rapist, tiptoeing so as not to wake the virtuously sleeping world, squinting at a slit in a stranger's door, preparing to slide a foreign object through it. What if the door should open suddenly, to reveal Magnus, still naked and warm from his bed, rubbing his eyes? Or what about the dog? Surely he would go berserk at the sound of her fumblings at the mail slot! Siân steeled her nerves for an explosion of barking as she fed the books and pamphlets, one by one, through the dark vent, but they dropped softly onto the floor within, and that was all. Hadrian was either uninspired by the challenges of being a guard dog, or asleep. Asleep on the bed of his master, perhaps. Two muscular males nestled side by side, different species but both devilishly handsome.

For goodness' sake, she sighed to herself, turning away. *When will you grow up?*

Bag empty and weightless on her shoulder, she hurried back to the hotel.

Siân had never been fond of weekends. They were all very well for people with hobbies or a frustrated desire to luxuriate in bed, but she would rather be working. Half the reason she'd switched from paper conservation to archaeology was that it required her to show up, no matter what, at the appointed hour, and dig. It wasn't easy, especially in raw weather, but it was better than wasting the whole day thinking about the past—her own past, that is.

Saint Benedict had the right idea: a community of monastics keeping to a strict ritual seven days a week, helping each other get out of bed with (as he put it) "gentle encouragement, on account of the excuses to which the sleepy are addicted." Siân knew all about those.

To prevent herself moping, she spent most of her weekends wandering around Whitby, back and forth across the swing bridge, from pier to pier, from cliff to cliff. She'd walk until she tired herself out and then lie on her bed in the Mary Ann Hepworth room with a book on her lap, watching the rooftops change colour, until it was time for her to go to sleep and get what was coming to her.

This week, Saturday passed more quickly than usual. Her early-morning excursion to the house in Loggerhead's Yard had been quite thrilling in its stealthy way, and afterwards she fell into a long, mercifully dreamless doze. She woke quite rested, with only three-quarters of the weekend left to endure.

In the afternoon, while she had a bite of lunch at the Whitby Mission and Seafarer's Centre, a gusty breeze flapped the yellowing squares of paper pinned to the notice board near the door. "Don't leave Fido out in the cold," said one fluttering page. "We have a separate coffee lounge where pets are always welcome." Siân left the ruins of her jacket potato consolidating on her plate and walked over to the opposite lounge to have a peek inside. Her nose nudged through a veil of cigarette smoke. Strange dogs with strange owners looked up at the newcomer.

On her way out of the Mission, Siân paused at the bookcase offering books for fifty pence each and rummaged through the thrillers, romances, and anthologies of local writers' circles. There was a cheap, mass-produced New Testament there, too. What a comedown since the days when a Bible was a unique and priceless object, inscribed on vellum from an entire flock of sheep! Siân closed her eyes, imagined a cloister honeycombed in sunlight, with a long rank of desks and tonsured heads, perfect silence except for the faint scratching of pen nibs.

"Now here's a blast from the past!" brayed the disc jockey on the radio. "Hands up anyone who bopped along to Culture Club when they had this hit—come on, 'fess up!"

Siân fled.

★   ★   ★

141

Early on Sunday morning, not long after getting her throat slit, Siân was out and about again, her hastily washed hair steaming. She couldn't be bothered blow-drying it, and besides, now was when she ought to be going—at exactly the same time as she'd set off for work on Friday. If Magnus and Hadrian were creatures of habit, this would send them running after her any minute now.

She walked along Church Street, quite slowly, from the hotel façade to the foot of the hundred and ninety-nine steps and back again—twice—but no chance meeting occurred.

Tantalised by the thought of the man and his dog running high up on the East Cliff, in the wild grasses flanking the abbey ramparts, she climbed Caedmon's Trod until she could see the Donkey Field. No chance meeting occurred here, either, at least not with Magnus and Hadrian. Instead, she met a bored-looking boy and his somewhat frazzled dad, returning from what had clearly been a less than inspirational visit to the abbey.

"Another really interesting thing that monasteries used to do," the father was saying, in a pathetic, last-ditch attempt to get the child excited, "was give sanctuary to murderers."

Siân saw a flicker of interest in the kid's eyes as she squeezed past him on the narrow monks' trod.

"Has Whitby got McDonald's," he asked his dad, "or only fish and chips?"

★   ★   ★

It was Monday afternoon before Siân saw Magnus again. In the morning, she loitered around the town centre before work, in an irritable, shaky state. Her nightmare hadn't yet receded, and her throat was sore where, in a befuddled attempt to deflect the knife, she had hit herself with her own hand. The lump in her thigh throbbed like hell.

In the town's deserted market square, on a bench, someone had discarded a copy of the current *Whitby Gazette.* With half an hour still to kill before 8:00 A.M., Siân settled down to read it. For some reason though, every single article in the *Gazette* struck her as monumentally depressing. Not just the sad stories, like the one about the much-loved local janitor dying of cancer ("He never moaned about his illness and was always cheerful", according to a colleague—a chip off Saint Hilda's block, then). No, even the stories about a holidaymaker being struck by lightning and surviving, or a charity snail-eating contest, or the long-overdue restoration of Egton Bridge, brought Siân closer and closer to irrational tears. She flipped the pages faster, through the property section, until she was on the back page, staring at an advertisement for a beauty clinic on the West Cliff. "Sun-dome with facial and leg boosters' it said, and to Siân this seemed like the most heart-breakingly sad phrase she'd ever read this side of the Book of Ecclesiastes.

Get a grip, she counselled herself, and laid the paper aside. She noticed that someone had joined her on the bench: an obese, spiky-haired punkette, an unusual sight in Whitby—almost as unusual as a monk. Siân goggled just a few seconds too long at the infestation of silver piercings on the girl's brow, nose, and ears, and was given a warning scowl in return. Chastened, she looked down. At the punkette's feet sat a dog, to help the girl beg perhaps. Apart from the pictogram for "anarchy" doodled on his wheat-coloured flank in black felt-tip, he was a very ordinary-looking dog, a Labrador maybe—nowhere near as beautiful as Hadrian.

Face it: compared to Hadrian, every other dog was plain.

At ten to eight, Siân began to climb the hundred and ninety-nine steps, and gazing for a moment across the harbour, she suddenly spotted Hadrian and Magnus on the other side, two tiny figures sprinting along Marine Parade. Her melancholy turned at once to a sort of indignant excitement. Why would they choose there to run instead of here on her side? They must be avoiding her! Surely nobody could prefer the stink of raw fish and the pierside's dismal panorama of amusement parlours and pubs to what lay at the foot of the church steps . . .

Her sudden, fervid impulse to jump up and down and wave to Mack, despite the fact that there was no chance of him noticing, alarmed her—clearly, she was farther gone than she'd thought and should make an immediate start on restoring her sanity before it was too late.

I am here, she reminded herself, to work. I am not here to be torn apart. I am not here to be treated like dirt.

She imagined her emotions embodied in the form of a hysterical novice nun, and her judgment as the wise and kindly abbess, counselling restraint. She visualised the bare interior of one of Saint Hilda's prayer cells lit up gold and amber with sunbeams, a merciful ebbing away of confusion, a soul at peace.

When Siân reached the burial site, Pru was already lifting off the blue tarpaulins, exposing the damp soil. Towards the edges of the excavation, the clay was somewhat soggier than it needed to be, having absorbed some rainfall over the weekend in addition to its ritual hosing last thing Friday afternoon. Siân was glad her appointed rectangle was towards the middle of the quarter acre. All right, maybe Saint Hilda wouldn't have approved of her desire to keep her knees dry at the expense of her fellow toilers, but the sheath of Tubigrip under her tights lost some of its elastic every time she washed it, so she'd rather it stayed clean, thank you very much.

"Sleep well?" asked Pru, rolling up another tarpaulin, exposing Siân's own appointed shallow grave.

"No, not really," said Siân.

"Lemme guess—you stayed up to watch that movie about the robbery that goes wrong. The one with . . . oh, what's-her-name?" Regurgitation of facts was not Pru's forte. "The one who's gained so much weight recently."

"I'm sorry, I haven't a clue," said Siân.

Jeff was next to arrive, a wizened old hippy who seemed to have been on every significant dig in Britain since the war. Then Keira and Trevor, a husband-and-wife team who were due to lay down their trowels and mattocks tomorrow and flee to the warmer and better-paid climes of a National Geographic dig in the Middle East. Who would replace them? Very nice people, according to Nina, the supervisor. Coming all the way from north Wales.

By ten past, everyone was on site and working, distributed like medieval potato harvesters over the subdivided ground. Fourteen living bodies, scratching in the ground for the subtle remains of dead ones, peering at gradations in soil colour that could signal the vanished presence of a coffin or a pelvis, winkling pale fragments into the light which could, please God, be teeth.

The skeletons exhumed so far had all been buried facing east, the direction of Jerusalem, to help Judgment Day run more smoothly. Four years from now, when the research would be completed and the bones reburied with the aid of a JCB and vicar to bless them, they'd have to sort out their direction for themselves.

Today, one of the girls was in a bad mood, her mouth clownishly downturned, her eyes avoiding contact with the young man working next to her.

Yesterday, they'd been exchanging secret smiles, winks, *sotto voce* consultations. Today, they did their best to pretend they weren't kneeling side by side; separated by mere inches, they cast expectant glances not at each other but at Nina, as if hoping she might assign them to different plots farther apart. A cautionary spectacle, thought Siân. A living parable (as Saint Hilda might call it) of the fickleness of human love.

"I think I may've found something," said someone several hours later, holding up an encrusted talon which might, once it was X-rayed, prove to be a coffin pin.

At four-thirty, as Siân was walking past Saint Mary's churchyard on her way down to the hundred and ninety-nine steps, she spotted Hadrian's head poking up over the topmost one.

"Hush!" he barked in greeting. "Hush, hush!"

Siân hesitated, then waved. Magnus was nowhere to be seen.

Hadrian ran towards her, pausing only to scale the church's stone boundary and sniff the base of Caedmon's Cross. Deciding not to piss on England's premier Anglo-Saxon poet, he bounded back onto the path and had an exuberant reunion with Siân.

By the time Magnus joined them, she was on one knee, her hands buried deep in the dog's mane, and Hadrian was jumping up and down to lick her face.

"Excuse me, I'm just going overboard here," she

said, too delighted with the dog's affection to care what a fool she must look.

Mack wasn't wearing his running gear this afternoon; instead, his powerful frame was disguised in a button-down shirt, Chinos, and some sort of expensive suedy jacket. He was carrying a large plastic bag, but apart from that he looked like a young doctor who'd answered his beeper at a London brasserie and been persuaded to make a house call. Siân had trouble accepting he could look like this; she'd imagined him (she realised now) permanently dressed in shorts and T-shirt, running around Whitby in endless circles. She laughed at the thought, her inhibitions loosened by the excesses she was indulging in with Hadrian. Casting her eyes down in an effort to reassure Mack that she wasn't laughing at him, she caught sight of his black leather shoes, huge things too polished to be true. She giggled even more. Her own steel-capped boots were slathered in mud, and her long bedraggled skirt was filthy at the knees.

"You and Hadrian better not get too friendly," Mack remarked. "He might run off with one of your precious old bones."

It was such a feeble joke that Siân didn't think anyone could possibly blame her for ignoring it. She heaved herself to her feet and, fancying she could feel his eyes on her dowdiness, she sobered up in a hurry.

"Have you read any of the books and pamphlets?" she said.

He snorted. "You sound like a Jehovah's Witness, on a follow-up visit."

"Never mind that. Have you read them?" Be firm with him, she was thinking.

"Of course," he smiled.

"And?"

"Very interesting," he said, watching her straighten her shapeless cagoule. "More interesting than my research, anyway."

As they fell into step with each other towards the town, Siân rifled her memory for the subject of his paper. It took her a good fifteen seconds to realise she'd never actually asked him about it.

They'd reached the bench on the resting place near the top of the hundred and ninety-nine steps, and he indicated with a wave of his hand that they should sit down. This they did, with Hadrian settled against Siân's skirt, and Mack carefully lowering the plastic bag onto the ground between his lustrous shoes. Judging by the sharp corners bulging through the plastic, it contained a large cardboard box.

"That's not your research paper in there, is it?" she asked.

"No," he said.

"What is it?"

"A surprise."

Michael, one of Siân's colleagues from the dig, walked past the bench where they were sitting. He nodded in greeting as he descended the steps, looking slightly sheepish, unsure whether to introduce himself to Siân's new friend or pretend he

149

hadn't trespassed on their privacy. It was a gauche little encounter, lasting no more than a couple of seconds, but Siân was ashamed to note that it gave her a secret thrill; how sweet it was to be mistaken for a woman sharing intimacy with a man! Let the whole world pass by this bench, in an orderly procession, to witness proof incarnate that she wasn't lonely!

For God's sake, get a grip! she reproached herself.

"My research," said Mack, smirking a little, "examines whether psittacosis is transferable from human to human." His smirk widened into a full grin as she stared back at him with a blank expression. Siân wondered if he'd make her ask, but, commendably, he didn't. "Psittacosis," he explained, "is what's popularly called parrot fever—if popular is the right word for a rare disease. It's a virus, and you catch it by inhaling the powdered . . . uh . . . faeces of caged birds. In humans, it manifests as a kind of pneumonia that's highly resistant to antibiotics. It used to be fatal, once upon a time."

Siân wondered just how long ago, in his view, "once upon a time" was. She, after all, had had to convince herself, after reading the "Health & Safety" documents covering archaeological digs, that she wasn't frightened of catching anthrax or the Black Death.

"And this disease of yours," she said. "Is it transferable from human to human?"

"The answer used to be 'Maybe.' I'm aiming to change that to a definite 'No.'"

"Hmm," said Siân. Now that she'd been sitting for a minute, she was suddenly rather weary, and her left leg ached and felt swollen. "Well, I'm sure that'll put some people's minds at rest." It sounded condescending, and she had the uneasy feeling she was being a bitch. "No, really. With diseases, it's always better to know, isn't it?" An inane comment, which reminded her of the lump in her thigh she was so determined to ignore. Irritably, she wiped her face. "Sorry, I'm tired."

"Another long day exhuming the dead?"

"No, I just didn't sleep so well last night."

Again to his credit, he didn't pry. Instead he asked, "Where do you keep them all, anyway? All the skeletons, I mean. Sixty of them, I read somewhere." He nodded towards the East Cliff car park. "Enough to fill a tourist bus."

Siân giggled, picturing a large party of skeletons driving away, taking their last glimpse of Whitby through steamy coach windows as they began their long trip home.

"We've only found a few complete skeletons," she said. "Usually we find half skeletons, or bits and pieces. Clay isn't as kind to bones as people imagine; in fact, they'd last longer just about anywhere else. Stuck in the ground, they crumble, they soften, they dissolve. Sometimes we'll find just a discoloration in the clay. A tell-tale shadow. That's why we have to be so careful, and so slow."

"And these people you've dug up—who were they?"

A single word, Angles, sprang to Siân's mind, which made her feel a pang of guilty sorrow. How ruthless History was, taking as raw material the fiercely independent lives of sixty human individuals—sixty souls who, in life, fought for their right to be appreciated as unique, to earn the pride of their parents, the gratitude of their children, the loyalty of their colleagues—blending them all into the dirt, reducing them to a single archaic word.

"They were . . . Angles, probably," she sighed. "Difficult to be sure, until we do carbon-14 dating on them. They lived after the Romans, anyway, and before the Norman Conquest."

"Any treasures?"

"Treasures?"

"Gold, precious jewels . . . Bracelets and swords that can be buffed up to a sheen for the English Heritage brochures . . ."

Siân was determined not to be goaded by his tone. Be firm with him, she counselled herself. Firm but dignified.

"These people were early Christians," she reminded him. "They didn't believe in taking anything with them when they died. You know: 'Naked came I into the world, and naked—'"

"Ha!" he scoffed, hoisting up a stiff index finger in a theatrical gesture of triumph. "I've read up on this stuff now, don't forget! What about all those fancy trinkets they dug up in the 1920s, eh? Brooches, rings, and whatever? Saint Hilda's nuns were rolling in it, weren't they?"

Siân leaned down, scorning to look at him, but instead stroking Hadrian tenderly. She spoke directly into the dog's furry, trusting face, as if she'd decided there was a great deal more point talking to Hadrian than to his master. "People nowadays would love to believe the nuns were as corrupt as hell," she murmured. "Did you know that, Hadrian?" She ruffled his ears, and nodded emphatically as though the shameless cynicism of humans was likely to beggar the belief of an innocent canine. "It makes people feel smug, you see. Gives them a warm glow, to think of those religious idealists betraying their vows of poverty and swanning around in fancy gowns and jewellery."

"And didn't they?"

Siân turned her attention to Magnus, looking him straight in the eyes while her hands carried on stroking. "I prefer to give them the benefit of the doubt. Abbeys weren't just for monastic orders, you know; they were places of prayer and seclusion for . . . well, anybody really. All sorts of rich people ended up in them—unmarried princesses, widowed queens . . . They'd retire there, servants and all. I like to think it's those powerful ladies that left behind the rings and brooches and buckles and whatnot."

"You'd like to think," he teased.

"Yes, I'd like to think," she said, barely able to keep a sharp hiss of annoyance out of her voice. "If there's no way of proving anything, why be cynical? Why not choose to think the best of people?"

His eyes twinkled with mischief.

"That's what I'm trying to do!" he protested mock-innocently. "These old nuns sound as if they had a pretty dismal time. I want to cheer 'em up with a bit of the good life."

Siân was imagining the twelfth-century ruins she knew so well, trying to reconstruct, in her mind, the lost seventh-century original that the Vikings had destroyed.

"Funny what 'the good life' means now . . ." she said wistfully. "And what it used to mean . . ."

"Back in the Middle Ages when *you* were a nun?" he ribbed her. Then, sensing he'd gone too far, he hoisted up his plastic bag and carefully removed the cardboard box from it.

"Anyway, I want to show you something. Something I'm sure you'll appreciate more than anyone else, being a—what was it again?—a conservationist?"

"Conservator," she said, intrigued despite herself as Mack opened the box to reveal, in a nest of crumpled toilet paper, a glass liquor bottle without any label, discoloured and dull, clearly antique. Inside the bottle was a large candle—no, not a candle, a tight scroll of papers. Water damage, evidently followed by ill-managed drying, had fused the layers of the scroll into a puckered cylinder. There was handwritten text on the outermost layer, and the few capital letters Siân could make out at a glance were unmistakably nineteenth- or even eighteenth-century.

I want, I want, I want, she thought.

Mack held the bottle up close to her face, turning it slowly so the scroll revealed its text like the beginning of a Web page stored in the world's most ancient VDU.

"Look," he said. "You can still read it."

Confession of Thos. Peirson, in the Year of Our Lord 1788
In the full and certain Knowledge that my Time is nigh, for my good Wife has even now

That was as much of the text as was visible before it swallowed itself inside the roll.

"Where did you find this?" Too late, she heard the tremor of excitement in her voice, and—damn!—he noticed, too, and grinned.

"I didn't find it, my dad did. It turned up in the foundations of Tin Ghaut when the town planners demolished it in 1959. He took it home before the bulldozers came back."

Siân watched him replace the bottle in its nest of toilet paper. She took a breath, priming her voice for what she hoped would be a casual, matter-of-fact tone.

"That scroll—it could be unrolled, you know. We could find out what this man was confessing."

"I don't think so," said Mack, fingering the glass regretfully. "I've tried to get the papers out. With forceps, even. But the paper's gone rigid, and it's wider than the neck of the bottle. Of course I could just break it open, but the thing is, the glass never got broken all this time, even when it was dug up by bloody great earthmovers. My dad thought that was a miracle, and it is kind of cool, I must admit. Smashing it now would be . . . I don't know . . . wrong somehow."

Siân was touched by this glimmer of rudimentary morality when it came to preserving ancient things, but also impatient with his ignorance.

"We have tools to slice the bottle open without smashing it," she said. "We could open the bottle, extract the papers, gently separate them, read them . . ."

"Who's 'we'?" he challenged her gently. "You and me?"

Siân smiled, keen to stay on the right side of him. The thought of him closing the lid on his treasure box and carrying that scroll out of her life was hard to bear. *Give it to me, give it to me, give it to me,* she was thinking.

"There's a man I know at the University of Northumbria who could do the bottle for me," she said. "The papers I could do myself, right here."

"Mm." He sounded noncommittal. Hadrian had wandered off, restless, miffed that the humans had allowed both the stroking and the running to lapse. He was in Saint Mary's churchyard again, pondering the bas-relief horses stabled at the base of Caedmon's Cross—horses that looked puzzlingly like toy dogs in a kennel.

"So . . ." said Siân. "What do you think? May I?"

Mack reached into the box, and lifted the prize back into view.

"Are you sure you can put it all back together? Just the way it is now?" He handled the bottle firmly but with great tenderness. *You'll make a good doctor,* Siân thought.

"Sure," she replied. "A thin seam in the glass, that's all you'll see. And we'll do it where hardly anyone would think of looking."

He raised one eyebrow dubiously. "We will, will we?"

But, God bless him, he handed it over. One moment it was in his hands, the next she had received it into hers. Flesh brushed against flesh during the transfer.

"Trust me," she said, as a thrill passed through her from wrist to toe, like a benign electric current looking for earth.

It was very late that night before she could begin. Neville, her pal at the University of Northumbria who could cut the bottle open, was unavailable to see her until he'd finished giving his evening lectures, and then he had some story about his wife expecting him at home. Siân forced him to call his wife on his mobile and tell her he had a quick job to do. Then she flattered him about his way with a laser.

"Honestly, Siân, can't it wait till tomorrow?" Neville had complained as he led her into his sanctum, switching on lights he'd only recently turned off.

"This thing has been waiting for me since 1788," she replied.

Hours later, in the privacy of the Mary Hepworth Room, Siân fondled the paper scroll with gloved fingers. It was light, as she'd expected from its loss of moisture, but also much more brittle than she'd hoped. Any fantasies she might have entertained of simply unrolling the sheets and smoothing them out flat were out of the question. Progress would be slow, methodical, painstaking—as always when rescuing anything from the ravages of time. Nothing ever came easy.

This paper had clearly been sized with a lot of gelatine—and a rich gelatine at that, involving generous amounts of animal skin, hooves, bones. A nice smooth glossy paper it must have been, in its day—but water damage had turned the gelatine to glue. And whatever had dried the soggy paper out again had hardened it into something very like papier-mâché. She prodded it gently with tweezers, and it responded with all the pliancy of driftwood.

She should, she supposed, count her blessings: this treasure had survived, when it could easily have disintegrated altogether. But why did the process of retrieving anything from the distant past always have to be making the best of a bad job? Why couldn't anything spring from antiquity fresh and intact? Why must all documents be blemished and brittle, all vases broken, all skeletons incomplete, all bracelets rusted, all statues vandalised?

Why should only tiny scraps of Sappho's poetry survive—why not *all* of it, or none?

She chewed her fingernails, knowing her irritability was really just nervousness: excitement about what she might disclose, fear that she'd bungle the job. She threw on her jacket and went out to the garage near the railway station and bought four different chocolate bars. By the time she returned to her hotel room, she'd already eaten three of them and her pockets were crackling with the wrappers. She paused in the doorway of her bedroom to take a long swig of complimentary mineral water. Then, highly alert and faintly nauseous, she laid out the tools and equipment for her surgery.

By 3:00 A.M., she was nudging the confession of Thomas Peirson into the light of the twenty-first century. For hours, she'd been humidifying the scroll, rolling it gently back and forth on a metal grid suspended over a photographic tray of warm water, then resealing it inside a garish placenta of blue plastic. The paper had finally absorbed enough vapour to relax a little, and the gelatine was loosening its grip. Now, with a palette knife, Siân began peeling the outermost sheet from its companions.

Confession of Thos. Peirson, in the Year of Our Lord 1788
In the full and certain Knowledge that my Time is nigh, for my good Wife has even now

159

*closed the door on Doctor Cubitt & weeps in
the room below, I write these words.*

The fibres of the paper were exceptionally frail;
the rags from which the paper had been made
must have been shabby stuff indeed, poorly
pounded. The brown ink of Thomas Peirson's
handwriting stood out tolerably well against a
background that hadn't discoloured much, but
then the paper's whiteness had less to do with
thorough washing of the rags than with an expe-
dient douse in that brand-new invention (well,
brand-new in 1788, anyway) chlorine bleach.
Inevitably, the bleach had left its own acid legacy,
and with every gentle nudge of Siân's knife, the
weakened grain of the humid surface threatened
to disintegrate. The words themselves were
fragile, the gallic acid and iron sulphate in the
brown ink having corroded little holes in the *e*'s
and *o*'s.

*below, I write these words. In my fifty years of
life I have been*

Been what? A thread of the paper had come loose,
damaging the crown of one of the words in the
line below. Siân paused, dabbed her eyes with her
sleeve. She ought to give the paper longer to relax,
get some sleep while it did so.

Outside in the street, a drunken male voice
shouted an ancient word of contentious etymology,

and a female voice responded with laughter. The act from which all humans originate, evoked in a word whose own origins were long lost.

Siân laid her head against her pillow, one leg hanging off the bed, the other twitching wearily on the mattress. She closed her eyes for just a moment, to moisten them before getting back to the task.

"I love you—you must believe that," the man with the big hands whispered into her ear. "I'll risk my soul to save yours."

He sounded so sincere, so overwhelmed by his love for her, that she pressed her cheek against his shoulder and hugged him tight, determined never to be disjoined from him.

Within minutes, of course (or was it hours?), her head was disjoined from her neck, and the seagulls were screaming.

Later that same morning, when the sun was high over Church Street and the hundred and ninety-nine steps were glowing all the way up the East Cliff, Siân stood poised at the foot of them, breathing deeply, getting ready for the climb. The sharpness of the sea air was sort of restorative and yet it was making her dizzy, too, and she was finding it hard to decide if she should keep breathing deeply or cut her losses and get moving. She still hadn't begun the climb when, half a dozen breaths later, she was jolted from her underslept stupor by the shout:

"Kill, Hadrian, kill!"

It was Magnus's voice ringing out, mock-imperious, but she couldn't see where it was coming from. All she knew was that a large animal, barking raucously, fangs bared, had sprung into her path, ready to knock her sprawling.

"Hey!" she yelped, half in fear, half in recognition. Hadrian leapt back on his haunches, panting with pleasure. His cream-coloured snout was still twitching, his teeth still bared, but in a whimpery, goofy grin.

"Show 'er no mercy, boy," said Mack, jogging into view. He was taller and better-looking than she remembered, stripped down once again to athletic essentials, his bare legs glistening in the sun, his T-shirt stained with a long spearhead of sweat pointing downwards.

"You scared me," she chided him, as he drew abreast of her and continued to jog on the spot, his limbs in constant motion.

"Sorry. Cruel sense of humour. Blame it on my father."

Though his face was flushed and she was regarding his pounding feet and pumping fists with disdainful bemusement, he seemed unable to stop running on the spot. It was an addiction, she'd read somewhere. Exercise junkies.

"For goodness' sake, stand still."

"It's a glorious day!" he retorted, throwing his arms wide to the sun as he continued to pound the stone under his feet. "Come on, let's run up the steps!"

"Be my guest," she said.

"No, together!" He leapt onto the first step, sending Hadrian bounding ahead in a fit of joy; then after scaling a few more, he ran back down to her.

"Come on—show me how fit you are!"

Siân was sick with embarrassment, dumbstruck by his rudeness. If he noticed her distress, it only spurred him on.

"Come on—slim young woman like you," he panted, "should be able to run up a few stairs."

"Please, Mack . . ." His flattery was crueller than insults. "Don't do this."

"It's all about pacing yourself," he persisted, his face flame-red now, suggesting he was ashamed, but had gone too far to retreat now. "You take a breath . . . every three stairs . . . sixty-six breaths . . ."

"Mack," she said. "I'm an amputee."

For a moment he paced on, then abruptly stopped.

"Christ," he said, his fists dangling loose at his sides. "I'm sorry."

Hadrian had scampered down to join them again, bearing no grudge for the way they'd teased him. He looked up at Siân and his master's faces, back and forth, as if to say, *What next?*

Mack wiped his huge palm across his face, then did a more thorough job with the hem of his T-shirt. A little boy finding a pretext for hiding his face from an angry parent. A beautiful young man baring his abdomen, muscled like a Greek statue.

You bastard, thought Siân. *I want, I want, I want.*

"Which leg?" asked Mack, when he'd recovered himself.

She lifted her left leg, wiggled it in the air for as long as she could keep her balance.

"It's a good prosthesis," he said, adopting his best physicianly tone.

"No it's *not*," she retorted irritably. "It's a Russian job, mostly wood. Weighs a ton."

"You haven't considered upgrading to a plastic one? They're really light, and nowadays—"

"Magnus," she warned him, caught between bewildered laughter and bitter fury, "it's none of your business."

To her relief, he dropped the subject, swallowing hard on his no doubt encyclopaedic knowledge of artificial limbs—if "encyclopaedic" was the correct word for a professional acquaintance with the glossy promotional brochures that prosthetics companies sent to doctors.

"I'm sorry," he said, sounding genuinely chastened. Hadrian, impatient for action, fidgeted between them, his downy black forehead wrinkled in supplication. Siân stroked him, and it felt good, so she knelt down and stroked him some more.

Mack knelt too, and since her hand was busy with the head and mane, he stroked the flank, hoping she wouldn't pull away.

"How did you lose your leg?" he said gently, not like a doctor quizzing a patient, but like an average person humbled by curiosity to know the gory details.

Siân sighed, not angry with him anymore, but struck by how absurdly inappropriate the verb "lose" was in this context, how coy and, at the same time, judgmental. As if she had absentmindedly left her leg on a bus and it was still lying unclaimed in a lost property office somewhere. As if, when the pain inside her was ready for the kill, she would "lose" her life like an umbrella.

"I lost it in Bosnia," she said.

He was instantly impressed. "In the war?" he suggested. She knew he was picturing her doing something exotically heroic, like pulling wounded children out of burning wreckage and being blown up by an enemy shell.

"Yes, but it had nothing to do with the war, really," she said. "I was there because my boyfriend was a journalist. And we were stepping out of a bar in Gorazde when a car knocked me down, right there on the footpath. It was a drunk teenager behind the wheel." She frowned irritably at Mack's look of disbelief. "They have drunk teenagers everywhere, you know, even in Bosnia, even during wars."

"And your boyfriend?"

"What about my boyfriend?"

"Was he . . . injured?"

"He was killed—"

"—I'm so sorry—"

"—four weeks later, by sniper fire. He'd already dumped me by then. Said he just couldn't see it working out, him and a disabled person. He'd have to devote his whole life to taking care of me, he thought."

Mack grimaced, tarred with the guilt of a fellow male he'd never even met.

"You've done brilliantly, though," he said.

"Thank you."

"No one would know."

"Not unless they tried to make me run up a hundred and ninety-nine steps, no."

"I'm really sorry."

Siân patted Hadrian's head. It was as far as she was willing to go towards letting the dog's master off the hook. *Let him sweat*, she thought. Metaphorically speaking, of course. Every muscle on his torso seemed already to be defined with the stuff.

"Speaking of contrition . . ." she said. "Your message in a bottle . . . your confession . . ."

"Yes?" He seized the change of subject gratefully, his head cocked in deference.

"The job is trickier than I thought. You're going to have to decide what's more important to you, Mack: knowing what that document says, or keeping it the way you like it. The shape of it, I mean. If I succeed in peeling those pages apart, I'll be doing well. I can't give them back to you in the form of a nice tight scroll inside a bottle."

"So what are you suggesting?"

"I'm not suggesting anything," she said, manoeuvring him gently towards where she wanted him. "It's *your* heirloom, Mack. I can glue

166

the bottle shut again, return it to you tomorrow."

She turned away to acknowledge Michael coming up the steps, greeting the poor little duffer with a cheery wave. Michael nodded back, squinting, almost tripping over his own feet in his attempt not to intrude. She could tell that in his myopic eyes, she and Mack were the enigma of romance, stumbled upon, unearthed, only to be handed over to experts for analysis. Sweet, shy little man—how she despised him . . .

"I don't know," Mack was saying. "There's something magic about it, just the way it is . . ."

"Well, there is one thing we could do," she said, figuring she'd softened him up enough. "I could make you a new scroll out of papier-mâché, and stick a facsimile of the outermost page on the outside. I know how to make things like that look old and authentic. The original papers could be mounted on board, preserved properly, and you could have a replica that'd look pretty close to what your dad found."

He laughed.

"More historical fakery, eh?"

She looked him square in the eyes.

"Do you want to know what the confession says or not?"

He pondered for no longer than three seconds. "I do," he conceded.

That afternoon, Siân and her colleagues at the dig said good-bye to Keira and Trevor, who were decamping to the Middle East. In their place, the "very nice people" from north Wales had already settled in—another married couple who'd been together forever. They wore matching jumpers and identical shoes. They whispered to each other as they worked, and kissed each other on the shoulder or on the side of the head. Siân knew very well they were adorable, but disliked them with an irrational passion. They smelled so strongly of happiness that even on the exposed headland of Whitby's East Cliff, the odour was overpowering.

I want, I want, I want.

At three-thirty, the heavens opened and the site supervisor declared the day's digging at an end. Thirteen of the fourteen archaeologists hurriedly dispersed into the downpour, hunched under nylon hoods and plastic habits, like a herd of monks fleeing a new Dissolution of the Monasteries. The younger ones sprinted down towards the town, free to embrace the unimaginable luxuries of the modern world.

Siân, without a raincoat or umbrella, walked gingerly on the slick and treacherous terrain, watching where she put her feet as the rain penetrated her scalp and trickled down the back of her neck.

Every few seconds, she cast a glance towards the hundred and ninety-nine steps, hoping against hope that Mack and Hadrian would be coming up to meet her. They weren't, of course. Still she cherished a forlorn fantasy of Mack surfacing from the horizon, running up the steps, one arm holding

168

aloft an umbrella. Pathetic. Saint Hilda would be shaking her head despairingly, if she knew.

The car park between the abbey ruins and Saint Mary's Church, which ordinarily failed to register on Siân's consciousness at all, annoyed her intensely today as she crossed it. What was it doing here, littering a sacred space with automotive junk? Buried somewhere underneath this dismal moat of concrete, this petrol-stained eyesore, lay oratories and other buildings erected by simple Christians more than a thousand years ago. What would it take to clear away this garbage, short of a bomb?

Siân winced at a flash of recollection—the sound of the shelling she'd experienced in Bosnia, the blasts and rumbles that drove her deeper into the crook of Patrick's arm as they lay in bed, a few miles from the action.

"Pretend it's a thunderstorm," he'd advised her. "It can't hurt you."

"Unless it hits you," she'd said.

"Then you won't feel anything," he'd said, almost asleep.

A lie, of course. Nothing dies painlessly. Even a limb that's long gone keeps hurting.

For more than an hour, Siân traipsed around the streets of Whitby, searching for something to eat. She was in one of those perverse moods where nothing seemed appealing except what was patently not on offer. A lively Greek or Turkish restaurant, with lots of different dips and delicacies and peasant

waiters hollering at each other across the room—
that would do. Or a Chinese buffet, with spiced
noodles and tiny spring rolls and hot soup. She was
most definitely not in the mood for fish and chips,
which, in Whitby, was an unfortunate way to be.

Window after window, street after street, she
peered through foggy panes of glass and read
menus that offered her cod and potato in its
various disguises, served with mushy peas, pickled
egg, curry sauce, gravy. A sign on the front door
of the Plough Inn said "Sorry, no food today". A
bistro that looked promising wasn't open till the
evening. The Tandoori place near the station was
good, but she'd eaten there yesterday, and besides,
she wanted something instantly.

She ended up eating a banana-and-ice-cream
crêpe in a café across the river. They served it with
the ice cream folded inside the pancake rather than
on top, so the whole thing was already a lukewarm
mess even as she made the first incision with her
toothless knife. Chasing the disappearing warmth,
she ate too fast, then felt sick.

If she'd been one of Saint Hilda's nuns, she
reflected, she would have dined on bread and wine,
in the company of friends. She would have drawn
a circle in the air and someone would have silently
handed her something wholesome, and there
wouldn't have been this Top 40 gibberish blaring
into her ears.

Dream on, dream on.

She paid for her pancake and crossed the bridge

to her hotel, still haunted, to top it all off, by the fantasy of Magnus cresting the horizon with an umbrella held aloft.

Siân's nightmare next morning was an ingenious variant on the usual. In this version, she had just a few precious seconds to find where her severed head had rolled and replace it on her neck, before the quivering nerves and arteries lost their ability to reunite. Her consciousness seemed to be floating somewhere between the two, powerless to guide her headless body as it groped and fumbled on the floor, its gory neck densely packed with what looked like gasping, sucking macaroni. Her head lay near the open door, inches from the steep stairwell, its eyes fluttering, its lips dry, licked by an anxious tongue. With a bump, Siân woke up on the floor next to her bed.

I really am losing my mind, she thought.

Still, looking on the bright side, she'd slept quite well, and for an uncommonly long stretch of hours. Buttery-yellow sunlight was beaming through the velux window, flickering gently as seagulls wheeled over the roof. The screaming was over, and breakfast would be served downstairs. Most cheeringly of all, she'd made good progress last night on Thomas Peirson's confession.

Before going to bed, she'd managed to liberate the whole of the outermost page. Aside from those *o*'s and *e*'s already lost to the corrosive ink, there'd been no further mishaps; she'd proceeded with the utmost

171

gentleness, ignoring the pangs of indigestion and . . . and whatever that lump in her left thigh might be. The lump was more palpable and more painful all the time, but she refused to let it terrorise her. She'd made a solemn vow, when she'd finally walked out of that hospital in Belgrade, feeling each clumsy step reverberating through the cushioned mould of her prosthesis, that she would never lie in a hospital bed again, ever. She would keep that vow. And if she was condemned to die soon, at least she'd die knowing she'd done a good job on this confession.

A hastily scribbled transcript of what she'd unwrapped so far was lying on the spare pillow of her double bed. Pity it had to be written on a cheap little notepad with a *Star Wars* actress on the cover, but that was the only writing paper to hand last night, and she was so impatient to share Thomas Peirson's secrets with Mack that she simply couldn't wait. He would be in seventh heaven when he saw this. He was just the sort of guy who'd be keen on murder mysteries, she could tell.

She scooped yesterday's skirt off the floor and held it up to the sunlight. It was well and truly ripe for the laundromat; she would wear something fresh today. To celebrate the first page.

All the way to work, the cheap little *Star Wars* notepad burned a hole in Siân's jacket pocket, and her ears were cocked for the sound of Mack's voice, or the heavy breathing of Hadrian. Neither sound came to her, however, and she joined her colleagues at the dig, tilling the soil for human remains.

At lunchtime, she wandered down to the kiosk and had a peek out into the world beyond the abbey grounds. Nothing. She considered going down to Loggerhead's Yard and actually visiting Mack at his house, but that didn't feel right.

After all, he might kill me, she thought—then blinked in surprise at the idea. What a thing to think! Nevertheless, she'd rather wait until he came to her.

She strolled back to the abbey remains. The fine lunchtime weather was luring visitors to the site— not just tourists, but also the children of English Heritage staff. Bobby and Jemima, the son and daughter of one of the kiosk workers, were running around the ruins, shrieking with laughter. At seven and six years old respectively, they weren't worried that their scrambling feet would erode the stonework of the pedestal stubs littering the grassy nave. They were so young, in fact, that they could even kiss each other without worrying about the consequences.

"Hi, Bobby! Hi, Jemima!" called Siân, waving.

The children were mucking about near the vanished sacristy, lying down flat and jumping up in turn, pirouetting gracelessly.

"What are you doing?" said Siân.

Jemima was swaying on her feet, dizzy after another spin; Bobby was lying in a peculiar hollowed-out depression in a rectangle of stone, staring up at the sky.

"We're tryin' to see the wumman jumpin'," he explained.

"What woman?"

"The ghostie wumman that jumps off the top." Bobby pointed, and Siân followed the line of his grubby finger to the roofless buttresses of the abbey. "You spin three times, then you lie in the grave, then you see her."

"Have you seen her?" said Siân.

"Nah," said Jemima. "We've not spinned 'ard enough."

And the two of them ran off, laughing.

Siân looked down at the hollow in the stone, wondering what it used to be before it served as a toy sarcophagus for superstitious children. Then she peered up at the abbey buttresses, imagining a woman moving along them, a young woman in a flowing white gown, her bare feet treading the stone tightrope with all the sureness of a sleepwalker.

"*HUSH!*"

Siân almost jumped out of her skin as the dog shouted his greeting right next to her. She staggered off balance and did a little dance to regain her footing, much to Hadrian's delight.

"Honestly, Hadrian," she scolded him. "Who taught you *that* trick?"

"My dad, I suppose," said Mack, ambling up behind. He was dressed in black denim trousers and a grey Nike sweatshirt with the sleeves gathered up to his elbows; he looked better than ever.

"That's right, blame the departed," said Siân.

"But it's *true*," he protested. "I'm just a foster carer, stuck with a delinquent orphan. Aren't I, Hadrian, eh?" And he patted the dog vigorously on the back, almost slapping him.

"You didn't need to pay £1.70 to meet me," said Siân. "I would've come out eventually."

He laughed. "Sod that. I want to know what that confession says."

"One page a day is the best I can manage," she cautioned him.

"I'll take what I can get."

She pulled the notebook from her jacket pocket, flipped Princess Whatsername over and immediately began to read aloud:

> *Confession of Thos. Peirson, in the Year of Our Lord 1788*
>
> *In the full and certain Knowledge that my Time is nigh, for my good Wife has even now closed the door on Doctor Cubitt & weeps in the room below, I write these words. In my fifty years of Life I have been a Whaler and latterly an Oil Merchant; to my family I have given such comforts as have been allow'd me, and to God I have given what I could in thanks. All who know me, know me as a man who means harm to no one.*
>
> *Yet, as I prepare to meet my Maker, there is but one memory He sets afore me; one dreddeful scene He bids me live again. My hands, though*

175

cold now with Fever, do seem to grow warm, from the flesh of her neck—my beloved Mary. Such a slender neck it was, without flaw, fitting inside my big hands like a coil of anchor rope.

I meant, at first, no more than to strangle her—to put such marks upon her throat as could not be mistaken. Despoiled tho' she was, I was loath to despoil her more; I would do only so much as would spare her the wrath of the townsfolk, and secure her repose among the Blessed. So, I resolved only to strangle her. But

She looked up at him.

"But?" he prompted.

"That's it, so far. A page-and-a-bit."

Mack tilted his head back, narrowed his eyes in concentration.

"Maybe he thought she was a vampire," he suggested after a minute. "Maybe he strangled her while she was sleeping, thinking she was going to sprout fangs when the sun came up."

"I don't think so," sighed Siân.

"Well, Whitby is the town of Dracula, isn't it?"

"Not in 1788," she said, restraining herself from a more fulsome put-down.

"I know damn well when the novel was written," he growled. "But maybe Bram Stoker was—what's the word?—*inspired* by how everybody in Whitby was vampire-mad."

"I don't think so. I think the people of Whitby were worried about their menfolk drowning in the

North Sea, not about Transylvanian bloodsuckers running around in black capes."

"They were pretty superstitious, though, weren't they, these eighteenth-century Yorkshire people?"

"I wasn't alive then, believe it or not. But I think we can be pretty sure our man Thomas Peirson, if he strangled someone, wasn't doing it because of a story that hadn't been written yet by a novelist who wasn't even born here."

Mack's eyes went a bit glazed as something came back to him. "My dad showed me Count Dracula's grave once, in Saint Mary's churchyard. I must have been six."

"Naughty man. Were you scared?"

"Bloody terrified; I had nightmares for days. I adored it, though. Nothing more thrilling than fear, is there?"

She looked down uneasily. "I don't know about that."

"OK, maybe *one* thing," he conceded. His voice was soft, deep, good-humoured; the tint of bawdiness in it was unmistakable.

"Tell you what," said Siân, blushing. "Why don't you show me the grave?"

The East Cliff churchyard may have been the final earthly resting place for hundreds of humans, but for Hadrian this grassy expanse of headland was heaven. He dashed across the green, leaping over tombstones as if they were sporting hurdles provided especially for him, rather like those handsome black receptacles on the seashore embossed *DOG WASTE*. With such a huge playground to explore, he was quite content to let his master and mistress get on with whatever they were here for.

"I don't know if I can find it, after so many years," said Mack, shielding his eyes under the visor of his massive right hand.

"Put yourself back in that little boy's shoes," she suggested.

He laughed, and lifted up one size twelve foot. "You've got to be joking."

They both, at exactly the same time, recalled the moment when she'd lifted her prosthetic leg for him on the hundred and ninety-nine steps. The moment when the scales fell from his eyes, and she knew with perfect certainty that he was imagining her body and wondering how he'd feel about it if it were stretched out naked beside him.

He reached out to her, cupped her shoulder in his palm.

"Look, it's all right," he said.

She walked ahead of him, face turned away.

"Lots and lots of these graves are empty, did you know that?" she declared, in a brisk, informative tone. "Sailors would be lost at sea, and the families would have a funeral, put up a headstone . . ."

"Ah, historical fakery again . . ."

"Not at all. It preserves a different kind of history—the reality of the loved ones' grief."

He hummed dubiously. "I'm not a grief kinda

guy, Siân. Bury the dead, get on with living, that's my motto."

She shivered without knowing why. She couldn't remember if he'd ever spoken her name before today. The way he voiced it, exhaled it at leisure over his tongue, "Siân" sounded like a noise of satisfaction.

They wandered around for another five minutes or so, but failed to find the unmarked grave Mack's father had told him was Dracula's. What they did find was something Siân had read about in a book: an adjacent pair of gravestones—one oval and flat to the ground, the other a tiny upright miniature—which countless generations of children had been assured marked the graves of Humpty Dumpty and Tom Thumb.

"My dad never told me that," said Mack.

"Well there you are: another black mark against him."

They went to fetch Hadrian, who was merrily digging up clods of earth all over the place. Siân glanced at the weathered tombstones as she walked, reading the odd name here and there if it was still legible. Sea-spray and the wind of centuries had erased the finer details, and she wasn't in the mood to study the stones closely, as she was getting peckish. But suddenly she did a double take and stumbled backwards.

"It's our man!" she cried. "Mack! It's our man!"

He bounded to her side—he and Hadrian both. Standing somewhat skew-whiff on the ground before them was a tall headstone clearly inscribed THOMAS PEIRSON, WHALER AND OIL MERCHANT. According to the remainder of the text, he was the husband of Catherine, father of Anne and Illegible. He died, as he'd anticipated in his confession, in 1788, but there was no hint of him having done anything to warrant remorse. Not so much as a "God have mercy on his soul."

The discovery of Peirson's headstone galvanised Mack, sending him sniffing around the other graves, squinting at the inscriptions. It was as if it hadn't occurred to him before now that his treasure-in-a-bottle was something more than a bizarre relic—that it was still intimately connected with the world at large.

"I wonder if his victim's here, too?" he was muttering, as he moved from grave to grave. "Mary . . . Mary . . . If only she'd had a more unusual first name . . ." He bent down to peer at an epitaph, reciting the bits he considered interesting. "'. . . in the thirty-fourth year of her age . . .' No cause of death listed, though . . . Shame . . ."

There was something about his attitude that Siân found provocative.

"Well, Dr. Magnus, this is a churchyard, not a hospital mortuary. These headstones are commemorations, they're not here to satisfy your curiosity."

"What do you mean, *my* curiosity?" he retorted, stung. "Of the two of us, who's digging up dead bodies, poking around in people's bones?"

Siân turned on her heel and began to walk away. How instinctively, how helplessly they argued with each other! The last person she'd argued with so much, she ended up declaring her undying love to—not to mention following him to a war zone and shielding him from the impact of an oncoming car. There was no hope for her; she was doomed.

"Let's not make a big thing of this," he said, catching up to her. "Can I take you out to lunch?"

She tried to say no, but Hadrian was at her side now, rubbing his downy snout against her skirt as she walked, snuffling in anticipation of her touch. She allowed her hand to fall into his mane, felt his skull arching against her palm. Her stomach rumbled.

"We could have a cup of tea at The Mission," she said. "They let dogs in there."

"The Mission?"

"The Whitby Mission and Seafarer's Centre. They run a coffee shop."

"Don't be silly—I'll drop Hadrian off at home and take you to a proper restaurant."

Determined not to argue, she said, "OK, then: Indian."

But his brow wrinkled into a frown. "Let me think . . ."

"What's wrong with Indian?"

"I'd rather something more . . . um . . . unusual."

She took a deep breath as they began to descend the hundred and ninety-nine steps.

"From a historical point of view," she said, trying

181

to convince herself she wasn't arguing but only making an interesting observation, "you surely can't get much more unusual than Punjabi food in a Northumbrian fishing town."

"*You* know what I mean," he said. "The small-town Indian restaurant . . . it's so . . . provincial."

"Well, we're in a *province*, for goodness' sake!" she snapped. "We're not in London now."

"Wow," he said. "You're the only person I know who says 'for goodness' sake,' even when she looks ready to clock me one."

"So? Does that make me cute?"

"Yes, it makes you cute. And by the way, you're dressed very nicely today. You're looking fantastic."

Siân felt herself colouring from the hairline down. As his compliment sank in, so did the realisation that, God help her, she really *had* dressed and groomed herself with unusual care this morning. Her skirt, tights, and boots were classy coordinates and, as her blush travelled further down her body, she was reminded that the neckline of the top she'd chosen was, for the first time in years, low enough to show off her collarbones.

"Uh . . . look," she said, only a few steps shy of Church Street, "I've just realised: I don't have time to go to a restaurant. I'm supposed to be back at work in five minutes."

He stared at her, mouth open, clearly and sincerely disappointed.

"This evening, then."

She thought fast; there was a tightness in her

throat, like hands pressing on her neck. "I'm going to be working on the next page of your confession this evening," she said breathlessly.

For a few moments they stood there, eye to eye. Then he smiled, dropped his gaze down to his shoes in good-humoured defeat, and let her go.

"Another time," he said, as he stepped onto the cobbled street and motioned Hadrian to accompany him into the town. Hadrian looked around once at Siân, then trotted to join his foster carer in a fast-flowing stream of tourists, native Northumbrians, and less adorable dogs.

In Siân's dream next morning, there was, for a change, no knife. The man was cradling her in his arms, both his hands safely accounted for, one supporting her back, the other stroking her hair. It wasn't what you'd call a happy dream, though: her hair felt wet, slick with a shampoo-like substance which she realised after a while was her own blood. In fact, she was covered in it, and so was he.

"I will carry you up the hundred and ninety-nine steps," he was crooning to her, in a broken voice. His eyes were almost incandescent with love and grief, and there were droplets of blood twinkling on his eyebrows. He looked like Magnus, except he wasn't. "I will carry you up the hundred and ninety-nine steps," he kept promising.

She tried to speak, to reassure him she understood why he had done what he had done, but her windpipe blew blood bubbles, and her tongue was growing stiff.

No particular climactic event woke her, only thirst and a pressing need to go to the loo. She'd drunk half a bottle of wine last night, to kill the pain in her "innermost parts", and it seemed to have done the trick: her headache was so bad she wasn't aware of the lump in her thigh at all.

Her hair felt tacky, and smelled of alcohol; she washed it in the bathroom sink, half expecting the water to run crimson. The veins in her temples went *whumpa whumpa whumpa* as she rinsed the shampoo out and groped for a towel. Only then did it occur to her that she may have been sozzled when she was working on the confession.

The second page was still lying on the table, pressed flat under a rectangle of transparent plastic. She examined the wrinkled leaf of paper and the curlicues of ink closely, anxiously. As far as she could tell, there was no damage that hadn't already been done before she came along.

Next she consulted the little *Star Wars* notebook in which she'd jotted the transcript. It was perfectly lucid—neater, if anything, than her handwriting tended to be when she was stone-cold sober.

She wandered back to the bathroom to dry and style her hair.

At lunchtime, in the same West Side café where she'd made herself sick on pancake, Siân read aloud from her little notebook while Mack listened intently. He leaned very close to her, his cheek almost brushing her shoulder, but then it was quite noisy in the café, as the staff and other customers were watching American soap operas on an elevated TV.

"*So, I resolved only to strangle her,*" she declaimed, while third-rate actors spat fake bile at each other overhead.

> *But, God help me, my thumbes became weak, & made no mark upon her flesh, or none that did not fade straightway afterward. These same hands, which have slashed deep into the hide of a Whale, which have lifted barrels heavier than a man; these hands which, even in my latter years of feebleness, could cleave a log in twain with a single ax blow—these hands could not put upon her pale and tender neck the bruises that would save her. I fancied I could hear her voice, already condemn'd to inhabit the wilds of Perdition, crying to me, imploring me to act afore the alarum be raised, and she be found, naked and ripe for Damnation. Nothing, only I, stood betwixt her helpless soul and the worst of Fates. I did but pause to cover her with a blanket, then hurried to fetch my knife*

Siân put the notepad down, lifted her coffee cup to her lips.

"Wow," said Mack, grinning broadly. "Talk about coitus interruptus . . ."

She sipped the hot brew, troubled by her inability to judge the aptness—or offensiveness—of this remark. Seen in one light, it was a flash of wit only a prude would object to (and after all, he *was* a doctor), but in another light, it was gruesomely, outrageously off. From one light to another she veered, and the moment passed, and she was silent. With Patrick, too, she'd become unable to stop her morality dispersing into his.

"You know what we should do?" he said, stabbing his fork into a wodge of chocolate cake. "We should sell this story to the press."

We? she thought, before replying: "The press? What press? The *Whitby Gazette?*" Only a few minutes before, he'd been leafing through the café's free papers, chortling, in his smug London way, at local place names like Fryup, and inventing preposterous news stories for the *Gazette*, such as an outbreak of psittacosis amongst homing pigeons. "Chief Inspector Beaver is investigating claims that the deadly bacterium was purchased from an unscrupulous doctor," he'd intoned, poker-faced, "by Mister Ee-Bah-Goom of the Whitby Flying Club, as part of a cunning plan to employ germ warfare against his rivals." She'd laughed despite herself.

"You do think small, don't you?" he gently disparaged her now. "I'm thinking of a big colour-feature in one of the major national supplements—the *Sunday Times*, maybe, or the *Telegraph*."

She was pricked to anger by his condescension; she felt that, after all she'd seen at Patrick's side, she wasn't a total innocent in the big bad world of newspapers.

"Do you think they care? Look at the way they've ignored our dig at the abbey! To get a major newspaper interested nowadays, you virtually have to dig up King Arthur's round table, or a previously unknown play by Shakespeare."

"Not at all. This is murder. Murder sells."

She knew he was right, but felt compelled to keep arguing anyway. The thought of her beautiful eighteenth-century manuscript, which she was so lovingly unpeeling from itself, being splashed across the pages of a throwaway Sunday supplement, made her sick.

"It's a very, very out-of-date murder," she said, hoping a cynical, jocular tone would score with him. "Way past its use-by date."

He laughed, and leaned across the table, staring straight into her eyes.

"Murder never goes off," he said, and, leaning farther still, he kissed her on the cheek, right near the edge of her lips.

Siân closed her eyes, praying for guidance as to how to respond. Slapping his face would be so frightfully old-fashioned, and besides, she was afraid of him, and also, it might spoil her only chance of happiness before the cancer decided that her time was up.

187

"Hadrian will be getting lonely," she said. "You'd better go and rescue him."

That afternoon, Siân left the dig early, telling Nina she thought she might be coming down with flu.

Nina scrutinised her face and said, "Yes, you don't look well at all," which was rather discouraging, since the flu story was a lie. In reality, the lump in Siân's thigh was so painful she could barely work, and she was hoping that if she stopped kneeling at her appointed excavation and putting so much pressure on her stump hour after hour, the pain might ease off.

"I'm getting a sore throat myself," said Nina. "Let's hope it's not the Black Death, eh?"

Siân walked stiffly back into town. Her whole pelvis was aching: a subtle network of pain radiating, it seemed, from the lump inwards. A kernel of malignancy haloed with roots and tendrils, like a potato left too long in a cupboard, silently mutating in the dark. Fibrosis. Metastasis. Dissemination. Words only a doctor should be intimately familiar with.

On her way to the White Horse and Griffin, she bought a bottle of brandy, a box of painkillers and, as an afterthought, a king-size block of chocolate. In the privacy of her hotel room, she consumed some of each, at regular intervals, while working on the next page of Thomas Peirson's secret testament.

★　★　★

188

"OK," said Mack the following day, leaning forward expectantly. "Carry on where we left off, yes?"

"Yes." She took a long deep breath, filling her lungs with sea air.

She'd arranged to meet him halfway up the hundred and ninety-nine steps, on the same bench where they'd first sat together. It was more convenient than a café or a restaurant; she wouldn't have so far to walk back to the dig, and she was quite content to eat the apple she'd pocketed that morning in the hotel's breakfast room. Fruit was probably quite a sensible thing to lunch on after a hangover, and she'd already promised herself that chocolate would never again pass her lips—in *either* direction.

Also, it was brilliant sunny weather today, and being out in the fresh air meant that Hadrian could be here with them, and she'd missed Hadrian so badly yesterday.

Also, Mack was less likely, she imagined, to kiss her on a public thoroughfare. Thus postponing the inevitable.

"*I did but pause to cover her with a blanket, then hurried to fetch my knife,*" recited Siân from her little notebook. Hadrian promptly laid a mendicant paw on her knee—the right knee, the one that was flesh and blood—to alert her to the fact she'd stopped stroking him. "Oh, Hadrian, I'm sorry," she crooned, ruffling his mane. "What a *bad* mother I am . . ."

"Come on, come on," growled Mack impatiently. "He'll survive. *Read.*"

189

She raised the notebook, savouring her modicum of power over him—the only power she had left, before she surrendered completely.

I did but pause to cover her with a blanket, then hurried to fetch my knife—that same knife I have used for a thousand innocent purposes—cutting rope, gipping fish, paring fruit, carving blubber. Believing myself to be alone in the house, I came down the stairs without caution, and was surpriz'd by our Anne in the parlour, crying, Father, what is the matter? Go catch your Mother up at market, I says. We are not needing a ham after all, for I mind now that Butcher Finch said he would give us one in lieu of payment for his oil. So she runs off, God bless her.

I found my knife, and returned to the room upstairs—the same room where I now write these words. It seemed to me that Mary had moved away from where I put her down—crawled towards the door—but when I spoke her name, she lay still. Once more I gathered her close to my breast, cradling her like a bairn. How I yearned to spare her the knife! Had I the nerve to beat her black and blew instead, to stave in her soft skull with my fists, and splinter her ribs like kindling? I owned I had not. So, without pausing any more, I lowered her into the wash-copper, and hewed the blade deep into her neck,

190

cleaving her flesh to the bone. Her blood flowed out like a wave, like a wave of shining crimson, clothing her nakedness.

Siân looked up. Mack's eyes were bright with excitement, his great hands clasped white-knuckled against his chin. In her eagerness to bring him the latest instalment, she must surely have known he'd respond like this, but now that she saw that look in his eyes, she felt ashamed.

"That's all," she said, with an awkward smile. "That's all I could get done. If you knew what it took . . ."

He leaned back, letting it all sink in. "Wow," he sighed. "This guy was a genuine, authentic eighteenth-century psycho. Hannibal Lecter in a frilly shirt."

"Who's Hannibal Lecter?"

"Come on! The world's favourite serial killer! You mean you've never seen *The Silence of the Lambs*?"

"Lovely title," she said, responding to Hadrian's urgent pleas for stroking at last. "Sounds like a pre-Raphaelite painting by William Holman Hunt or someone like that."

"Who's William Holman Hunt?"

They sat in silence for a few seconds, while Siân petted Hadrian and Mack watched the dog go demented in her hands.

"Anyway, our man Thomas Peirson," he declared, when finally, to his bemusement, Siân's face disappeared in Hadrian's flank. "He's a star, can't you see? He could really put Whitby on the map—the *modern* map."

Siân surfaced, blinking.

"Don't you ever get tired," she challenged him, "of this ever-so-*modern* fascination with psychopaths and sick deeds? It can't be good for us—as a culture, I mean. Filling ourselves up with madness and cruelty."

"Face it, Siân, when was it ever different? Madness and cruelty have always been the staple diet of history." And he smiled, secure in the knowledge that he had, among many other things, Hitler and de Sade on his side.

Siân looked away from him, towards the headland, for inspiration. "Think of Saint Hilda founding the original monastery here," she said, "long before Whitby was even called Whitby. Think of the devotion, the sheer strength of spirit invested in this place. A little powerhouse of prayer, perched on a clifftop next to a wild sea. I find that thrilling—much more thrilling than serial killers."

"Jolly good, jolly good," he said, in a fruity mockery of an upper-class relic. "But honestly, Siân, I'm sure your Saint Hilda was as twisted as they come."

Violently, she jerked to face him, startling Hadrian with the sudden movement.

"What would *you* know?" she snapped, as the poor dog cowered between them.

"Oh, I've read plenty," Magnus shot back. "Did

192

you know that in the middle of the night, friendly elves drop history books through my letterbox? It's like the Open University, it's amazing what you learn. The complete rundown on religious fanatics in England, with colour illustrations. Step-by-step instructions for flagellating yourself."

"You're making no effort to understand these people! Just because they weren't driving around in cars, talking into mobile phones . . ."

He threw his hands up, just like Patrick used to do, and exclaimed, "Christ almighty: the arrogance! You're assuming that if I were only a bit more educated, I'd realise what total *darlings* these lunatics really were. Well, I *have* read my history books and my glossy brochures, thank you very much. And these monks and friars and abbesses, *some* of them may've believed in what they were doing, but their philosophy *stinks*. Hatred of the human body, that's what it boils down to. Hatred of natural desires, hatred of pleasure. Think of their routine, Siân: knocked out of bed at midnight, walk to a horrible gloomy hall, kneel down on a hard floor, start praying in the freezing cold, pray and chant all night and all day. Wear rough clothes specially designed to stop you feeling too comfortable. Nice food forbidden, just in case you're tempted to gluttony. Conversation forbidden, in case it distracts you from being a zombie. And if you dare to break the rules, you get flogged publicly. It's *sick!*"

He pointed up towards the abbey, his thumb and forefinger as rigid as a gun.

"*That's* why those ruins are ruins, can't you see that? It's got nothing to do with hurricanes, or Henry VIII, or German warships taking potshots at the abbey in 1914. It's got to do with society growing up—evolving to the point where we realise we don't *need* a bunch of sad old perverts telling us we'll go to hell if we enjoy life too much. It's the twenty-first century, Siân, wake up!"

"You're yelling at me," she said, miserable with déjà vu. Screaming rows with Patrick, heads turning in crowded places, furious tussles finally won and lost under rumpled bedsheets.

Magnus folded his arms across his chest and glowered.

"For Christ's sake." He was making a strenuous effort to keep his voice down. "The Dark Ages are over, haven't you noticed? People enjoy taking a peek at the ruins, they'll buy a postcard of Saint Hilda at the kiosk, but that's as far as it goes. Sooner or later, the last few walls will fall down, and it'll be *adios*, ta-ta, good *night*."

"Those walls," said Siân frostily, "will still be standing when people like you are long gone. None of your . . . huffing and puffing can change that."

He glared at her, thrusting his massive shoulders forward as if bracing himself to punch her. Instead, with a groan of frustration, he suddenly threw his arms around her and pulled her close to him, crushing her against his chest.

"You drive me crazy," he murmured, his breath hot in her ear, his heartbeat pervading her bosom. "I want you." And he kissed her full on the mouth.

Siân squirmed, embarrassed for him, loath to reject him so publicly, in front of anyone who might be passing by—and besides, she was aroused, intensely aroused. She pulled her mouth away, but wrapped her arms around his waist, clinging hard, her cheek pressed against his jaw. If they could only hold each other like this, breast to breast, for the rest of her life, it would be enough. Nothing else would need to happen.

He began to stroke the back of her head, one palm smoothing her hair; his hand felt big enough to hold her skull inside it, and she was electrified with fear and desire.

"Give me time," she whispered—and he let her go.

"All the time . . . in the world," he reassured her, breathing harder than if he'd just run up and down the steps. "Just say you'll see me again."

She laughed shakily, delighted with the high drama of it all, despising it, too. Hadrian only made it worse, looking from her to Mack and back again, with that absurd wrinkle-browed *What next?* expression of his.

"Of course," she said. "Tomorrow, lunchtime. I'll have the rest of the confession for you."

"Of course," he said, perspiring with relief. A semblance of normality settled in the air around them; the world expanded to include passersby on the church stairs, seagulls, the harbour. The town and its environs had held its breath while they were kissing; now it was letting it out.

"Where shall we meet?" said Mack.

Siân thought for a moment.

"The Whitby Mission. They let dogs in there."

He opened his mouth to argue, then grinned.

"The Whitby Mission." His right hand, whose warm imprint still tingled on her back, reached down to Hadrian, grabbing the dog by the scruff of the neck. "They'll let *you* in there, did you hear that?" he announced, pulling the handful of hair teasingly to and fro. "And we'll find out what that bad man did with the body, eh? Won't that be exciting?"

Hadrian wasn't convinced, baring his teeth and twisting his head in frustrated pursuit of the badgering grip.

"Rough!" he complained.

The inner layers of the scroll were, contrary to Siân's expectations, the most damaged. Something had leaked into them at some stage in their two-hundred-year confinement, something more corrosive than simple moisture or the intrinsic hazards of the gelatine and the ink. Try as she might to peel the pages apart with no damage to the integrity of the fibres or the calligraphy, there were small mishaps along the way: an abrasion of the paper surface here, a comma or a flourish lost to impatience. She took a swig of brandy straight from the bottle, and worked on, sweat trickling into her eyes.

"Come on, you!" she muttered, as she laboured to unfasten, millimetre by millimetre, the page she already knew from the page she hadn't read yet. "Explain yourself." There must surely be a reason behind Thomas Peirson's actions, a better reason than mere evil. Decent, godfearing eighteenth-century men were not psychopaths, plotting their motiveless murders for the future delectation of Hollywood.

But with every word that came to light, Thomas Peirson's soul emerged darker and more disturbing. Sentence by sentence, he painted himself to be exactly the remorseless monster she'd seen reflected in Mack's excited eyes.

When the deed was done, I was in a frenzy of haste. Mary's body I swaddled in waxed sailcloth and hid in a chest; then I washed clean of blood my self, the copper, the knife, and the floor; whereupon I took my place at table downstairs, affecting to be busy with accounts.

The remainder of that day, and the next day after it, were a torture greater than any I expect to suffer in the Time-To-Come, even if it should please God to banish me from his mercy and cast me to the Devil. While Mary's carcase lay stiffening in my sea-chest, I joined my worried wife and daughter, all throughout the streets of Whitby, searching for our lost lamb. We questioned folk on the East side and the West side; we walked till we were weary.

She has run away with that William Agar, my wife says. He has taken her, the blackguard.

So, we visited William's mother & axed her what she knew, and she replied with such a skriking as set our ears ringing. My boy is gone up to London, she says, and you are deceived if you think he would dream of taking your daft daughter with him. My boy has been fair driven away, to get peace from all her fond stories & her lies—I have had the poor lad beating his brow, saying, Mother, are all girls so cack-brained, to see love where none was ever offered? Now he is free of her mischief at last, and if she means to follow him to London, I pray her wiles get her no farther than a whorehouse in York!

After this exchange, I took Catherine home in a terrible anger, and indeed this gave her a certain courage for a while, but then we fell again to waiting for Mary to come home. Hour upon hour, all three of us strained our ears for the footsteps I knew would not sound. She has come to harm! my dear wife wept, wringing her hands. She has come to harm, I know it! Nonsense, woman, I said, inventing a dozen comforting stories with happy embraces for endings.

On the third night, my family at last took

to their beds and slept deep, and I carried my beloved Mary out into the night—being newly in the oil trade then, I had the strength of a whaler yet, & bore her in my arms as easy as a thief bears a sack of candlesticks. Under cover of darkness I ran down the ghaut to the riverside, and there I discharged her poor body into the restless waters.

Next morning, she is found, and fetched up on Fish Pier. The cry of MURDER! spreads throughout the town, from mouth to mouth, until it reaches my door. Still I dissembled—You are mistaken, It cannot be, &c. But then they brought her carcase to me, and the streets of Whitby did echo with the clamour of my weeping.

Siân staggered among the gravestones on the East Cliff at midnight, drunk as a skunk. An immense full moon worthy of Dracula's demon lovers lit her way—that, and a dinky plastic torch with faltering batteries.

"Where are you, you sick bastard . . ." she muttered, sweeping the feeble ray of torchlight over the headstones.

Her mission, as far as she could have explained it if someone had collared her on her way out of the White Horse and Griffin, was revenge. Revenge on a man who would murder his own daughter for falling short of some hateful religious ideal. Revenge on Mack for being so sickeningly right about everything, for seeking out the soft under-belly of her own faith in human nature and injecting it with a lethal dose of cynicism. Revenge on Saint Hilda and all her kind for being so pathetically impotent to stop anything tragic happening to anyone ever. Revenge on the eternal, unfathomable badness of human beings. Revenge on the whole damn Godless universe for deciding she must die when, really, if it was all the same to whatever damn random cellular roulette decided these things, she would rather live.

Revenge on THOMAS PEIRSON, whaler and oil merchant, whose headstone tilted before her now. Husband of Catherine, father of Anne and Illegible. Poor illegible Mary: given the cold shoulder by her lover, butchered by her father, erased from her pathetic few inches of memorial stone by two centuries of North Sea winds. Siân knelt on the ground and attacked the grave plot with a trowel.

VIOLATED! MYSTERY GHOULS STRIKE IN CHURCHYARD, that's what the *Whitby Gazette* would say.

Drunk as she was, it took her almost no time to realise that her grand plan of digging up Peirson and flinging his bones into the sea was a nonstarter. The combination of her fury and one small trowel was not sufficient to send voluminous cascades of earth flying skyward; she was barely penetrating the grassy topsoil.

With a cry of disgust, she abandoned the attempt; she even threw the incriminating trowel away—let the police trace her and arrest her if they had nothing better to do! Bumbling provincials! She lurched back onto the hundred and ninety-nine steps, and promptly fell over, grazing her palms and wrists.

AMPUTEE BREAKS NECK ON CHURCH STEPS. No, not that; anything but that.

She forced herself to sit down on a bench and breathe regularly. Ten breaths of sea air were probably equal in sobering power to one sip of coffee; she would inhale lungfuls of salty oxygen until she was capable of walking safely back to the hotel.

For several minutes she sat on the bench, breathing in and out, trying to brush the sharp grains of grit from her bloodied hands. All the while, she stared down at the stone landing on which generations of coffin-bearers had rested their burden one last time before proceeding to Saint Mary's churchyard. Her feet—foot—feet, shoes, whatever, damn it—were occupying the same space as hundreds, maybe thousands of Whitby's long-vanished dead.

"I promised you," whispered a male voice at her shoulder. "I promised I would carry you up here, didn't I? And here we are."

All the hairs on Siân's body prickled up, and she turned her face into an eerie brightness that had flowed up the hundred and ninety-nine steps like a car's headlight on full beam. A man was bending at her side, a man with a translucent white head and torso. Right through his glowing skin, faintly but unmistakably, she could see the dark windows and tiled rooftops of the houses below.

Instinctively she swung at him with her fist, and he was gone.

It was midday the following day before Siân even considered attempting anything more ambitious than rinsing her mouth with water. Mostly she just lay in bed, watching the slow progress of a shaft of sunlight through the velux window; it started pale and diffuse, on the skirting boards at the far end of the room, then moved inch by inch along the floorboards, growing in intensity, gradually enveloping the table and the blue plastic bag. Had Siân been upright and praying instead of slumped and groaning, she might have been a Benedictine nun in a prayer cell, aware of nothing outside her cloister but the sun making its stately progress through the unseen heavens.

Mack and Hadrian would be waiting for her at the Mission soon, but there was no way she was going to be able to keep that appointment. They would have to try again tomorrow, perhaps, when she was back in the land of the living.

She wondered if she should phone the site supervisor, to explain her nonappearance at the dig. Politeness aside, it seemed a pointless gesture, since her absence was surely obvious to everyone, and what would she say, anyway? *I've got the flu.* Or how about, *I'm massively hung over.* Or, if she was feeling really confessional, she could say, *Maybe you should find a replacement for me now. I'm thinking of killing myself while I'm still well enough to manage it.* Siân lay very still, imagining herself walking to the callbox at the foot of Caedmon's Trod and speaking these words into the telephone receiver. Then she remembered it was Saturday. No one was expecting her to be anywhere in particular.

Except Mack and Hadrian.

She looked at the alarm clock. Half past twelve. Mack surely had better things to do than wait for her: she could sense in him that typically male combination of hunger for female companionship and impatience with women for wasting men's valuable time. Perhaps he would go so far as to wander up the church steps, hoping to run into her. Perhaps he would even pay £1.70 to look for her at the abbey. Or perhaps, contrary to her instincts, he was head-over-heels in love with her, and would wait in the Mission coffee lounge until it closed and the Christian ladies shooed him out into Haggersgate, a sad young man with only a dog for company.

All she knew was that she was relieved she'd never told him where she was staying. She needed a sanctum, even if it was a hotel room that smelled of booze.

Strangely, despite feeling that there were toxic fumes rising from her body and that she must breathe very shallowly to give the pain in her head all the skull room it demanded, she was a lot less miserable than she'd expected to be today. She hadn't had any nightmares, for a start, unless you counted the hallucination on the summit of the hundred and ninety-nine steps. For the first time since her accident, she'd survived a night's sleep without being pursued or mutilated. The notion of a few hours of benign unconsciousness, so taken for granted by other humans when they laid their heads on a pillow, was a novelty for Siân, and she hoped it might happen to her again sometime.

The despair she'd felt last night, the extremity of disgust and disillusionment with human nature, seemed to have faded too. She felt purged, hollow and airy inside, as if everything she'd ever known was no longer stored there. Like an infant, she knew nothing much about anything, and must wait for some clues from the universe before she could make any judgment of what sort of world she was in.

It was the strangest feeling, but not unpleasant.

As the afternoon progressed, Siân got herself ready for going out. She washed her hair, dressed nicely, applied Band-Aids to the abrasions on her palms and wrists, even though she knew they'd peel away in no time. Setting off from the White Horse and Griffin at three-ish, she thought she might go to the East Cliff and throw herself off the edge, hopefully dying instantly on the Scaur below, but instead she crossed the bridge to the West Side, walked to Springvale Medical Centre, and asked to see a doctor.

"I thought you'd decided you never wanted to see me again," said Mack, when he found her waiting for him in the Whitby Mission & Seafarer's Centre on Monday, forty-eight hours after their original appointment.

"Thanks for coming," she said, choosing her words with care. "It was bad of me not to show up on Friday. I really wasn't well enough, though."

He scrutinised her face, clearly unable to decide whether he should respond as a doctor or a lover, torn as he was between voicing professional concern and praising her feminine charms regardless of how ghastly she looked.

"You look very tired," he said, after some deliberation. He himself was in the usual fine shape, though so immaculately groomed and blow-dried today that he reminded her of a male model. She pictured him doing the rounds of hospital wards, accompanied by more nurses than strictly required. Or what about when he graduated to private practice? Female patients would discover hitherto unsuspected talents for hypochondria, no doubt. "And I have to say . . ." he told Siân hesitantly, "your face is rather flushed."

"Oh, I really am sick," she assured him, dabbing at her cheeks with the cool back of one hand. "It's under control, though. Nothing for you to worry about."

They were sitting in the Mission's alternative coffee lounge, the one with the sign above the door saying, "Customers wishing to smoke or accompanied by a pet please use this room". Hadrian was snuffling and whining under the table, doing his best not to bark, beating his tail loudly against the floor and the table legs, and laying his head repeatedly in Siân's lap, for her to pat. Despite the animal-friendly sign above the door, he was the only dog in the room just now, and flirting shamelessly. Mack seemed nervous, rolling a cigarette from a crackling plastic pouch of amber tobacco.

"I didn't know you smoked," said Siân.

"I don't—much," he replied, indicating, with a shrug of his eyebrows, the slightly hazy atmosphere created by the folk at the other tables. "I just get the occasional urge, when there's a lot of it in the air." A sly, disarming grin spread slowly on his face, as though he were the town's most respectable schoolboy caught puffing on a fag behind a rubbish bin. "Not a very good example for a doctor to set, eh? But at least I don't smoke the mass-produced kind."

"Your big moral stand," she remarked drily.

The sparring between them was beginning again, only a few minutes after their reunion. Magnus relaxed visibly, perhaps taking heart from this—or perhaps it was the nicotine.

"I've missed you," he said.

She licked her lips, opened her mouth to reply.

"Hush!" said Hadrian, his skull clunking against the underside of the table.

Mack lifted the tablecloth and peered underneath, half-amused, half-annoyed. "Hadrian disgraced himself here on Saturday, you know that?" he said, grabbing at the animal's tail to force him to turn around. "Whimpered the place down, didn'tcha, eh, boy? That's the last time I take *you* anywhere."

"Rough!" retorted Hadrian, as softly as his canine vocal cords allowed.

Mack allowed the tablecloth to drop, and Hadrian returned to Siân, only his tail showing, a thick plume of white plush sweeping the smoky air. The other diners, mainly elderly couples, were smiling and nudging each other; this dog was better than the telly.

"Are you hungry?" said Mack.

"The ladies are making some warm milk for me," said Siân. "They're going to bring it when it's ready."

He stood up and walked to the main coffee lounge to study the menu. Siân knew perfectly well that nothing would be to his liking. He would, she predicted, come closest to considering the slabs of quiche, but then reject them because the choice of "flavours" was described, in the Mission's bluff un-Londonesque fashion, as "cheese & onion" and "bacon & egg".

While waiting for him to return, she alternated between stroking Hadrian and flipping the pages of *Streonshalh*, the Whitby Parish magazine. The hot news was the latest ecclesiastical Synod—not the one Saint Hilda hosted in 664, obviously, but a forthcoming one. There were advertisements for videos and colour laser copies, but also long articles about the merits of the alder tree and the willow-herb. Since last month, a startling number of parishioners had died—more females than males, too, despite the supposedly superior life expectancies of women. Four different funeral directors offered Siân their services.

On a positive note, a mixed-voice choir called the Sleights Singers, founded in 1909, serenaded her thus: "New lady-and-gentleman members always made welcome". Sure it was quaint, but behind the quaintness she sensed the genuine tug of human welcome, a reminder that if she were to show up at a particular house in Sleights on a particular night, she could have new friends instantly, and start singing with them. Siân committed the address to memory. If she was still alive next Thursday between 7:15 and 9, maybe she'd drop in.

Mack ambled back to the table and sat down.

"Nothing for Magnuses?" said Siân, deadpan.

"Nothing for Magnuses," he agreed. "Look, I know you've been ill and everything, but have you had a chance to . . . ah . . ."

She pulled her *Star Wars* notebook out of her jacket and held it up to her mouth, enjoying the loudness of this silent action. Indeed, she was thinking that all the words they'd spoken up to now had been superfluous, an elaborate verbal game, and could have been replaced with a few decorous hand gestures.

"I've got the whole thing now," she said. "It's all done."

A matronly woman came to the table and set a tall glass of warm milk in front of Siân. She also laid down a cold pasty wrapped in a paper napkin.

"Wow," murmured Mack when she'd walked back to the kitchen. "If you pay extra, do you get a plate?"

"I told her the customer wouldn't need one," said Siân, immediately conveying the pasty under the table, where Hadrian scoffed it noisily.

Mack squinted at her in bemusement. "Were you so sure we'd come?"

"No, I wasn't," she said, and took a careful sip of her milk while, at her feet, the dog went *gronff, snuffle, flupp,* and so forth. "But I liked the idea of giving Hadrian this treat so much, that I bought it for him and hoped it would happen. And it has."

He frowned, as if her rationale were a mystic riddle too thorny—or too stickily sentimental—for him to wish to grasp.

"OK—read," he said, motioning towards the notebook. "Please."

She leaned forward, and he did, too, so their faces were close together, causing a murmur of gossip behind them. Siân delivered the testament of Thomas Peirson in a soft voice, softer still during the more sensational bits, pausing every few sentences for a sip of milk. When she reached the part where Mary's body had been fished out of the River Esk, and her father was weeping for all he was worth, Magnus shook his head in admiration.

"Wow," he said. "Thomas Peirson, take a bow. Hollywood awaits."

"I don't think so," said Siân. "There's more. I did the final page and a half last night. It's going to disappoint you, Mack."

She cleared her throat, and continued reading, in the same soft tone as before. But these were new words, words she had uncovered in the wee small hours, when her sober hand had wielded the knife for the final time and she had wept tears of pity onto the frail old paper.

> Of the events that followed, I have not the time to write. This Confession must be hid in the earth while I have yet strength to bury it. I will say only, that our Mary's funeral was one of the grandest this town has ever seen. She had a coach, drawn by six coal-black horses, and a long train of mourners bearing torches, for in those days burials were done after dark. When we carried her up the Steps, she had servers all dressed in white, carrying a maiden's garland afore her coffin, with ribbons held by all her friends. The Vicar spoke with full sureness of her place in Heaven.
>
> Now, in my own dying days, I know not if I shall meet my daughter again. If she be in Hell, I pray that God finds reason to send me there; if she be in Heaven, I beg His forgiveness. These last years, folk have taken to calling me Bible Thomas behind my back, for I have read the Scriptures more than

most Clergie-men, and there are some who say, He should have been a Monk, & a host of Whales would be the happier for it! None can guess why I have studied the Holy Book so earnestly, leaving not a word of it unturned—but I must be certain that no case like mine was ever judged before!

Under the strict terms of Scripture, I broke no Commandment—this much I know. I can also be sure of one other thing: that if I had left my daughter even as I found her, with the powder of poison on her dead lips, and the name of her faithless lover writ on her belly, she should have been buried in unhallowed ground with a stake through her heart. Now she lies among the Blessed, and soon I shall join her. For how long? Only at the Last Trump shall we know.

You who find this; You who read this—Pray for her, I beg of you!

Thomas Peirson,

father and Christian, as best he could be.

Siân laid the notebook on the table, and drank the rest of her milk. Hadrian had settled down to sleep on her feet, his warm flank breathing against her left shin. Magnus was frowning even more than before, his dark eyebrows almost knitting together.

"I don't get it," he said. "Was she a vampire after all? This stake-through-the-heart business . . ."

"It's how they used to bury suicides," said Siân.

"Mary killed herself, Mack. She was already dead when her dad found her."

His frown only deepened. "So . . ."

"So he did what he had to."

"Slashed his own daughter's throat so she'd score a place in the correct patch of dirt?"

Siân picked up her empty glass and shifted it to one side of the table, as if clearing the way for an embrace—or an arm wrestle.

"Magnus," she said as calmly as she could, "I'm starting to wonder if you have everything it takes to be a good doctor. Can't you see that for our man Thomas, defending his child with a bit of twenty-first-century sarcasm just wasn't an option? As a suicide, she'd've been an object of disgust and shame; instead, he managed to get her buried with love and respect. You can't blame him for that."

Mack leaned back in his chair and ran his hands through his hair, flustered, it seemed, from the effort of understanding such rank idiocy.

"But . . . what difference does it make? God's not fooled, is he? If Mary killed herself, she goes to hell, right?"

"Maybe Thomas was hoping God would turn a blind eye." Siân winced at the ugly vehemence of the sound Mack interjected—something between a sneer and a snort. "Please, Mack: just once, try to put yourself into the mind of a person who believes there's an afterlife and a loving and just God. Imagine the end of the world, when the last trumpet sounds and all the dead rise from their graves, all the millions of people who've ever lived. Imagine God looking down on Whitby, at Saint Mary's churchyard, and there, in amongst all the resurrected souls, there's Mary, standing hand in hand with her father and mother and sister, all of them blinking in the light, wondering what happens next. Imagine. God and Mary's eyes meet, and suddenly each of them remembers how she died. The door to eternal life is open, the other townsfolk are walking through, all the drunkards and the gossips and the men who broke women's hearts. But Mary hesitates, and her father puts his arms around her. Now, tell me, Mack. If *you* were God, what would you do?"

Magnus pouted, scarcely able to believe what she was asking him, discomfited by the shiny-eyed intentness of her stare. "I wouldn't've taken the job in the first place," he quipped. "I would've told the Deity Registration Board to go shove it."

He flashed a grin, a pleading sort of grin painfully at odds with his sweating forehead and haunted eyes. He was evidently hoping the wisecrack would break the tension and restore an atmosphere of warm banter, but that hope died in the chill between them.

"Well," said Siân with a sigh. "It's a good thing nobody asked you, then, isn't it?" And she folded the notebook back into her jacket.

Alarmed at the prospect of her preparing to leave, Mack searched for a reentry point, a way to prolong if not redeem their conversation.

"The bit . . . the bit about Mary having her lover's name written on her belly is weird, isn't it? Do you think she may have been mentally ill?"

Siân rested her chin on her clasped hands, half-closed her eyes. "I think she was very, very unhappy."

"That's what I was getting at. Clinically depressed, if she'd been diagnosed today."

"If you like."

"Or maybe she'd found out she was pregnant?"

"With a little test kit from the pharmacy?"

"I'm sure they had ways of knowing, didn't they, in the eighteenth century?" He looked at her hopefully, as if to call attention to his willingness to concede the wisdom of past ages.

"I don't think Mary was pregnant," said Siân. "Or if she was, she wasn't aware of it. I think this William Agar fellow deflowered her, and then rejected her, and she couldn't cope with the loss of her honour."

"Wow. That's so Victorian. Or Romantic. Or something."

"We all need a sense of personal integrity, Mack," she said, finally pulling her feet out from under Hadrian's sleeping body. "These days more than ever. There's far more people committing suicide now than at any time in history. What have all those people lost, if not their honour?"

"Yeah, but come on . . . To link whether you live or die to being dumped by a boyfriend . . ."

"Oh, I don't know," said Siân. "Who we give

ourselves to is very important, don't you think?"

"Oof," came a voice from under the table.

Siân shifted in her chair, and started laughing—ticklish, involuntary laughter. Her right leg, having gone to sleep some time ago, was suddenly buzzing with pins and needles; the lump in her thigh was giving her hell; in fact, the only part of her that didn't feel lousy was the part that was manufactured by Russian technicians.

"Are you all right?" said Mack, smiling nervously, keen to share the joke.

"No, I'm *not* all right," she groaned, and giggled again. To make matters worse, Hadrian had woken up, and was pawing gently against the leg whose nerve endings were going berserk. "Have you ever been dead, Mack?"

"*What?*"

"Have you ever been clinically dead? You know, in an accident, before they revive you."

He shook his head, dumbfounded.

"*I* have," she went on. "And you know what? I saw the light that people always talk about, the shining light on the other side."

Before he could stop himself, Mack blurted, "Yes, I've read a couple of investigations into that: it's actually the brain's synapses flaring or something . . ."

This, for Siân, was quite enough, and she rose from her seat.

"Sorry, Mack," she said. "I have to go now."

★   ★   ★

A week later, when Siân had just been released from hospital, she walked gingerly up the hundred and ninety-nine steps to the abbey. The ruins were still standing, large as life, despite a summer storm that had damaged roofs and satellite dishes on Whitby's more modern buildings. Siân walked all the way around, making sure nothing was missing that hadn't been missing already, then stood for a minute in the shadow of the abbey's towering east front, enjoying the Gothic symmetry of the great tiers of lancet windows and the scarred perfection of the ancient stonework. Maybe God still had plans for this medieval skeleton after all.

When she wandered over to the dig and said hello, her fellow archaeologists treated her like a returning heroine, everyone downing tools to crowd around her. Even the lovey-dovey couple from Wales were distracted from their industrious serenity long enough to ask how she was getting on. To be honest, everyone seemed extravagantly relieved that she was upright and walking around. This surprised Siân; she'd told no one she was going into hospital, only that she was ill and needed some time off work, but her colleagues made such a fuss of her, she could have been Lazarus. Perhaps, in those agonised last few days before she'd gone to the medical centre and burst into tears in the arms of a nurse, the fear of death had been showing on her face, naked and ghostly pale, for anyone to see.

Then again, perhaps the fear had been showing for years.

The site supervisor told her that a handsome young man had been asking after her every day. Siân took the news pensively, as if calling to mind a host of men who might possibly be the one, then enquired if this guy had a beautiful dog with him. More a miserable-looking, whiny sort of dog, was the reply.

Warmed by the brilliant afternoon sun, Siân walked down to Saint Mary's churchyard, to the very edge of the cliff. She could tell that some of the soil had crumbled away during the storm, and fallen off the headland to the rocks below. Erosion was nibbling at the East Cliff, a never-ending natural labour to equalise the disparity between land and water. With every clod of earth that fell into space, empty air encroached closer to the great community of graves. At some stage in the future, sometime between tomorrow and when the sun turned super-nova, Thomas Peirson's remains, and the remains of his loved ones, would tumble down to the shore of the North Sea.

Siân walked back from the edge onto the firmer terrain, found the Peirson headstone, and stood staring at it. She swayed a little on her feet, dopey with painkillers and antibiotics and the lingering aftereffects of anaesthetic. The marks on the ground where she'd hacked with her trowel were barely perceptible, like scratches from a dog's claws.

Suddenly, out of the corner of her eye, she glimpsed something hurtling towards her, but before she could brace herself against the impact, she was knocked reeling. She didn't quite fall, though, and her assailant wasn't a car—it was Hadrian, bouncing back from her torso like an over-sized soft toy thrown in a tantrum. While she was staggering and windmilling her arms, he danced around her and offered woofs of encouragement.

A man's deep voice shouted, "Hadrian, no!" just as Siân managed to steady herself against Thomas Peirson's headstone. Magnus leapt to her side, his hand extended, and she grasped hold of it, even though it wasn't strictly necessary now.

"Christ, I'm sorry . . . !" said Mack. They stood locked in an absurd handshake over the graveplot, he dressed like a corporate businessman, she all in black like a Goth—the modern kind. Hadrian was bouncing up and down between them, panting and snuffling, and although his manic behaviour was annoying at first, it gave them a convenient excuse to let each other go.

"Maybe he's desperate for exercise," Siân suggested, fondling the dog's sumptuous flank with both hands. "Have you given up running?" And she aimed a nod at Mack's classically formal suit, the trousers of which were the kind she could imagine the wearer fastidiously inspecting for evidence of dog hair. The memory of this man plastered with a dark arrowhead of sweat, scantily clad in T-shirt and shorts, was difficult for her to retrieve now, so faded had it become.

"It got a bit . . . unmanageable," he said, jerking

forward in an abortive attempt to assist her as, with a grunt of pain, Siân knelt next to Hadrian and started stroking the dog in earnest. "Hadrian wouldn't run with me anymore, you see. He'd just shoot ahead like a missile. Totally out of control."

"And this is what drove you to dress up like a sales executive for an insurance firm?"

But his appetite for sparring seemed to have deserted him; instead of firing off a witty rejoinder, he only winced.

"I've got a meeting today, a conference," he explained, his already rather pained eye contact with her faltering. "In fact, I'm leaving. Leaving Whitby."

"Oh yes?" she said, after only a moment's pause in her stroking. "Going back to London?"

"Yes."

"Research paper finished?"

"Yes."

"Proved what you wanted to?"

He shrugged and looked down towards the town, in the general direction of the railway station. "That's for my examiners to decide."

Siân had her arms around Hadrian's neck, her chin nudging his bony, downy skull. She waited a few more seconds to see if Mack would oblige her to ask, or if he'd have the courage to put her out of her suspense.

"What's going to happen to Hadrian?" she enquired at last, in the silence of the headland.

Mack blushed crimson, an ugly inflammation

from the roots of his hair to the collar of his creamy-white shirt. "I don't know. I'll take him with me, I suppose, but . . . I can't see myself being able to manage him in central London." Sweat glistened on his great blushing forehead, and he began to stammer. "Still, he . . . he's a pure-bred, isn't he, and I'm sure he's worth a mint, so I expect there'll be . . . experts, you know, connoisseurs, who'd . . . ah . . . take him."

"How much do you want for him?" said Siân. She'd no doubt he would respond badly to this overture; braced herself for a shamefaced display of something horrible—craven retaliation, evasion, anger. She was wrong. He was enormously, unmistakably relieved.

"Siân," he declared, clapping a palm to his brow, "if you want him, you can *have* him."

"Don't be silly," she said. "He's worth a mint, as you so . . . *bluntly* put it. How much do you want?"

Magnus smiled, shaking his head. "I've owned him long enough, Siân. Now I want *you* to have him as a gift—like those history books you dropped through my letterbox."

"Don't be patronising."

"No, no!" he protested, as animated and confident now as she'd ever seen him. "You don't understand—I was thinking of offering for ages! It's just that I . . . I didn't know where you lived—whether you'd be able to have a dog there. I had an idea you might be staying in a hotel . . ."

"I might be," she said. "But I could move

220

somewhere else, if I wanted to. If there was a reason to." *Yes, yes, yes,* she was thinking, hiding her daft grin of exultation inside the dark fur of Hadrian's back. *Mine, mine, mine.*

"I just don't want you to be left," Magnus was saying, "with the wrong impression of me, that's all. Like I didn't have a generous bone in my body . . ."

She giggled, hugging Hadrian tighter to keep a grip on her own hysteria, her own longing to weep and wail. The wound in her thigh was throbbing; she wondered if it had burst its stitches when she was staggering off balance.

"Don't want to go down in history misunderstood, eh?" she said.

With a flinch he acknowledged she'd scored a direct hit. "Yeah."

Siân stood up, using Hadrian as a four-legged prop, which the dog seemed to understand instinctively. She noticed Mack cast a furtive glance at his watch; only now did she twig that he probably had a train to catch, and a roomful of people somewhere in London waiting to be impressed by a man in an immaculate suit.

"I'm making you late, aren't I?"

"Nothing a few grovelling apologies to a bunch of medical registrars won't fix." And he enclosed one giant hand gently inside the other, in an attitude of prayer, bowing his head like a penitent monk. "*Mea culpa, mea culpa.*"

Time accelerated suddenly, as Siân realised this really was goodbye.

221

"I'll have to return your confession," she said. "And the bottle. Not through your letterbox, though."

"Don't worry about it," he said wearily. "Keep it."

"It's worth a hell of a lot more than a Finnish Lapphund, you do realise that, don't you?"

Her attempt to speak his language missed its mark; he smiled ruefully and looked away. "Not to me. I liked it the way it was, before . . . before I understood it. When it was a mystery, a mysterious object my dad rescued from the ruins of Tin Ghaut when he was a kid. Something he'd take out to show me if I was good, and then put back in its special place."

"I'm sorry, Mack," said Siân. "*Mea culpa.*"

"It's OK," he said breezily. "I'm sure you'll write an academic paper on it one of these days. Then you can thank me in the acknowledgments, eh?"

She stepped forward and embraced him, pressing her hands hard against his back. He responded decorously at first, then allowed himself to clasp her tight, uttering a deep and protracted sigh. He smelled of toothpaste, deodorant, aftershave and, very faintly, mothballs—a combination which somehow got past her defences and, despite her vow to avoid a melodrama, made her cry after all.

"I don't even know your surname," she said.

He groaned, and a hiccup of laughter passed through his breast into hers. "Boyle."

"Can't blame your father for that."

"And yours?"

She hugged him tighter, suppressing a tiny fear, left over from the nightmares, that his hand would cease stroking her hair and seize her by the throat. "It's a secret," she said, and, pulling his head down to her lips, she whispered it in his ear.

When Mack was gone, Siân took shelter behind Thomas Peirson's gravestone and lifted her skirts to inspect her bandaged thigh. The gauze was clean and white, wholly devoid of the spreading stigma of blood she'd envisioned. Overactive imagination, as always.

Tentatively, she prodded the site of the surgery; it hurt less than before, and the pain was localised now, no longer a web of soreness throughout her innermost parts.

"It seems you've been carrying a little chunk of Bosnia around with you for quite a few years," the doctor had said, when the X-rays were ready. She'd been slow to catch on, assumed he was making some smug, oh-so-penetrating comment about her relationship with the past. All he meant was that a fragment of stone, ploughed deep into her flesh when the car was dragging her mangled body twenty yards across a street roughened by tanks, had managed to escape detection in the desperate attempts to mend her afterwards. Overworked military surgeons saved her life, did their damnedest to save her knee, were forced by monstrous swelling and infection to sacrifice it. Somehow, though, in all the drama, an embedded crumb of tarmac had been overlooked, and had spent all these years since, inching its way— millimetring its way, more like—to the surface.

"That's not possible, surely?" Siân had said. But her conviction that she must be the eighth wonder of the world was gently undermined by medical statistics. The tendency of foreign objects to work their way out of people's bodies had been recorded, the doctor assured her, as far back as the Renaissance; there was, historically speaking, a lot of it about.

Siân stood at the top of the hundred and ninety-nine steps, fingering the morsel of rubble in her pocket, wondering if Magnus, running at the top speed that his suit and stiff black shoes allowed, had reached the railway station yet. She wondered how much older he might need to be, how much he might need to live through, before Time weathered him into the right man for her—counselling herself that he was sure to have found somebody else by then. The stone in her pocket was smooth as a pebble, as if her flesh had sucked it like a toffee for years, hoping to digest it. Overactive imagination again.

How odd to think that Whitby's sleepy harbour was twinkling here below her, obscured by a mushroom proliferation of typically English rooftops, while nestled inside her palm was a relic of a war-torn Balkan street thousands of miles away. She considered tossing it down the steps, just to see how long she could keep her eye on it before it became, irreclaimably, part of the British landscape. But, on balance, she preferred her original idea of getting a jeweller to fashion it into a pendant. A silver chain would be nice; Saint Hilda would have to forgive her.

She reached the abbey just as the last of the day's visitors were leaving. Homeward-bound American tourists looked at her in pity as she made her way towards the ruins; she wondered why, then realised they must think she'd just arrived on a late-running coach and was only going to get five minutes' worth of antiquity before being evicted by the English Heritage folks.

She walked to the sacristy and found the stone rectangle where Bobby and Jemima had shown off their superstitious spinning game. The vaguely human-shaped depression in the stone was, she had to admit, very inviting to lie in, even though its grey austerity had been tarnished by the words I WAS HERE graffiti'd in yellow felt-tip. Tomorrow, with pious diligence, those words would no doubt be erased.

Siân looked right and left, to confirm that the tourists were all gone, and then she balanced herself carefully on one foot and, after a deep breath, began to spin. Her intention was to spin thirty-four times, but physicalities got the better of ritual and she found herself deliriously dizzy after only ten. With the land and sky revolving before her eyes, she laid herself down in the stone hollow, settling her shoulders and head in the proper place. For what seemed like ages, the turrets and piers of the abbey moved to and fro on the turf of the East Cliff like giant sailing ships made of rock, then finally glided to a standstill. Up there on the buttresses, the ghostie woman not only failed to jump, but failed to appear.

Siân gasped in surprise as her cheek was touched by something rough and wet and rather disgusting; Hadrian was licking her. She opened her mouth to scold him, but his preposterous name stuck in her throat.

"I think I'll call you Hush," she said, elbowing herself up a little.

"Hush," he agreed, nudging her to get to her feet.

THE FAHRENHEIT TWINS

In memory of Panda

At the icy zenith of the world, far away from any other children, Tainto'lilith and Marko'cain knew no better than that life was bliss. Therefore, it was bliss.

Certainly they had plenty of space to play around in—virtually unlimited space. All around their house, acres of tundra extended in all directions, unpunctuated by fences, roads, or other dwellings. A team of huskies could easily pull a sled with the little bodies of Tainto'lilith and Marko'cain on it, for miles, without even losing the frisk in their step. Time was also no problem: in almost perpetual Arctic twilight, there weren't any rules about being back by sunset. The only thing the children's mother absolutely insisted on was that they never leave the house without a compass, since the tundra looked much the same in all directions, especially when the snows were fresh. During the darker months, even the uncannily keen vision of the Fahrenheit twins was strained by the gloom, and navigation by the light of the moon on a sea of grey snow was impossible.

Still, however dark and treacherous, all that they

surveyed was their domain. Nominally, the island of Ostrov Providenya was part of an archipelago that belonged to the Russians, but in reality no law extended far enough to include this barren wasteland encircled by a shifting morass of ice. The Fahrenheits were monarchs here, and their two children prince and princess.

"What lies beyond?" the twins once asked their father.

"Nothing special," Boris Fahrenheit replied without looking up from his journals.

"What lies beyond?" they then asked their mother, knowing she tended to see things rather differently.

"Oh, darlings, too much to explain," she teased. "You'll see it all when you're tired of this little paradise." And she ruffled their unwashed hair, in that distantly affectionate way she had.

Physically, there was little in common between parents and offspring. Boris Fahrenheit was a tall thin German, grey of face and silver of hair, walking always slightly stooped as if the weight of his over-sized knitted pullovers was too much for his skeletal frame to bear. Una was also tall, a blue-eyed, rosy-cheeked Aryan beauty with dyed black hair cut short in a between-the-wars style. She walked erect, keeping all the flesh firm. She was fifty-nine years old and had produced her children well past the age where such things were considered feasible.

Tainto'lilith and Marko'cain were small, even for their age, which was somewhere between nine and eleven. No one had recorded the birth, and it was now too long ago for Boris and Una to recall the exact date. The children were clearly not adolescent yet, anyway. They tumbled around below the furniture, giggling, rounded with puppy fat. They smelled sweet. They wore without demur the embroidered sealskin jumpsuits sewn together for them by their mother. They conversed with the huskies as equals.

Their hair was naturally black, hanging long over their ivory-white faces. Each pair of cheeks was sprinkled with cinnamon freckles, as well as a scattering of tiny puckered scars from a mysterious disease that had thankfully run its course without needing medical attention. Their brown eyes were large, with something of the seal about them: all dark iris and no whites, or so it seemed. They resembled neither their father nor mother, despite the fact that the Fahrenheits were, at the time of the twins' conception, already long exiled from past friends. But Boris and Una had been shaped and coloured by the Old World, and their children by a subpolar archipelago, whose glacial contours could not even be mapped.

More than anything else, the twins' characters were formed by benign neglect. To their father, they were an indulgence of their mother's which he tolerated so long as it didn't interfere with his research. To their mother, they were like robust little pets, pampered and cooed over when she was in a frivolous mood, forgotten about utterly when she had better things to do. Typically, she might spend hours bathing them and massaging whale oil into their skin, scolding them for spoiling their beautiful young flesh with so many calluses and scars; then for the next week she might scarcely notice their existence, nodding absentmindedly as they tore away into the icy night.

In any case, Boris and Una Fahrenheit were themselves often away from home, advancing the progress of knowledge. Specifically, they were away visiting the Guhiynui people, on whom they were the world's foremost authorities. The Guhiynui being mistrustful of strangers, however, progress was slow, at least on fundamental issues. Una's book on Guhiynui handicrafts had already been published and she was compiling another on their cuisine, but there was no end in sight on Boris's long-awaited history, and despite the Fahrenheits' best efforts the dark secrets of the Guhiynui's sexual taboos had not yet been illuminated.

Of course, it was the Fahrenheits who must travel to the Guhiynui, not the other way around. And, because Boris and Una always travelled together, it transpired that Tainto'lilith and Marko'cain were often left alone in the house, with only the dogs for company, for days or weeks on end. This made them uncommonly self-sufficient, in a way that would have astounded visitors—if there had ever been any visitors.

The existence of Tainto'lilith and Marko'cain was in fact a secret from anyone in the green parts of the world. Few people had even heard of the island where the Fahrenheits lived, let alone the specifics of its invisible, unreachable population. Una had given birth at home, midwifing herself. Stoical in the face of the duplicated results, Boris had constructed a second cot identical to the first, the memory of how it was done still fresh in his mind.

The indistinguishable cots were apt. In all respects except genitals, Tainto'lilith and Marko'cain were identical twins. Their expressions were the same. There was even the same amount of light inside their eyes, a difficult thing to reproduce exactly.

One day their mother told them a story—a true story, she insisted—about how a future would come when their bodies would change beyond recognition. Tainto'lilith would grow teats, and Marko'cain would sprout a beard.

"Oh ho!" they chortled.

But their mother's seriousness sewed a needle of anxiety through the tough skin of their hearts. From that moment on, the challenge of arresting the advance of time became a priority for Tainto'lilith and Marko'cain. The years must not be allowed to pass: they must be kept in check, securely corralled in the present. But how?

The answer must lie, the twins felt sure, in ritual—ritual being a concept that was much discussed in the Fahrenheit household, in reference to the Guhiynui. But Boris and Una were mere observers, too European to understand ritual in its visceral origins. Their black-maned, seal-eyed children were already devising a way to control the workings of the universe with such ready-to-hand materials as Arctic fox and knife.

Tainto'lilith and Marko'cain had never met the Guhiynui, but their minds seemed to work similarly—as Una always remarked whenever she saw her children setting off for some solemn ceremony, sled laden with improvised talismans, fetishes, and jujus.

"Ah, if it was *you* two trying to unlock the Guhiynui's secrets," she'd flatter them, "instead of old Boris, you would get results in a hurry, wouldn't you, my little angels?"

In fact, the twins were capable of great patience when it came to ritual. Certainly, like all children they were impetuous and never walked if they could run, but magic was a different thing from play. It was grand and elemental and couldn't be rushed. You could wolf your dinner or jump recklessly into the embers of a bonfire, but picking at the threads of the fabric of time required more caution.

To crack the "teats and beard" problem, for example, Tainto'lilith and Marko'cain planned a ritual which could only be performed once a year, at that potently magical moment when the summer sun rose above the horizon at last. Shortly beforehand, they would trap a fox, and make a cage for it—well, they'd have to make the cage first, perhaps. Then they would take the fox to the horizon and fasten it in position, its head facing where the sun was going to rise. Taller than their captive, the children were sure to spot the first glow of light coming, and, just as the fox was about to see it, Marko'cain would pinion the animal's head with his knees while Tainto'lilith stabbed out its eyes.

Afterwards, they would kill it, although this wouldn't be an essential part of the ritual—merely a gesture of mercy. And every year, they would repeat the ritual with a fresh fox, an eternally re-incarnated fox that would always close its eyes rather than witness the changing of the season.

"Do you think it will work?" said Tainto'lilith.

"I'm sure of it," Marko'cain assured her. "I feel it in my testaments."

Having said that, there could be no doubt.

The great house where the Fahrenheits lived stood out from the landscape like an abandoned space-ship on the moon. It was a domed monstrosity of concrete, steel, and double-glazed glass, attached umbilically to a generator and humming gently all the time. Inside, it was decorated and furnished in the schmaltziest Bavarian style, with intricately carved cuckoo clocks, chocolate-brown tables and chairs, embroidered tapestries, glass cabinets filled with miniature poppets of all nations. A massive oil painting of golden reindeer in a forest of broccoli hung above the fireplace, which was never lit because the central heating took care of all that. There was no vegetation outside anyway, so nothing to burn except (if need ever be) the furniture and the Fahrenheits' books and papers.

The kitchen was a Baroque wonderland of

polished wood and brass; dozens of weirdly shaped implements and utensils hung in neat rows on the walls. Few of them were ever used. All the Fahrenheits' food came from a freezer the size of a Volkswagen, and Una boiled or baked it either in the grey pot with the cracked wooden handle or the singed pink ceramic oven dish, according to what it was. She was a pathologically forgetful cook and any meal not prepared by the children was likely to be a challenging affair, though occasionally she did get into moods when she would create elaborate pastries or even soups.

"You need vitamins, minerals, and all those mysterious little trace elements," she would enthuse, serving each of her children some extraordinary treat on the special plates with the silver rims. "You can't live on rubbish all the time, you know."

The twins' bedroom was painted mauve, as a bisexual compromise between pink and blue. Very little of the walls showed through, though, because of the density of prints and bookcases and shelves piled thick with knickknacks. All these things had belonged to Una when she was a child; she had insisted on taking them with her to the island for her own personal, sentimental reasons, long before she had conceived of Tainto'lilith and Marko'cain. Over time, more and more of it was passed down to the children. Her eyes would mist over, and she would rush to fetch something from a locked cabinet or even a suitcase.

"Here, I want you to have this," she would say,

brandishing some ancient ornament or faun-coloured book. "If you promise to take care of it."

From careful study of these things—the little wooden horses with real manes and tails, the crystal baubles with cherubs inside, the music boxes that played Alpine melodies, the stuffed mouse with the Tyroler hat, green velvet jacket, and lederhosen—Tainto'lilith and Marko'cain pieced together an impression of who their mother might be.

Conversation was considerably harder to come by. Una addressed perhaps a hundred sentences a year to her children, or even less if repetitions weren't counted.

In view of this scarcity, the twins were compiling a "Book of Knowledge", in which they faithfully recorded all the things their mother said to them. Not the halfhearted scoldings or the offhand domestic instructions, but anything more pregnant. The book—a hundred or so blank pages bound in stiff, intricately patterned covers—was a sacred object and mistakes were not allowed. Every word, every letter proposed for inclusion in it was discussed by the twins beforehand, practised on scrap paper, then inscribed onto the creamy white pages with great care. Appropriately enough, the first thing written into the book was what their mother had told them about the book itself when she'd presented it to them.

"This book was once a tree."

It was an intriguing thought. The Fahrenheits' house was infested with paper—hardbound texts, maps, German romances, very old newspapers, glossy magazines flown in from Canada, plus, of course, Boris and Una's own mountains of notes and journals. All these, if mother was to be believed, had once been trees. The notion was doubly potent because the children had never seen a tree, except in books.

Their own attempt to grow such a miraculous thing for themselves, by pulping a book into paste and burying it in a compost of excrement and yeast, had not been successful.

Disappointed, they'd worked up the courage to knock at their mother's study, to ask her the exact recipe for trees.

"Not now, darlings," she warned them, leaning farther into the pearly light of her desk lamp.

One day, Boris and Una Fahrenheit returned from yet another visit to the Guhiynui, landing their grimy blue-and-silver helicopter just outside the house as usual. From the dining-room window, through the trickling shimmer of condensation, Tainto'lilith and Marko'cain watched them disembark. Four cuckoo clocks, in various rooms of the house, started cooing simultaneously. In the snows outside, a chaos of huskies swirled around the returning grown-ups, barking and snuffling.

It was obvious, even before Boris and Una reached the front door, that they were in an unusually subdued mood. They were neither arguing like bitter enemies nor (as was equally common) discussing their findings like affectionate colleagues on the brink of a breakthrough. Instead, Una walked into the house silent and pale, pausing only to let her coat fall to the floor before disappearing into the bedroom.

Boris, a few steps behind, followed her to the bedroom door, then thought better of it. He left the house again, and busied himself putting the helicopter away. Tainto'lilith and Marko'cain watched him through the glass, wiping the condensation away with their pyjama'd elbows, *pwoot woot woot*.

Eventually their father was ready to give them an explanation.

"Your mother has eaten something that disagreed with her," he said. "Don't be surprised if this ends badly."

This was the sum of his thoughts on the matter, but it was enough to galvanise the twins into action.

For the next three days, Tainto'lilith and Marko'cain put aside all childish things in order to nurse their mother in her bed. Holding back offers of nurture only during those arbitrary hours of "night" when their parents were actually sleeping together, they devoted every remaining minute to a routine of snacks, cold compresses, warm towels, fizzy pills, and hot-water bottles.

"Oh, you are such little darlings," Una beamed at them, her face glowing like a gas flame. "My own mother couldn't have nursed me better than you two are doing."

Pride in this distinction didn't blind the twins

to the fearsome obstinacy of their mother's illness. As the days passed, they grew stoical in their acceptance of the prophesied "bad end," which in their minds was their mother having to be transported hundreds of miles to the nearest hospital.

Instead, she died.

Bringing the breakfast as usual, the twins found their father loitering outside her bedroom, fully dressed.

"She's dead," he said, then smiled a ghastly smile as if trying to reassure them that he would not let a thing like this cast a shadow over their welfare.

"But we have her breakfast," said Tainto'lilith.

"It's all right, you weren't to know," said Boris.

Seeing that the twins were not taking his word for it, he stepped aside to let them into the bedroom where, at some uncertain time during the night, his wife had finally left him. The event seemed to have rendered him oddly lenient, almost tender.

Tainto'lilith put down the tray of tea and oatmeal just outside the door and followed her brother in. Una Fahrenheit was lying horizontal in the bed, sheets pulled up to her chin. Her flesh was the colour of peeled apple. Her mouth hung slackly open, her eyes were only half shut. There was nothing happening inside her skull; it was deserted.

Boris stood in the doorway, arms loosely folded, waiting for Una's children to confirm the correctness of his judgment.

Tainto'lilith and Marko'cain dawdled around

238

the bed, sobbing and snivelling softly. Then, briefly, they wailed. In time, they stopped moving and made a little space for themselves on the edge of the mattress next to their mother's body. They sat there, shoulder to shoulder, breathing in turns. Outside the bedroom, the tongues of dogs slurped at oatmeal and cold tea.

"What happens to her now?" Marko'cain asked the shadowy figure in the doorway.

"Burial," said their father. "Or cremation."

"Oh," said Marko'cain. He was thinking angels might still come down from the snowy sky and scoop his mother's body up to heaven. Hidden somewhere far beyond the featureless gloom of the polar atmosphere, there might be an exotic paradise of teak and lace, laid out ready for Una Fahrenheit. Perhaps only the reinforced concrete of the ceiling was keeping the angels from getting in.

"I'll leave the final decision to you," said Boris, with a heavy sigh. "Don't think too long about it, though."

Left alone with their thoughts, Tainto'lilith and Marko'cain wept a little longer, then began to plan for the future.

They were angry, of course, that the opportunity of saving their mother had not been offered them. Had they seriously imagined she might die, they would certainly have done something to stop it. The universe was not above agreeing to bargains of various kinds, providing enough advance warning was given.

But she was dead now, and that was that.

"We are orphans now, like in the storybook of *Little Helmut and Marlene*," suggested Tainto'lilith.

"Well . . . not really," frowned Marko'cain. "We have a father."

"For how much longer?"

"He looks quite well."

"That's not what I meant."

"You think he will leave us now that mother is gone?"

"It's possible," said Tainto'lilith.

"Ours is the only house on the island," objected Marko'cain.

"He may go and live with the Guhiynui. He knows them a lot better than us, and some of them are bound to be women."

Marko'cain considered this for a minute, then said, "We are talking about the wrong things."

Behind them on the bed, the body of their mother was waiting.

"True," said Tainto'lilith.

The important question was, what ritual would be the right one for their mother—not simply in the matter of removing her body, but also in commemorating all she had been in spirit. She was, after all, no mere piece of refuse to be disposed of.

"We buried Snuffel," recalled Marko'cain. Snuffel was the children's pet name for Schnauffel, one of the huskies who had died a couple of years before. They had buried him near the generator, in the lush soft earth surrounding the hot-water pipes. An elaborate ceremony had accompanied the burial, involving recitations, toys, and raw meat.

"Snuffel was a dog," said Tainto'lilith. "Our mother isn't a dog."

"I'm not saying we should do it exactly the same. But we could bury her along with her favourite things."

"She would hate to have her things buried. Whenever she gave us something, she was always upset if we got it dirty."

"But won't she be in a box?"

"I don't know. Father didn't say anything about a box. And you remember when we asked about making the fox cage, he said he had no wood to waste on such foolishness."

Marko'cain sat slumped in thought. Outside the door, the dogs' tongues stopped lapping and their soft clicking footfalls faded away. These things and more were made audible by the silence of their mother on the bed behind them.

"I think," said Marko'cain at last, "Mother should be buried in very deep snow. Then, if after a time we decide we have done the wrong thing, we can fetch her out and she will still be good."

For some reason this made Tainto'lilith cry again. Her brother put his arm around her convulsing shoulders. The bed shook gently, its three burdens bobbing up and down.

"She wouldn't *like* to be buried in snow," sobbed Tainto'lilith.

Marko'cain bit his lower lip and frowned.

"Dead people don't feel anything, do they?"

"Don't they?"

"It's in the Book of Knowledge, I'm sure."

They went and fetched the Book of Knowledge and found the relevant page. Sure enough, there it was: *Dead people don't feel anything.*

The physical act of fetching the Book of Knowledge, quite apart from what was in it, helped the twins feel a little better somehow. It got them out of their mother's bedroom for a minute, allowing their accumulated grief to escape like harmful fumes into the hallway. When they returned, the bedroom seemed airier and more benign. Una Fahrenheit was lying exactly where they had left her, unchanged to the smallest wisp of hair and glint of tooth. So clear was it from this that her spirit had departed, that the children lost much of their terror of the body she'd left behind. It was a husk, no longer truly their mother—more like their mother's most treasured possession, which had been given to them as a parting gift.

All they had to do was decide how best to pass that gift on to the universe. There was, after all, a possibility that their mother was taking a lot more interest in her children now that she was dead and her splendid body was in their care. Always so well preserved in life, she might be watching them anxiously from somewhere up above to make sure she wasn't mistreated or neglected in death.

"I still don't like to think of her frozen," said

Tainto'lilith, "even if she can't feel it. She is our mother, not a piece of lamb in the freezer."

Marko'cain nodded, accepting this, but then an instant later he frowned, stung in the forehead by a new idea.

"Perhaps we should eat her," he said.

"Oh! What a horrible bad thought!" cried his sister.

"Yes, so there must be power in it," he reasoned.

Tainto'lilith bit her lower lip, thinking. All ideas must be considered carefully. The universe knew what was best for everyone, even if the way to its heart might sometimes be hard to understand.

Gamely, she tried to imagine the universe smiling down on such a hideous ritual, tried to imagine being brave enough to sacrifice her own feelings to it. Certainly there was a potent appeal in the idea of making their mother disappear inside them, rather than abandoning her body to parasites or the elements.

"She is too big," said Tainto'lilith at last. "If I could eat her like an apple—or half an apple—I would do it."

"We could eat a little of her for the rest of our lives," suggested her brother. "Eat nothing else, ever. That would be a very strong thing to say to the universe."

"This is silly talk," sighed Tainto'lilith. "I am feeling sick. Think of the hair."

"We could do something else with the hair."

"This is silly talk."

"Yes, you are right."

Crestfallen, they sat on the edge of the bed, the Book of Knowledge lying closed on the floor at their feet.

"Well . . . what is left?" said Tainto'lilith after a while.

"The best thing," said Marko'cain.

"What do you mean?" said Tainto'lilith.

"All that we have thought of so far is no good," said Marko'cain. "So, the best thing is still left."

That was cheering. They pondered with renewed vigour.

"Father seemed most in favour of cremation," remarked Marko'cain. "That is, burning her."

"How do you know?"

"It was the way he spoke the word."

"He said he would let us decide, though."

"But not to take too long."

"What time is it?"

"I don't know. The cuckoos will tell us soon."

"I don't like the thought of burning mother," fretted Tainto'lilith. "It is worse than eating her. It's like starting to cook her and then forgetting, and coming back to find her all black and ruined."

"The Guhiynui burn their dead people, I'm sure I heard father say."

"Every tribe has its own rituals," Tainto'lilith said, struggling with hand gestures to make him understand. "The universe knows we are not Guhiynui. The universe isn't stupid. We have to do something that is right for the tribe that we are."

"You think we are a tribe?"

"Of course we are a tribe."

"Just the two of us?"

"There are more of our kind where our mother and father came from. That's our tribe."

"Father says they are all imbeciles and backstabbers there. And mother said once that they let the streets get dirty, and another time that the trains are always late and full of rude people who will not stand up for a lady."

"Still, they are our tribe."

Marko'cain had become agitated, picking at little scabs on his knuckles and shuffling his feet.

"I can't remember why we are talking about these things," he said despondently.

"Neither can I," admitted Tainto'lilith.

"If only mother could tell us what she wants done."

"Perhaps she will send us a sign."

"Perhaps father will come back soon, and tell us we've run out of time."

As if to confirm this, several cuckoo clocks went off at once, filling the house with the sound of mechanical birdsong.

After much discussion, the twins finally worked up the courage to tell their father they wanted to take their mother away with them into the wilderness. Once they were far enough out there, they would wait for a signal from the universe as to the best thing to do with the body.

Surprisingly, Boris Fahrenheit agreed.

"You are little primitives, aren't you?" he commented, with new respect. "I had thought of commissioning some sort of Christian minister to fly out here and do the job, but I'm sure you would do better. You are blood, after all."

Uncharacteristically, he began running about like a maniac, gathering together the necessaries for their journey.

"With the extra weight, the dogs will be slower, and will get hungry and thirsty sooner: you must allow for that," he cautioned, filling a large canister with boiling water.

"You must take a hamper of food for yourselves," he went on. "And food for the dogs. And fuel for a fire, if . . . if you need to make a fire. And I will fetch the compass for you. That is essential."

Within half an hour he had organised them, hamper and all, and escorted them out of the house. In all those thirty minutes, from the moment the twins had announced their intention right up to the moment they stepped onto the snows, he scarcely stopped talking, reminding them of all the things they must do to keep safe. It was a totally unprecedented and, in the circumstances, bizarrely maternal display of fuss. Had there not been an important mission to accomplish, the twins might have considered inaugurating a whole new Book of Knowledge, merely to contain all the advice and instruction their father was shovelling onto them now.

They stood together in the chill wind and the

horizonless gloom, the three remaining members of the Fahrenheit family. The huskies were harnessed and ready, their breath clouding silver in the tungsten porch light. The corpse of Una Fahrenheit, wrapped in furs and bound with leather straps, was secured on a long sled, shackled behind the twins' buggy like a tenacious seal.

"And remember!" Boris shouted after them as they slid away towards the wasteland, "If you need to send up a flare, avert your eyes as you fire!"

Faces blushing hot with mortification and fear, Tainto'lilith and Marko'cain urged the dogs to go faster, to escape from the avalanche of unwanted love.

For what seemed like eternity but was probably only an hour or two, the twins raced full-pelt across the sugary tundra.

"Faster!" shouted Marko'cain.

"Quicker!" shouted Tainto'lilith.

Of course the dogs were wild with enthusiasm at first, but then their pace slackened, not so much from exhaustion as from anxiety—the need to be reassured that there were fellow mammals behind the reins and not some sort of unfeeling machine. Flicks of the whip against their flanks goaded them back up to speed.

Even as they ran, the dogs tried to turn their heads, straining to catch a glimpse of the children they loved so dearly, who had never driven them so hard for so long before. But Tainto'lilith and Marko'cain ignored the appeal, identically determined, hunched down low in their buggy, blinking stoically against the upflung snow.

It was as if they feared that if they stopped or even looked around, their father would still be running after them, clutching a thermos flask or an extra pair of gloves.

"It's mother's death that has done this to him," said Marko'cain when they finally stopped to let the huskies rest. "He will feel better when he has had a sleep, don't you think?"

"I don't know," said Tainto'lilith, blinking in the steam from the panting dogs. "Perhaps he will be like this forever."

Glum, they turned to look at their mother on the bier behind them. Her face, which they had not been able to bring themselves to wrap up like the rest of her body, was snow-grey in the twilight.

"She looks worried about something," fretted Tainto'lilith.

"It's because you are looking at her upside down," suggested Marko'cain.

Tainto'lilith contorted her head to test this theory. Her black mop of hair swung free from under her furry hood, and she palmed it tight against her cheek while examining her mother's physiognomy.

"No, she still looks worried," she concluded.

"The cold has made her complexion paler," said Marko'cain, secretly afraid of where this line of enquiry might be leading them.

"No, it's in her expression," said Tainto'lilith. "In her brow."

"She has a few wrinkles there, that's all," explained her brother, as if the subtle workings of ageing held no secrets for him. "In life, she kept them moving around so we wouldn't spot them. Now, they're still."

"It's more than that," insisted Tainto'lilith. "I hope she wasn't worried about something as she was dying."

"What would she have been worried about?"

"Us, for one thing."

"We are two things."

"Precisely."

"She knew we would take care of each other."

"You think so?"

"She must have, or she would have done more for us herself while she was alive."

For several more minutes they sat there, their seal-coated forearms resting on the back rung of their buggy, their faces pensive, staring down at the glacial upside-down face of their mother. Then they got up to stretch their legs and to pour some of the hot water from the canister onto the snow, so that a tepid pool formed from which the dogs could drink.

All round them, in all four directions (but why only four?—in all three hundred and sixty thousand directions!), the landscape looked exactly the same. Only the sky differed, varying from greyish indigo to pale purple.

"Where are we going, exactly?" enquired Marko'cain.

"We've been going south, I think," said his sister, stroking her favourite husky, allowing the bewildered animal to lick her furry fingers. "Is the direction important?"

"The universe hasn't taken any notice of us so far," said Marko'cain. "Maybe if we go to where the land ends, it will understand that we need help."

Tainto'lilith had knelt down in the snow, butting her cheek and nose playfully against the snout of the husky. The dog leaned close into her face, almost wetting himself with relief.

"Our island is only small," Tainto'lilith said, as the other dogs began to pant for their turn. "We are bound to get to one of its edges soon."

Marko'cain fetched out the compass and consulted it, turning round and round as if playing a game, his black boots trampling a hollow in the snow.

"Ho!" he said. "This is a strange thing: the compass is pointing to a different north whichever way I turn."

Tainto'lilith gazed up into the stratosphere.

"Perhaps we have reached the Pole," she murmured.

"The Pole is the other way," said Marko'cain, frowning. "I think this compass is broken."

His sister sidled close, examining the pristine-looking instrument nestling in the grubby palm of his glove.

"The glass is perfect, and the arrow is wobbling just like normal," she pointed out.

"It's broken inside," declared Marko'cain, "where we can't see."

He shuffled around in a circle again, to demonstrate how north had lost its meaning. Tainto'lilith shuffled with him, and the huskies, smelling a new kind of play, paced around them in a wider circle.

"You are right," she said. "But it doesn't matter. The dogs know the way home."

And they stowed the compass somewhere safe, for their father to mend when they returned.

It took longer to reach the shore of Ostrov Providenya than the twins expected. A whole day's worth of hours, perhaps more. Perhaps two entire days. There was a feeling the twins always got when they had neglected to sleep, a feeling as if their eyeballs had been carelessly left lying about somewhere, and had dried out. Then again, maybe this time it was the weeping that had caused it. Maybe they had only been travelling for a day after all.

And yet they really hadn't thought their island big enough to permit such a long journey as they had made. At their first glimpse of the sea, when it was still a long way off, the twins wondered whether perhaps they'd passed the end of the land a long time ago, and had ever since been traversing an appended halo of frozen seawater.

However, when at last they were drawing near to the strand, all doubt was swept away. They could see the waves breaking against an undeniably substantial shore of stone, an igneous corona around the rim of the softer earth.

The twins whooped in unison, waving fists in the air as if their advance towards the sea were a battle charge.

Even from a distance, it was obvious that this strip of Ostrov Providenya's shore was only very narrow, and yet it seemed to have some influence inland: the ground on which the twins were travelling grew deceptive beneath them. Oh, the snowy tundra *looked* the same as all the terrain they'd been sliding over from the beginning, but it wasn't the same. Violent bumps and scrapes under the skis of the buggy warned them that the crust of snow was hazardously thin. They glanced behind them: two long lines of dark earth trailed in their wake, and the frozen body of their mother was jolting against its straps.

Hastily, Marko'cain and Tainto'lilith reined the dogs in. If the seashore was the place where the universe intended to give them its verdict, they would have to travel the rest of the way there on foot.

With the sleds at a standstill, quiet descended—or what would have been quiet a few miles back: instead, the air was abuzz with the sound of waves. This was an awesome novelty for the Fahrenheit twins; not the vastness of the ocean, because they had grown up with vastness, but the sound of it. All their lives, circumambient silence had suggested to them that their little family and its machines must be the only animated things in the world: everything else just lay there, still. Even the occasional storm seemed nothing more than a stirring of white dust, a redistribution of lifeless snow by the careless opening of some big door in the universe. As soon as that open door was noticed by whoever was responsible for these things, it would be shut, and silence and inertia would be restored. Here by the sea, however, the illusion was shattered. The great waters were in constant motion, bawling and hissing to each other. Their hubbub was fearsome and relentless, and next to it the voices of the Fahrenheit twins were feeble, barely audible, swallowed up by a larger life.

All this the twins observed and understood in a moment, but even in their newfound humility they found reason to hope. Perhaps the grand restlessness of the sea, its deafening roar of collective purpose, only served to prove how much power it had to help them.

Tainto'lilith and Marko'cain had stopped thirty yards or so from the shore. Dismounting from their buggy, they stumbled around, stiff-limbed, calming the huskies. The ground beneath their feet crackled and sighed. Here and there, sparse vegetation poked through the thin snow, like limp green beans emerging from an inedible expanse of mother's powdered potato. In the near distance, tortured rock formations—volcanic froth frozen in time—fringed a stony shore. Startled by the arrival of the

Fahrenheit twins' little cortège, a colony of white birds billowed into the air, a swirling cloud of wings.

"This is the place," affirmed Tainto'lilith.

The dogs were very hungry by now, and so the Fahrenheit twins fetched out the tins of food from either side of their mother's body.

"There is a tin opener, I hope?" said Marko'cain, holding one of the tins aloft from the slavering jaws of Snuffel Junior.

"Of course there is," Tainto'lilith reassured him, bringing the glittering tool to light. "Father has thought of everything."

Disappointingly, however, the contents of the unlabelled cans, when the lids were cut off, did not appear to be dog food—at least no dog food the twins had encountered before.

"What is this stuff?" frowned Tainto'lilith, peering into the tomato-red goo.

"I'm not sure," admitted her brother. "Let's see what the dogs think."

They tipped two canfuls of the substance onto the ground, where it spread into a globulous pool of gore, enriched with pale seeds. The huskies approached eagerly, sniffed, then looked up at the twins in honest puzzlement.

"This is bad news for us," said Marko'cain.

"Worse news for the dogs," said his sister. "*We* have food, at least."

"Yes, but we need the dogs to get home. They

are hungry and cold. Soon they will get weak and bad-tempered."

"Let's make a fire, then, and cheer them up."

Tainto'lilith and Marko'cain walked to the shore, feeling the strange new pressure of stones against the soles of their boots. Accompanied by the cloud of cooing birds, the twins searched the rocky strand for something to burn. There was nothing. However, they did find a big bowl-like metal object, ochre with rust—a fragment of a ship, perhaps. They carried it back to where the sleds and huskies were, with the idea of filling it up with fuel like one of those flaming braziers in *Hansi and the Treasure of the Mongols*.

"Remember to stand well back," counselled Marko'cain as Tainto'lilith prepared to drop a lighted match into the oily pool.

The match fell into the liquid and was instantly extinguished. A second match did likewise. One after another, the little sticks of flaming wood were sacrificed to the same greasy fate. Eventually a faint aroma of singed fried food, familiar to the twins from their mother's meals, began to venture through the air.

"This is cooking oil," said Tainto'lilith.

A finger-dip's taste confirmed she was right.

"We should have packed our own supplies," said Marko'cain, putting his glove back on. "Father was not thinking very clearly."

"He certainly was in a state."

Perplexed, the twins perched themselves on the

edge of their mother's sled and considered their lot. The huskies whined and snuffled nearby, investigating every clump of vegetation and bird dropping in case it was edible. They were well behaved so far, but it wouldn't last. Soon they would realise that the twins, and the body of Una Fahrenheit, were the only meat for miles around.

In the skies above, contradictory messages were being sent. A subtle orange glow on the horizon promised the dawn, at long last, of the Arctic summer. Then again, there were massive clouds in the sky and the occasional flicker of light, threatening a thunderstorm.

"We are going to need some shelter," predicted Marko'cain.

"If we get too comfortable, the universe may think we don't need any help."

"I'm sure we will not be able to get too comfortable."

They harnessed the dogs again, then travelled along the shoreline at a funereal pace. The heavens were crackling with electricity, which made the animals uneasy and distractible, tugging against the reins. The waves crashed louder and louder, sending spray so far inland that it spattered the cheeks of the Fahrenheit twins.

After another mile or so, something extraordinary could be seen, sprouting up from a hillock.

"Is it a tree?" wondered Tainto'lilith, urging the huskies on. But it wasn't a tree. It was the giant blades of a helicopter, all on their own without a vehicle to be attached to. Someone had carried the great metal cross here, buried one of the blades deep in the ground, and thus created a monumental steel crucifix.

"We should be careful," said Tainto'lilith. "If lightning comes, it will probably strike that cross."

Marko'cain nodded, deep in thought.

"Perhaps this is the message from the universe," he said, as they drew nearer.

"About mother?"

"Yes. Perhaps we should stand her up against that cross, and invite the lightning to strike her."

As if in support of this idea, a bright tendril of electricity whipped across the sky, lighting up everything for a moment with tungsten clarity.

"Do you really think so?" said Tainto'lilith dubiously. "Don't you think it might . . . it might make her . . . come back to life?"

"Back to life?" breathed Marko'cain. "No! Do you think so?"

"I can imagine it happening."

Marko'cain stared at the cross, then into his embroidered lap, imagining it for himself.

"That frightens me," he admitted at last.

"Me too," said Tainto'lilith.

"Let's wait for a different message."

A few hundred yards farther on, they found the helicopter from which the blades had come. It was bigger than Boris and Una Fahrenheit's machine and in better decorative order, except, of course, for the missing blades and (on closer examination) its belly, which was all crumpled and ruined. Plainly, it had crashed, and failed to get up again.

The Fahrenheit twins went to investigate the wreck. They peered through the Perspex windows, then flipped open one of the doors. There were seats for six passengers, but no one inside, despite complex skeins of blood patterning the upholstery. No doubt at least one of the people who had lost that blood was buried beneath the great metal crucifix nearby. Those who had done the burying had moved on, seeing no point in staying with the husk of their flying machine. Tainto'lilith and Marko'cain would have done the same. After all (as they quickly ascertained), there was no food in the helicopter anymore, and all the flammable stuff had been taken out of it. The twins walked back towards the growling dogs, empty-handed.

"We could sleep inside it, maybe," said Marko'cain, looking back.

But next instant, a flash of lightning struck the steely hull, exploding the windows like the skin of a giant balloon, branding a helicopter skeleton shape on the twins' retinas. In terror they covered their eyes, but the flare of luminescence faded almost immediately, leaving only a blueish flicker fidgeting over the blasted paintwork.

They hurried back to their sleds, where the dogs were barking and howling frantically.

"Be calm! Don't fear!" they counselled the animals, too fearful themselves to extend their hands. Even Snuffel Junior looked as though he might bite instead of submitting to a placatory stroke.

"Good dogs!" cried the twins without conviction, taking a step towards the phalanx of snapping canine teeth and saliva, then taking a step backwards.

However, just as the children were on the brink of conceding they'd lost control, the tension was resolved from an unexpected quarter. One of the dogs, a little removed from the others, detected a hint of movement where no movement had been, and, with a yelp of glee, bounded away to investigate. All the other dogs stopped their barking and turned their heads, nostrils agape.

Over at the helicopter hulk, whose metal skin was still hazy with smoke, a small hole in the torn fuselage was apparently giving birth to a flurry of animal life: a family of voles, shrieking in distress. No sooner had the first one found its feet on the snow than it was snaffled up in the husky's jaws. An instant later, all the other dogs had pounced in unison, and the twins' view of the squirming litter of disoriented rodents was blotted out by a scrum of haunches and wagging tails. Furious growling quickly subsided when it became clear that there was enough for all.

"We are lucky," said Marko'cain as the dogs gnawed at their miraculous feast. "Such things can't happen very often."

"We should eat something ourselves," sighed Tainto'lilith, weak and shivery now that the crisis was past.

Marko'cain walked over to the sled and fetched the big bag of provisions out of it. He unbuckled it and peered inside.

"Ho! This is a puzzle," he exclaimed. "The hamper our father packed for us is empty."

"Empty!" cried his sister. "But it was full when we set off! Did the dogs eat it when we weren't looking? Did it fall out, maybe, as we were moving along?"

"No . . ." Marko'cain was pensive, grappling with ambiguities. "I shouldn't have said it was empty. It has some . . ."—he rummaged—"some big crumpled-up papers in it, and a heavy book called . . . *Principia Anthropologica*."

The Fahrenheit twins stood for a while with the hamper at their feet, warming their hands inside their armpits, listening to the waves on one side of them and the crunch of bone against gnashing teeth on the other.

"Do you think perhaps our father is trying to kill us?" said Tainto'lilith.

"Why would he wish to kill us?" said Marko'cain.

Both of them did their best to imagine, willing themselves to transcend the limitations of childish thought.

"He might think we are trouble to look after, now that mother can't do it anymore," suggested Tainto'lilith.

"But we've been looking after ourselves, haven't we?" protested Marko'cain. "He doesn't often notice we are there."

"Maybe that's the problem!" declared Tainto'lilith. "He doesn't notice us very often, so perhaps in his mind we are still babies, needing milk and love."

"Well . . ." frowned Marko'cain. "We will need *something* to eat soon, or we will die."

Warily, the Fahrenheit twins sampled the tomato-red gloop in the tins. It was, rather unsurprisingly, tomato. They spooned it into their mouths, glob after glob, crimson juice running down their chins.

"This will keep us going," said Tainto'lilith as cheerfully as she could.

"We need a message from the universe," retorted Marko'cain. "And we need it quick."

When they had eaten as much of the chilly, snot-textured fruit as they could stand, they sat at the edge of their mother's sledge again, facing the sea. A pearly glow was growing on the horizon. Summer was about to come up.

In normal circumstances, this would have been a cause for ecstatic celebration, but just now the Fahrenheit twins had other things to think about. With great earnestness, striving not to be distracted by their sleepy heads, sick stomachs, and the uneasy sense of their unfinished mission, Tainto'lilith and Marko'cain discussed their chances of survival—not just in the short term, but in the event that they were no longer welcome at home.

The discussion began well enough, with an accurate inventory of their meagre supplies and a head-count of the dogs, but when they moved on to speculate about more slippery intangibles—like their father's true desires or the reliability of supernatural aid—their tempers began to fray. Over and over, they were forced back to the same conclusion: that they had no one to rely upon but each other.

"We must each consider our strengths and weakneths," said Marko'cain.

"But we are both the same!"

"Not inside our underpants."

Tainto'lilith sighed in exasperation. Testaments and pee-holes were equally useless in the face of an unfriendly universe, as far as she was concerned.

"We are the same," she said, digging the heels of her boots through the crust of snow, gouging into the hard dark earth. "Same, same, same."

Unnerved by the intensity of his sister's conviction, Marko'cain swallowed hard, trying to keep his disagreement to himself. He gazed out across the swirling surf, as if soliciting the sea's ideas, but really he was comforting himself, sending confidential reassurances to his slighted genitals. Tainto'lilith smelled his estrangement instantly, of course.

"Why *shouldn't* we be the same, anyway?" she demanded.

Marko'cain kept his eyes on the sea, dignified in his appreciation of the wider picture.

"If there really is no difference between us, it would mean that neither of us can know anything that the other doesn't," he pointed out.

"Is that dangerous?" his sister wondered.

"It could be."

262

There was a pause.

"I can't imagine how."

"Neither can I," said Marko'cain solemnly. "That gives danger the advantage."

"Now you're just being silly," Tainto'lilith scolded him. "Like when you used to make me frightened in bed as we were about to fall asleep, by saying that a bear might come through the window and eat us."

"Bears came to our house all the time," retorted Marko'cain defensively. "You saw their footprints in the mornings."

"Footprints don't kill," sniffed Tainto'lilith, hugging herself. "All those years, all those bears, and what did our mother die of?"

The question, released as an innocent puff of rhetorical vapour, hung in the air, cloudier than expected.

"We don't know what she died of," said Marko'cain at last.

"No," admitted Tainto'lilith.

"It could kill us too."

"I don't think so."

"Why are you so sure?"

"I feel very well. You not?"

"I'm hungry and tired and cold."

"Me too, but those things can be fixed."

"I hope so." Marko'cain seemed unconvinced, even as the first ray of sunshine began to creep across the ocean towards them. Something—a suspicion—was nagging at him. "Perhaps father killed mother. He said she ate something that disagreed with her. Perhaps we have now eaten the same thing. A deadly poison."

"What nonsense you are talking!" grizzled Tainto'lilith, pointing to the discarded tins at their feet. "It's just tomato, from our own storehouse. Mother would have eaten something strange. Guhiynui food."

"Still . . ."

Wave by wave, the sea was turning from grey to silver. The birds were going mad with joy. Elongated black shadows were unrolling like tongues from the rocks on the shore, the sleds, the empty hamper, the tins. Even the blades of grass, prickling up through the increasingly slushy snow, cast magnified javelins of shade before them.

"What would father want to kill mother for?" said Tainto'lilith.

"They argued all the time," Marko'cain reminded her, waving his hands about to demonstrate.

"Not all the time."

"More than half."

Tainto'lilith's brow furrowed as she made a few calculations.

"Exactly half," she concluded.

Marko'cain, knowing she was right, slumped a little. Then he was pricked by another memory.

"Father told us once that he wouldn't trust her as far as he could throw her. She is as bad as the Guhiynui, he said."

"Yes, but another time mother said he couldn't

possibly manage without her. Without a woman, he's helpless like a baby, she said."

"Are you sure?"

"It's in the Book."

They sat in silence, picturing their father shambling to and fro in the Fahrenheit house, his uncut grey hair hanging in his eyes, his pullover full of holes, his heart in pieces, his coffee cold.

"So what will happen to him now that mother is gone?" murmured Marko'cain.

"We'll help him," said Tainto'lilith. "If it's true that he sent us out to die, I'm sure he's sorry by now. He'll be glad to have us home, you'll see. And every year we are bigger. If he can wait a little while, we can do everything mother did."

Having decided this, they made a fire with the *Principia Anthropologica*. Fed with five hundred and sixty-two dry pages one after the other, it burned hot and bright, but lapsed into substanceless ash as soon as the last page was added. The huskies, closely gathered around what had been such merry flames, raised their panting heads in disappointment.

"That's all, doggies," sighed Tainto'lilith.

The storm finally having passed over, the children took shelter in the blasted shell of the helicopter, sleeping in the cabin together with the dogs. The overcrowding helped to conserve body heat: a snug interleaving of fast-breathing furry haunches and gently snoring little humans.

While they slept, the sun raised itself from the

265

horizon. The snows glowed white, the heavens azure and pink. The temperature began to climb towards zero.

On waking, the twins extracted themselves groggily from their dense swaddling of hot flesh. The huskies slumbered on while Marko'cain and Tainto'lilith crawled out of the cabin, blinking in the sunshine.

The world had been utterly transformed by the advent of summer, and this in turn had its effect on the children's spirits. The golden-white light and long, clear views encouraged in them a placid, groundless optimism. The risk of imminent death from cold and hunger seemed, all of a sudden, oddly remote, despite the fact that they had only a few tins of tomatoes left, possibly frozen solid by now. They could imagine themselves catching seabirds, picking them out of the sky with a well-aimed pebble or even pouncing on them with the stealth of a superior species. They could imagine flinging a penknife straight into a polar bear's heart.

"Oh, look!"

In the clarity of day, the twins could now see, in the far distance along the shore, thin plumes of smoke rising from a cluster of dwellings. The bulbous, vaguely pyramidal shape of these dwellings was familiar to them from their parents' notebooks. These were the whalebone-enforced domiciles of the Guhiynui.

"But what about mother?" said Tainto'lilith as

her brother ran to fetch the dogs. "What about the message from the universe?"

"This *is* the message from the universe," Marko'cain replied, his enthusiasm inspiring the huskies to leap out of the helicopter one after the other, a fluid tumble of milky fur.

"How do you know?"

Marko'cain was already busy with the harnesses.

"I feel it in my testaments!" he yelled in triumph.

And so, the Fahrenheit twins set off for the Guhiynui village.

In strict mathematical terms, as it might be depicted on a map, the journey was three miles at most, but in practice the children had to veer several hundred yards inland to keep their purchase on the softening snow. A long thigh of land rose to shield them from the sound of the waves, and they travelled in silence and still air. This far away from the shore, the Guhiynui's settlement too was hidden from sight, though its plumes of smoke remained visible in the sky above.

With perhaps a mile and a half still to go, the land assumed a bizarre topography, all peaks and hollows. Grassy mounds erupted through the snow, and rocks the size of houses were scattered all about. The dogs negotiated these obstacles warily, needing flicks of encouragement from the whip. They whined softly even as they jerked to obey, pining, in their inbred doggy solidarity, for the flat environs and the well-known smells of home. Too much novelty was spooking them.

The children sympathised, but they too were being driven. The deceptively placid face of their mother, sweating its veneer of frost off in the sunlight, was exerting a powerful stimulus behind them. They must find a place for her soon.

Then, as yet another massive boulder was looming in front of them, and with the Guhiynui settlement still a fair way off, an unexpected sound made the twins' ears prick up inside their furry hoods.

"Ho!" cried Marko'cain. "Do you hear that?"

They reined the dogs to a halt. Ricocheting among the giant rocks was a faint but unmistakable music: the peal of mechanical birdsong.

"A cuckoo clock!" shouted Marko'cain in wonder.

"That isn't possible, is it?" said Tainto'lilith, as the cooing abruptly stopped. "It must be a *real* cuckoo."

"No, it is a cuckoo clock," Marko'cain assured her. "I even know what cuckoo clock it is. Didn't you recognise it?"

Tainto'lilith closed her eyes tightly, chasing the echoes through her brain.

"Yes," she said, almost at once, surprising herself. "It is the smallest one, with the two little hunters on either side, and the upside-down rabbits with the tied-up feet and the purple door."

"Yes," affirmed Marko'cain. "The one that went missing from our house a long time ago."

"Mother said it got broken."

"And we said, 'Can father not mend it?'"

"And she said, 'Don't bother your father about this, or I will be angry with you.'"

"Then she said, 'One less clock makes no difference to the universe.'"

"We wrote that down in the Book."

"Yes. It feels like yesterday."

"It was a long time ago."

Cautiously, they steered the dogs in pursuit of what could no longer be heard: the invisible sonic footprints of a tiny automated thrush, which might prove to be a figment of their own delirious memories.

Once the turn was taken, however, very little searching was required. In a small snowless clearing, hidden from the wider world by towering stones, stood a single Guhiynui dwelling. In all respects it was identical to the drawings their mother had made of such dwellings in her note-books: the whaleskin exterior, stiffened by tanning and tarring, the whalebone framework, interwoven with rope and metal, the absence of windows, the thong-tied entrance slit, and the thin central chimney, poking up like a smoke-blackened wick. Only, there was no smoke coming from the chimney just now, and no sounds of life within—no evidence at all, in fact, of the communal bustle and vigorous manly activity on whose attractiveness Una and Boris Fahrenheit had so often disagreed.

The children dismounted from their buggy and walked straight up to the house. There was no more need for caution. The universe had them in hand, after all. The entrance flap was knotted loosely, in a shoelace-style bow. Marko'cain tugged it free, and he and his sister squeezed inside.

"Ho!"

There was no-one at home. Instinct had told them there wouldn't be, but a quick glance confirmed it, for Guhiynui houses were simple things, undivided into separate rooms. This one didn't even feel lived-in, in the sense that there was no mess or clutter whatsoever. It was a place meant for visiting.

There was no furniture to speak of, only a bed and, in the centre of the room, a potbelly stove of burnished green iron. The rest of the floor space was bare, but because the walls tapered inwards rather sharply, the whole house was still scarcely big enough for a grown-up to walk around in, and far too cold to be cosy.

And yet, from the moment the Fahrenheit twins stepped inside, they were intoxicated by the mysterious potency of the place. This was unquestionably where the universe wanted them to be. This was the message, delivered not in a voice of thunder but in the barely audible fluting of a familiar automaton.

It wasn't just the presence of the missing cuckoo clock, defiantly keeping its exotic brand of time with its delicate pendulum. No, the mystique of this place went beyond that. The whole interior seemed to glow much brighter than the single ray of sunlight through the entrance slit could possibly explain, and the air, for all its chill, seemed aromatic with intimacy.

Perhaps, more than anything else, it was the paintings. Everywhere on the curvaceous walls, warmly hued cloth paintings were mounted, sewn close against the whaleskin with twine. There were images of adventure: top-heavy Guhiynui warriors sailing the seas on toy boats, or slicing each other up like sausages. There were images of hunting: seals and beluga whales spreading attenuated flippers in surrender to a hail of spears. There were images of birds, carrying tiny sleeping humans towards the sun. And, directly above the bed, there was the largest painting of all, a dynamic full-length portrait of a dark-skinned male and a slender, creamy-white female. From her stylised hairdo and the blush of rose on her cheek, it was quite obvious that this woman was meant to be Una Fahrenheit.

Admittedly the Guhiynui's style of illustration was very different from what the twins had grown up with in their mother's antique storybooks. Both bodies seemed to be floating in space, surrounded by an intricate pattern of stars or snowflakes. The feet were impossibly tiny, the legs bonelessly contorted and intertwined. No clothes had been attempted, not even underpants, leaving the figures naked but apparently impervious to the elements. The man had some kind of extra limb growing from between his legs, and Una had two mouths, one on her face and another, much larger one, on her belly. And yet, for all the primitive eccentricity of the image, its colours were lush and vibrant, and something of their mother's nature had been captured—the best side of her nature, the way she'd tended to look when she was in her happiest mood. On her face, here in this Guhiynui tribute to her, the twins recognised the expression that always came over her when she was about to wash them and pamper their skins with whale oil.

The bed was a big nest of seal skins, all different kinds: hooded, ringed, bearded. It looked supremely comfortable, especially with two fluffy pillows at the far end, each covered in a pastel-coloured pillow-case embroidered with tiny edelweiss. Tainto'lilith removed one glove, and stroked the satiny braille of the coloured cotton. Then she gathered up some stray hairs, fine black ones with grey roots where the dye had failed to penetrate. Pressing her nose into the pillow, she inhaled the scent of Idyl-Geruch and Hyacinthe-Gesang, the heady perfumes of a long-lost Bavaria. Meanwhile, farther down on the bed, Marko'cain allowed himself to test the softness of the seal skins under his sprawling body.

Both twins felt sick with desire to sleep in that bed, knowing very well that it was not intended for them. The perfect equation of two pillows and two children was almost impossible to resist, but resist they did. Troubled and enchanted, they struggled to their feet and looked away.

Kik-kik-kik-kik-kik, the little cuckoo clock was saying, securely mounted on the whalebone wall. *Kik-kik-kik-kik-kik* . . .

Venturing up close, the twins examined the clock's condition. Its fragile brass chain was unbroken;

indeed, it had been pulled up quite recently, giving the mechanism plenty of time before needing another tug. Care had been taken, in bracketing the clock to its cetacean rib, to keep the little birdhouse straight, despite the curve of the wall. The wrought-iron pine cone hung like a plumb line on the end of the chain, confirming the correct orientation of the whole machine. For the clock to be working as well as this, it must, during the long intervals between Una's visits, have been treated with the utmost respect and gentleness by the Guhiynui. Only the minuscule wooden barrel of one of the hunters' guns was broken off, but that might well have happened en route between the Fahrenheit house and this, Una's secret home away from home.

Without needing to confer on the decision, the twins helped each other unbuckle their mother's body from the sledge and carry her into the Guhiynui house. Reverently they inserted her into the bed, wrapping the seal skins around her, smoothing her penumbra of wet hair evenly over the pillow.

"Cuckoo!" carolled the clock, once only. It had used twelve of its cries to call them here, and must begin again.

After consulting the universe, the Fahrenheit twins decided they would go straight home, rather than visiting the Guhiynui settlement. There was, they felt, something not right about prolonging their adventures when their mission was accomplished, and the dogs seemed desperately keen to turn back.

Moreover, there was a long, comfortable sledge free now, in which Tainto'lilith and Marko'cain could slumber the miles away, basking in the sun while the huskies pulled their lighter load homewards.

So that is what they did.

In one of her rare outbursts of nostalgic story-telling, Una Fahrenheit had once told her children of the express trains which carried people across the borders of deepest Europe, whisking them from country to country without anyone having to give a thought to the steering. People could play card games, read books, or even sleep, and the trains would continue unerringly, drawn to the destination as if on a tight string. This was how the long journey back to civilisation felt to the Fahrenheit twins.

When at last they sensed themselves coming to rest in a warm, dark place, it might have been one of those fabled tunnels leading into a railway station, the like of which they had struggled to describe for the purposes of the Book of Knowledge. It was, in fact, the huskies' heated bunker, their concrete kennel, nestled behind the generator. The exhausted dogs were putting themselves to bed without even waiting to be untethered from their harnesses.

Tainto'lilith and Marko'cain prised themselves out of the sledge like a couple of imperfectly defrosted fish, falling onto the seagrass matting of the kennel floor. They were, they realised, half dead. Only their instinctive huddling together, nuzzling their faces into each other's furry hoods and locking torso to torso, had saved them from sleeping themselves into frostbitten oblivion.

"Oh, oh, oh," they said, crawling dizzily on their hands and knees on opposite sides of their mother's bier. Snuffel Junior lifted his head from his boneless slump, momentarily concerned for the twins' welfare. Then he nuzzled back to sleep. They would live.

Boris Fahrenheit was thunderstruck at the twins' return. A rowdy influx of polar bears would have surprised him less than the quiet reentry of his two small children, padding into the kitchen in their damp and filthy socks. He looked from one twin to the other, noting the trickly red stains on their chins and the breasts of their jumpsuits, the halo of animal hair all over them, the pink irritations in their luminous eyes.

"It's done, father," said Tainto'lilith reassuringly, but the old man's grey complexion only went greyer.

Perhaps his discomposure was caused by a difficulty in juggling two social challenges: that of welcoming his children home and that of entertaining a visitor. For Boris Fahrenheit was not a social creature, and the matronly looking woman who was sitting at the breakfast table, tea in hand, was surely the first visitor they had ever had.

"Oh, Bumsie!" she cried, apparently addressing Boris. "You didn't tell me you had children!"

Boris's jaw was shuddering like an abused motor.

"I—I was keeping it a surprise," he stammered. "They're no trouble, really. They're basically . . . self-caring."

"Oh, but they're adorable!" exclaimed the woman, springing up from her breakfast stool. She was a small thing, hardly taller than the twins themselves, and she had a fetchingly dishevelled abundance of blond hair. Her skin was so tanned it was almost caramel, contrasting vividly with her white bathrobe. Her face was uncannily similar to one of the many dolls their mother had given them over the years, an impish Scandinavian poppet intended (according to the Book) to dangle from the ceilings of automobiles. She radiated nurture.

"This is Miss Kristensen," croaked Boris Fahrenheit. "She will be living with us from now on."

"How do you do," said the twins in unison, resorting to the language of the stories they had read. It seemed to be what was wanted.

"Oh, very *well!*" beamed Miss Kristensen, extending her hands in friendship, one for each twin.

Hunched behind the breakfast table, Boris Fahrenheit exposed all his teeth in a startlingly unbecoming smile.

The twins ate themselves sick on a lavish meal prepared for them by Miss Kristensen. They were too weak to sit at the table with their father, so she fed them on the floor, where they helped themselves

276

to a cornucopia of steaming protein and starchy tidbits.

"You poor, poor things," she sang, bending down to serve them milk, not from the ample bosom that swung inside her bathrobe, but from colourful little cartons manufactured in Canada. Before they could thank her politely, she was back at the stove.

Miss Kristensen was in fact a dynamo of culinary energy, chattering in the steam of her own high-speed cooking, flipping eggs without even looking at them, happily bonding with all the utensils Una Fahrenheit had never used.

"Here you are, you secretive rogue," she said, setting a plate of sizzling cutlets in front of the bewildered Boris. Then, in a raucous whisper, "I'm dying to know what else you never mentioned in your letters!"

Tainto'lilith and Marko'cain excused themselves to go off and vomit.

Hidden away in their own bedroom, feverish, hunched over a big metal bowl, they puked all the colours of the rainbow for what seemed like an age.

"We smell bad," observed Marko'cain, during a little rest between exertions.

"It's all the tomato," sighed Tainto'lilith.

More than anything, they were desperate for a bath. This in itself was not a problem: they were well accustomed to bathing themselves, and washing their clothes, too. But unspoken between them was a bewildering new anxiety: the possibility of

Miss Kristensen volunteering to bathe them. The thought was terrifying—more taboo, somehow, than anything they had yet encountered. So, stealthily, they spirited themselves into the bathroom, locked the door, and filled the tub.

Whoops of feminine laughter and growls of paternal caution echoed through the house as the naked twins stepped into the water together.

"This is not our home anymore," said Tainto'lilith, facing her brother across the soily, steamy broth shimmering between them. "Things have changed."

Marko'cain nodded in agreement.

"We have changed, too," he said.

They glanced at each other, surreptitiously checking whether the threatened teats and beard were sprouting yet, but their outward appearances were still comfortingly identical. It was their insides that would never be the same. Something had happened to them, out there in the wilderness.

"I am angry at father," mentioned Marko'cain, saucing himself with shampoo. "Are you?"

"Very angry."

"Do you think it would make us feel any better if we killed him?"

"I think we should just run away," said Tainto'lilith. "But with proper food, this time."

Marko'cain ducked his head into the water, allowing his sister to paw the suds out of his scalp. When he surfaced, he said, "Perhaps we should kill father, *then* run away."

"What about Miss Kristensen?"

"Kill her as well," added Marko'cain glibly.

"We don't mean her any harm, do we?"

"Perhaps she *told* father to get rid of us," suggested Marko'cain. "So she could come and live with him."

Tainto'lilith sighed: a deep, doleful exhalation of regret.

"I wish our eyes had not been opened to these things," she said. "The world was so much nicer before."

Frowning, wedging her head between the taps, she made her very best effort to tell guile apart from innocence. Hot water droplets pattered onto her right shoulder, and cold onto her left.

"She honestly seemed surprised to see us," she reflected. "To see that there was such a *thing* as us, I mean."

"Perhaps she was just play-acting," said Marko'cain.

"I don't believe so."

"All right, then, we'll leave her be, and just kill him." There was a strange new tone in the boy's voice, a cocky impatience, as if the choice between life and death was too straightforward a matter to waste much discussion on. This, too, made Tainto'lilith sad. She racked her brains for a way to save her father, that poor old baby who was, after all, helpless without a woman.

"If we kill father," she said, "Miss Kristensen might get killed as well, without us wanting it."

"How?" The threat of complication was, as Tainto'lilith had hoped, putting a wrinkle on his brow.

"She might throw herself in front of him," she said. "Like the brave little squaw in *Sheriff Flintlock and the Rustlers*."

"One of us could kill father," suggested Marko'cain, "while the other engaged Miss Kristensen in conversation."

"That seems terribly unkind," sighed Tainto'lilith, glimpsing a long lifetime ahead of her of keeping her brother's inclinations in check. "Especially since she is a visitor. I think we should just run away."

"All right," he said, standing up in the bath abruptly, a tutu of froth clinging to his midriff. "But not with the huskies."

"On foot?" said Tainto'lilith.

"In the helicopter," declared Marko'cain, clambering out, with such a swagger of purpose that it looked as if he might stride naked to the hangar.

"But we've never flown the helicopter," protested Tainto'lilith, splashing out of the bath herself.

"We've read the book," her brother said airily, meaning the pilot's manual they'd often played with when it was too snowy to go outside.

"It's not the same."

"Of course it isn't. But there is a connection."

Wrapping towels around themselves, the twins walked to the laundry, where the massive front-loader washing machine was almost finished washing their jumpsuits. The house had gone all quiet, apart from the mechanised sloshing of the water. Boris Fahrenheit and Miss Kristensen had made peace with each other, it seemed.

"Where would we go?" said Tainto'lilith.

"A green place," enthused her brother. "Europe. Canada. Russia. Gre-e-e-enland."

"The names are good," admitted Tainto'lilith. Then suddenly she started weeping, a stream of hot tears rolling down her face, a lost and frightened look in her eyes.

Marko'cain, catching sight of her distress, was shocked. She had never wept without him before, particularly not in a situation where he himself could imagine nothing to weep about. Awkwardly, he patted her trembling shoulders. Now he, too, glimpsed a lifetime ahead of him, of trying, and failing, to comfort his sister in her secret sorrows.

"We might get to see a tree," he said, encouragingly. "And all the other things that mother used to talk about."

Tainto'lilith nodded, unable to speak, the tears still flowing down her cheeks. She would be all right in a moment. Behind the big glass porthole in the washing machine, their clothing had begun to spin, an inextricable, mesmerising ring of embroidered pelts. Soon they would be able to put it on again and cover their nakedness.

And yes, her brother was right, they had so much to look forward to, in the big wide world down below. The Book of Knowledge had a lot of blank pages.

ACKNOWLEDGMENTS

My thanks, as ever, to Eva Youren for her wise advice during the writing of these three novellas and especially for her help in creating the characters of Ben and Dagmar in "The Courage Consort."

"The One Hundred and Ninety-Nine Steps" owes its existence to Keith Wilson, who commissioned me to write a story set around the English Heritage dig at Whitby Abbey.

No animals were harmed or coerced in the making of these three tales.

—MICHEL FABER
March 2004